······

Eden

Dorothy Johnston grew up in Geelong and has lived in Canberra since the 1970s. Two of her novels – *One for the Master* and *Ruth* – have been shortlisted for the Miles Franklin Award. Her debut crime novel, *The Trojan Dog*, introducing security consultant Sandra Mahoney, was joint winner, ACT book of the year, and has been published in North America by St Martins Press, along with the second of her Sandra Mahoney mysteries, *The White Tower*.

. . . . . .

By the same author

Tunnel Vision
Ruth
Maralinga My Love
One For The Master
The Trojan Dog
The White Tower
The House at Number 10

Eden

A SANDRA MAHONEY MYSTERY

Dorothy Johnston

Wakefield
Press

Wakefield Press
1 The Parade West
Kent Town
South Australia 5067
www.wakefieldpress.com.au

First published 2007

Copyright © Dorothy Johnston, 2007

All rights reserved. This book is copyright. Apart from any fair dealing for the purposes of private study, research, criticism or review, as permitted under the Copyright Act, no part may be reproduced without written permission. Enquiries should be addressed to the publisher.

Cover designed by Liz Nicholson, designBITE
Designed and typeset by Clinton Ellicott, Wakefield Press
Printed and bound by Hyde Park Press, Adelaide

National Library of Australia
Cataloguing-in-publication entry

Johnston, Dorothy, 1948– .
Eden: a Sandra Mahoney mystery.

ISBN 978 1 86254 760 5 (pbk.).

1. Murder – Fiction. I. Title.

A823.3

. . . . . .

To Kim Johnston

One

Eden Carmichael died on a hot Tuesday afternoon in January. He was found lying across a double bed at one of Canberra's best-known brothels, dressed in a blue and white flowered silk dress and a blonde wig.

Carmichael's loyal constituents felt betrayed by a death of such robust indignity. Not that he had many loyal constituents left. He'd never fully recovered from a spectacular public heart attack, and was rumoured to be retiring before the next election.

Others, who'd never voted for him, were drawn to the politician's death by a mixture of boredom and revulsion. A photograph had been printed in *The Canberra Times* a few days afterwards, of Carmichael in his flowered dress and wig. He stared at the camera from beneath a mass of yellow hair, one hand clutching the top button of his dress, with a dazed and wondering expression. He could have been drunk. Some of the people who sent protest letters to the newspaper concluded that he was. The most bitter and accusing of them reminded readers how Carmichael had argued that the ACT should change its laws and make prostitution legal, as though being found dead in a brothel was a logical consequence of this, and no more than he deserved.

Others speculated about who had sold the demeaning picture to the paper, whether its publication constituted a breach of privacy, and if it been taken on the day he died. None of these questions was answered in the one editorial the *Times* ran on the subject, which concentrated instead on the issue of freedom of the press.

More interesting questions, to my way of thinking, were: who had Carmichael been mocking that hot afternoon, besides himself? How had the joke of his last moments been shared?

Details continued seeping out, though not ones that threw light on these particular concerns. I wondered if the published photo was the only one that had been taken, and concluded that it seemed unlikely.

Canberra was a small enough city for any untimely public death to be felt personally. Cracks opened in the minds of citizens whose lives had in no way touched that of the Independent MLA. Television interviewers dug out anyone who had, or could claim, a connection with the man, or the club in which he'd spent his final hour, and the subject of prostitution, which had received little public attention for a decade, was daily in the news.

I lingered over my breakfast, savouring the quiet, and staring at the photograph, attracted to it as so many others were. I hadn't cut it out, but folded the page over and left it at the one end of my kitchen table cleared of children's clutter.

Carmichael faced the camera squarely. His dress looked neat. It fitted him. He wasn't wearing make-up. The picture was cut off just below the knees, so I couldn't see his shoes. He appeared to be a little nervous, as though he was waiting for someone who'd been unaccountably delayed. There was nothing to identify exactly where he was. It was an arresting picture, though not, to my mind at any rate, a degrading one.

Later that morning, after I'd washed up my few breakfast dishes, and begun work on as dry-as-dust report, one of Carmichael's former colleagues at the Assembly rang.

He introduced himself as Ken Dollimore, a veteran of Canberra politics and Carmichael's oldest rival, then asked for my partner, Ivan Semyonov. When I explained that Ivan was in Moscow, he asked me to send him a copy of a report Ivan had written for an anti-censorship lobby group.

'It's on the net,' I told him.

Dollimore seemed to be waiting for me to catch on to something he hadn't explained, and apparently didn't want to explain.

'I'm interested in anything additional your husband did for them.'

'What might that have been?'

'Oh, come now. It hardly helps Electronic Freedom's image to suppress its own research.'

It was my turn to be silent.

'This company, *CleanNet* it's called, that your husband refers to in his report, it's important to know if there's any further information about

them, in informal notes, for example, that haven't yet been published.'
I had no idea what was in Ivan's notes, but I wasn't about to admit this to Ken Dollimore, much less offer to send them to him.

'I suggest you try Electronic Freedom directly, since you seem confident of their obligation to supply you with whatever it is you're after.'

Dollimore hung up.

I recalled the last occasion I'd exchanged words with the Canberra politician. It was during a case that had ended with a young radiographer at our major hospital being charged with murder. Dollimore had been Health Minister at the time, and had done all he could to block my access to the hospital's records, even those that were supposed to be publicly available. Now here he was expecting a favour from me, and not even bothering to be polite about it.

I remembered that a woman called Lucy who worked for Electronic Freedom had rung Ivan and asked if he'd look into *CleanNet*'s history. The lobby group was campaigning vigorously against the Internet censorship legislation that had just been passed, and looking for ways to discredit its supporters. *CleanNet* produced filter software, and the company had put out a press release in support of the legislation and of mandatory content regulation. Hardly a surprise, since they stood to make money out of it.

Ivan had been in two minds about the job, but had finally agreed to do what he could in the rushed couple of weeks before he'd left for Moscow with our three-year-old daughter, Katya.

We'd celebrated our fifth anniversary as business partners just before he left. Sometimes it seemed a small miracle that our consultancy had survived, that we'd managed to go on making a living. 'Computer security checks – fast, discreet, efficient', our ad in the yellow pages said. Our names were under it – Ivan's followed by a list of diplomas and degrees, mine, Sandra Mahoney, without any such obvious recommendation. Most of our work came from small firms and agencies who wanted to improve their security, or suspected that something fishy was going on, but were unwilling to call in the police. Electronic security was big business. Ivan and I hadn't succeeded enough to expand ours, but we'd hung in there, and that, I told myself, was reason to feel pleased.

I found the report. It was very short. *CleanNet* specialised in blocking technologies for filtering out undesirable material on the Internet – that much I already knew. They were based in Sydney and had begun life as a private company in 1996 with start-up capital of a modest half million dollars, going public with their first share offer just two years later. *CleanNet* looked like hundreds of computer companies, who so far had not made any money, but had managed to attract some reasonable-sized investors on the promise that very soon they would. The world was full of people investing in the Internet. The skill was in picking a winner, or trading on promises, then getting out before the crash, which Ivan said was just around the corner. *CleanNet* was making a play for sales to schools and libraries, and, like everyone else, fighting competition from America.

I didn't know a whole lot about filters, but I did know that the technology was at a pretty crude level of development. It might stop six-year-olds coming across couples having sex, but it stopped access to a whole lot of perfectly unpornographic sites as well.

I looked up Ivan's notes, and printed out a hard copy since I couldn't find one on his desk. Eden Carmichael's name appeared in connection with a presentation *CleanNet* had put on last November for Senator Bryant, the Minister for Broadcasting and Telecommunications. Carmichael seemed to have been in favour of *CleanNet*, and impressed by the product they'd come up with. Ivan had listed all the members of the Federal Parliament, and Canberra's Legislative Assembly, who'd been at the presentation, and had checked with a friend of his, who'd confirmed that Carmichael appeared to be giving the company his blessing.

There the notes came to an abrupt end.

It wasn't unusual for politicians to become more conservative as they grew older. There were famous examples, like Winston Churchill and Billy Hughes. But the idea that Ed Carmichael should suddenly take up a pro-censorship position conflicted with everything I knew about him – not least the circumstances of his death. Why that particular switch? Why not a religious conversion, which I was sure Ken Dollimore would have loved, and brought about if he'd been able to?

I was getting ahead of myself. Perhaps Carmichael had been moving away from his small 'l' liberal views on a number of issues. I recalled the drama surrounding his first heart attack, when he'd fallen over the Blackwood banisters at the old Parliament House, landing just inside the main entrance. I hadn't seen him fall, but I had seen him lying there. Like many others present, I'd thought he was dead.

In order to avoid going back to the report I was supposed to be writing, I logged onto the Australian Securities and Investment Commission website. It was a requirement for all companies to register with ASIC – names and certain basic details, such as year and place of registration, and their directors' names. *CleanNet* had only one director, Richard McFadden.

For more details, it was necessary to pay one of the brokers. I filled in my credit card details, and typed a list of questions.

. . .

A couple of hours later, the answers were there for me to download. McFadden was listed as the major shareholder, but I was disappointed there was so little information about him available under ASIC's rules. Apparently McFadden was not, and never had been, director of any other company, nor did he own shares in any company but his own. Only the top twenty shareholders had to be included in the information that was sent to ASIC. All were fairly minor, underlining the point that *CleanNet* was McFadden's company. The top three were a brewery, a real estate group, and another group called *Herman Marcus Limited*, which was registered with a Canberra solicitor. Carmichael's name was not among the shareholders, nor was Ken Dollimore's.

CleanNet's website, which I visited next, was a mass of kindergarten colours, big balloons and beach balls with large, naively formed words around them leading to different sections of the site – mission statement, investment news – *CleanNet Is Family Friendly*. The combination of images and words was a curious one, since the product was aimed, not at children, but their parents. What preschool-aged child, the kind I imagined being attracted by red and yellow letters leaning against each other, was going to go surfing for net porn? What person over the age of eight would think the design anything other than condescending? There was something suggestive, almost obscene, about the balloons and their configuration. Collections of swollen testicles, they could have been, or silicone-inflated breasts. I looked for the site designer's name, but couldn't find one.

I did a bit of site hopping between filter companies next. I hadn't realised how much of a censorship debate had been going on at the level of online marketing, with companies out to attract buyers for their products, and their shares as well. Many sites included investment advice and nicely coloured graphs showing beautifully rising prices. Their critics pointed out how faulty the technology was, how clunky and unreliable. The names and addresses of the blocked sites were encrypted, so consumers could never find out exactly what they, or their children, were being protected from, nor were the owners of the sites informed. If you were an AIDS sufferers' support group, and had your site blocked because it happened to contain the word 'penis', there was no way you could appeal.

No one was answering the phone at Electronic Freedom. They were probably taking a long lunch break at the beach. I looked for any additional notes Ivan might have made, but couldn't find any. Ivan followed his own filing system. You needed to be trained in his eccentric form of archaeology to make sense of it.

Ivan and I shared one house, office, bed and occupation, but the words husband and wife carried too much weight to use, or even think of. A part of my wariness was that we'd both been married before. I'd known early in my first marriage that it wasn't any good, but it had taken me a long time to pay attention to this knowledge, or to act on it, while Ivan had taken years to recover from a failed marriage. Sometimes I suspected that he hadn't recovered at all.

I sent him an email, asking about links between Carmichael and *CleanNet*, and whether he'd come cross any further information concerning *CleanNet*'s director, Richard McFadden.

It depressed me that it would be at least six hours before I could expect a reply, and probably longer. Ivan was checking his mail once a day at most. Mentally and emotionally, he was far away from Canberra, concentrating on our daughter and his sisters, re-weaving threads that had loosened almost to dissolving after his parents died.

I admitted to myself that I was wasting time, and might just as well be at the pool. I was doing what I despised others for doing, leaping at any connection with Eden Carmichael to give my day a bit of excitement.

I hadn't chosen to spend most of January alone. I had my son Peter's dog, Fred, for company, but I hadn't planned it this way. I'd intended to spend the time with Peter, while Ivan and Katya were visiting Ivan's sisters. Halfway through last year, Ivan's younger sister had been diagnosed with breast cancer. She'd had a partial mastectomy and recovered well. Ivan had begun to plan his trip. Then the week before school broke up, Peter's father, Derek, had announced that he and his second wife Valerie wanted to take him to Tasmania with them. There was no question of changing Derek's mind, and Peter had been happy to go. He'd spent the time between Christmas and New Year reading about convicts.

Peter and I had been going to stay with a friend of the family, and my particular friend, Detective Sergeant Brook, who'd rented a house at Broulee for two weeks. When I'd told Brook about the changed plans, he'd been annoyed, and had plodded off to the coast on his own.

. . .

By three in the afternoon, the office at the back of the house throbbed with a steady pulse of hot, dry air. It moved across scorched grass, through walls, paying no attention to drawn curtains or the fan on three.

I checked that Fred's bucket had plenty of water, and walked over to Dickson for a swim.

Fred was getting on, not so lively now, especially in the heat. He seemed content to spend his days stretched out on the kitchen floor tiles, occasionally padding down the corridor to say hello, or let me know he wanted to go out.

At Dickson Pool, I pulled a cap over my short hair, tensing the muscles in my legs and pretending for a moment that I was eighteen again. I joined the serious swimmers in their lap lanes, though not the fast one, which had a sign at the end asking swimmers to please be realistic when they chose it. Clouds were massing behind Mt Majura, but the forecast that morning had been the same as always – fine and hot.

Water, and the slosh of my slow but steady freestyle, woke me up. Each down stroke, I studied the blue-tiled bottom of the pool through my goggles. I stopped at the shallow end to rest my forearms on the burning concrete, and felt pleased at the prospect of a long, uninterrupted evening.

Dollimore's phone call had been strange, no doubt about it, too intense for an expression of general curiosity. Canberra was on holiday, absent from itself, but something was beginning. I could feel it. I realised that the mischievous part of me, which came to the surface when I was less than fully occupied, like now, would love the chance to slide a splinter under Ken Dollimore's skin.

I'd been waiting until the sun was almost gone behind O'Connor Ridge before taking Fred for a walk. I liked the moment when the lights came on along the bike path, then in the houses that straggled up the hill. Half an hour or so in the warm dusk seemed enough for him. He didn't stray far from me, and his interest in the high school rubbish bins was in abeyance until the kids went back in February.

I made myself a light meal, then jotted down what I knew about Carmichael. The coroner was expected to find that his death had been caused by heart failure. He'd been well known for his progressive views on prostitution and pornography, and had played, if not the key role then a significant one, in changing the laws in 1992, several years after the ACT gained self-government. It was due largely to his efforts that brothels were legal in Canberra's light industrial zones of Fyshwick, Hume and Mitchell, escort work was city wide, and X-rated videos and magazines could be sold openly to anybody over eighteen. Our small national capital had become a centre for mail-order distribution of pornography to states with stricter laws.

Two

Ivan's reply to my email arrived sooner than I'd hoped. He might have turned up more on *CleanNet* if he'd had the time, but nothing had looked dodgy as far as he could tell. Only someone reading his notes would have seen the mention of Carmichael's name. He hadn't talked to anyone about it, apart from Chris Laskaris at the Internet Industry Group. It had been Laskaris who'd confirmed that Carmichael seemed in favour of the filter package.

When I finally got onto Lucy at Electronic Freedom, she said Ken Dollimore had rung her to ask about Ivan's report. Before that, she'd never heard of him.

'What did you tell him?' I asked.

'Where to find the published stuff.'

'And the notes Ivan sent before he left?'

'Notes are a euphemism right? I didn't pass them on.'

The anti-censorship group was funded by membership levies. Lucy did a part-time shift in the office, answering phones and correspondence, on top of a better-paying job. When she picked up the phone, she always sounded as though she was in the middle of a crisis, and talking to me was a favour that, any second now, she'd be forced to withdraw. I'd never met her, but I imagined her having a face and body that went with the voice – short hair, loose-fitting shirts and trousers made from materials that never needed ironing. I could identify with that.

'Dollimore got up your nose?' I said. 'He got up mine as well.'

'I asked him what he wanted, but he wouldn't say.'

I told Lucy I'd been surprised to find that Eden Carmichael had been at *CleanNet*'s presentation. 'I wonder if Dollimore persuaded him to go.'

'He's on the religious right, isn't he? That's what frustrates me about these evangelicals. They don't understand the technology, what it can and can't do, but they're out there making promises to people.'

'Who saw Ivan's notes?' I asked.

'No one outside this office.'

'Someone must have told Dollimore about them.'

'All *CleanNet* cares about is making money,' Lucy said impatiently. 'They couldn't give a shit about what the legislation might do to the industry as a whole, or how it's going to stuff up the net.'

'The Carmichael connection would be what Dollimore is after.'

'You could be right.'

I enquired about payment for Ivan's report. Lucy said she hoped he might have got a bit further than he had.

There was a short silence, then I said, 'I wouldn't mind digging round a bit.'

'I'll run it past the committee. Your rates would be the same as your partner's?'

I confirmed this, then added, 'If you wouldn't mind paying for services already rendered? Ivan's currently supplying Moscow with about half its foreign currency.'

Lucy agreed to this, then told me she had another call.

I put the phone down, feeling pleased. Here was a job for me and no one else. Ivan was away. Ken Dollimore would certainly have insisted on speaking to him, if he hadn't been on the far side of the world. If there really was a link between Eden Carmichael and *CleanNet*, it was up to me to find it. At the same time, I wondered what I was letting myself in for. I was used to having Ivan to talk to. I was used to noise and children's chatter, not solitary thoughts echoing through hot, still rooms.

. . .

Herman Marcus Limited was registered with a firm of solicitors called *Benjamin Plant and Partners*. I rang them and asked if I could have a look at some annual reports. Then I rang Chris Laskaris and made an appointment to see him.

I bought *CleanNet*'s package from a local computer shop, had a bit of a play round with it, then made myself an early lunch and drove over the lake to the solicitors' suite of offices. I was shown into a small comfortable room, so comfortable that, once I'd been sitting in one of the dark-brown leather chairs for about ten minutes, I started feeling sleepy. I'd been given a stack of annual reports and left alone to read them.

Herman Marcus was a group of Canberra-based IT firms. I was surprised to find the group had chosen to invest in *CleanNet*. Representatives of several of the firms had given evidence to the Senate Select Committee On Information Technologies, and had expressed views that, if not quite at Electronic Freedom's end of the spectrum, were broadly against the legislation, and sceptical about whether filters would do any of the things that their manufacturers claimed.

Business is business? Maybe so. Maybe there was nothing remarkable in that. I'd learnt from *CleanNet*'s website that their shares had gone from $12 to $53 in the week they were released. They'd hovered in the $40 to $50 range ever since. I was no expert when it came to the stock market, but it seemed to me that investors looking to make money quickly would have made it and got out by now. I wondered if this meant that those who remained were in for the long haul, that they believed *CleanNet* had a superior product that could beat American imports and survive the impending crash. I pondered the ethics of it – saying one thing publicly, in front of a Senate committee, and putting your money in another.

I also wondered why none of the business journalists had picked up the anomaly. My friend at the *Times*, Gail Trembath, recently back from a year and a half in South-East Asia, wasn't a business journalist, but she might be interested.

I made a list of what was obvious, hoping to clear my mind of this, and allow room for more original thoughts to emerge. I glanced up at the Western Desert dot paintings on the walls, then gave in to my impulse to snoop. I opened desk drawers and scanned the spines of loose-leaf binders lined up in rows on heavy walnut bookshelves.

In the drawers, I found stationery, a hole punch and stapler that looked as though they'd never been used, packets of paperclips, pads of paper with the firm's logo at the top. The young woman who'd shown me into the office had taken down several volumes from a loaded shelf. I hadn't realised that so many computer companies were registered with *Plant and Partners*.

Ivan's report contained nothing that could not be gained from spending an hour going through the public records. It was no wonder that Lucy had been frustrated by how little he'd produced. Again, I asked myself what Ken Dollimore was looking for.

. . .

Chris Laskaris's office was on the third floor of Industry House. There was an intercom outside. While waiting to be buzzed in, I peered through double-glass doors at thick green carpet, a curved reception desk, framed small business awards sharing wall space with more dot paintings.

The office was open plan. Chris took me to an alcove with a desk, computer and two chairs. His smile said nice to see you. Chris and Ivan had met as students, though Chris was much younger, and obviously on the fast track even then. He'd started an ISP business with another young Greek guy, in a garage in O'Connor. They'd parted company, and I didn't know what had happened to his ex-partner, but Chris had gone from garage to office to bigger office to industry representative. He'd put himself on the record as opposing Internet censorship, and at the same time had got the best deal he could for the people who now paid his salary.

'I wanted to ask you about this censorship stuff, how it's panning out,' I said.

Chris was wearing the bottom half of a suit that I didn't think Ivan would ever be able to afford, a white shirt with the sleeves rolled up to the elbow, and no tie. He pushed his sleeves up further, a gesture that revealed his smooth tanned arms.

'You're in a difficult position,' I prompted, 'I mean, with your members having to supply filters when you don't believe they can do the job the politicians have promised Australian families they'll do.'

'Tell me about it.' Chris smiled, then made a deprecating face, head on one side. He looked as though he swam every evening, three kilometres to my half a one. He looked like he'd been born knowing how to play both sides against the middle.

The On-line Services Bill, Chris explained, which had come into effect on January 1, did two things. It set up a complaints mechanism so that people could object to offensive Internet sites, and the Australian Broadcasting Authority could order them to be taken down – a futile process, critics of the legislation said, since the owners of the sites would simply move offshore. In addition, Australian Internet Service Providers were required to provide filters, or other kinds of blocking software, to their customers. This was where *CleanNet* and their many competitors came in.

'What about *CleanNet*?' I asked. 'Is their package any better than the others?'

'Have you tried it?'

'It blocked the National Party site. Is that meant to be a joke?'

Chris laughed and said, 'It's not technically possible to produce a reliable filter.'

'Will it be, in the near future?'

'I don't believe so. I'm a programmer, and I know how these things work. The marketing people sell a product, then tell the programmers to make it. When the programmers say it can't be done, their opinions are swept aside as unnecessarily modest.'

'A compromise is reached?'

'Usually.'

'But usually without a political spotlight.'

'Usually without that, yes. We're between a rock and a hard place on this one. Consumer legislation states that companies must provide products that are fit for the purpose for which they are sold. So the consumers who need protection may end up suing the companies for not providing what we said *couldn't* be provided because it wasn't technically possible.'

Chris shrugged and spread his hands, palms downwards on the desk.

'The companies supplying the software aren't Australian for the most part,' he went on. 'Nor are they members of our association. But you can see how our members will be caught.'

'*CleanNet*'s Australian, though,' I pointed out.

'And the guy heading them up is very patriotic.'

I caught something in Chris's tone. 'You don't like Richard McFadden?'

'He was in town for the hearing. Someone set him up with a special presentation for the Minister.'

I made a mental note that Chris hadn't answered my question directly, then said, 'I've been told Eden Carmichael was impressed by what McFadden had to offer.'

Chris shrugged and said he'd seemed to be.

'Do you think Carmichael might have been changing sides, throwing in his lot with the pro-censorship lobby?'

'I wouldn't go that far necessarily. I didn't really know the guy. He didn't discuss his opinions with me.'

Sensing Chris didn't want to be pushed on Carmichael, and would clam up if I tried, I went back a step. 'So your association is the meat in the sandwich.'

'Our brief is to serve the interests of our members, not all of whom are going to be of the one political persuasion. That's one big difference between us and EF for instance. You don't join *them* if you're pro-censorship. Unless you're a mole.'

'But your group can have members who are both pro and anti.'

'In theory, according to our constitution.'

'And in practice?'

'In practice most of our members are anti-censorship, certainly in the form of the present legislation.'

'But you took part in the debate about it, you succeeded in getting it modified, and now your members are going to have to implement it.'

'That's right.'

'I heard a rumour that the Labor Party was about to toughen its position.'

Chris looked grim.

'Forcing ISPs to filter content, isn't that rather a turn-around for Labor?'

'I'm not sure I follow you.'

'Labor used to have a less severe position on censorship than the Coalition.'

But Chris refused to be drawn on the rumoured policy change. 'Strange times we live in,' was all he said.

'Is *CleanNet* a member of the Internet Industry Group?' I asked.

'I can't tell you that. You see,' Chris smiled to soften his refusal, 'if you look at the code of ethics we've been developing, through months and months of consultation and incredibly hard work I might say, there's a lot of emphasis on getting international agreement to ban certain sorts of traffic – child pornography, incitement to racial hatred – these things are covered by the Crimes Act in Australia. We don't need special legislation for them here. But getting international controls to work is another story. It's not that this government isn't aware of the international perspective. They know that controls applied within Australia aren't going to be all that effective.'

'What about *CleanNet*'s competitors? Aren't they going to be pissed off at what appears to be favourable treatment?'

'Most of them are American.' Chris paused, then added, 'There's the list, of course.'

'What list?'

'Senator Bryant's about to announce a short list of filters that will carry a government recommendation. There's even some talk of the government supplying them for free.'

'Is *CleanNet* on the list?'

'No one knows who's on it. Not officially.'

'Unofficially?'

'I honestly don't know.'

'When will it be announced?'

'The word is any day.'

'What's McFadden like?' I asked, realising Chris wasn't going to tell me any more about the list just then.

'Maverick,' Chris said.

'He runs his own show, you mean?'

'I mean Maverick with a capital 'M'. He grew up on American Westerns and people say that he's addicted to them. He used to get around in a black shirt, cowboy boots and stetson. And gambling. He was here to lobby, and he did a fine job there. But he spent most of his time in the casino.'

'Did he win?'

'Claims he did. Mind you, if he lost, I don't think he'd admit it.'

'What about you? Are you a gambling man?'

'Not that kind. McFadden loves Americans, and he loves to hate them. That's partly what this super-competitiveness is about. Beat the Yanks at what the Yanks do best.'

'What about his ethical position with regard to censorship?'

'I'd say it's pretty basic.'

'He's determined to make money out of it?'

Chris nodded.

'He and Senator Bryant must be quite a pair.'

'Know how he started off his presentation? Of the top ten websites accessed by employees of a company, the number one site will be something to do with stocks, and the second one with sex. So you can see what drives the human psyche.'

'That got a laugh from everybody present?'

'It broke the ice. We're all human, all in this together.'

'Maybe Bryant liked him because he's so up-front.'

'I think that's probably one twist too many. McFadden wants to win. He wants to beat the competition, and he wants the biggest possible audience to watch him doing it.'

'Was he dressed in his Western gear?'

'Definitely not. Dark suit, white shirt, short back and sides.'

'Sounds like a man selling religion.'

'The other side of the image, I suppose. Evangelism comes in all shapes and sizes.'

'Who else was at the presentation?'

'The usual suspects. Actually, someone I didn't expect to see. Stan Walewicz. You know him?'

'I know of him. He makes porn movies, is that right?'

Chris nodded again. 'Looking very prim and proper. Keeping in the background too.'

'He doesn't usually?'

'I don't know him personally, but when I *have* seen him in action – let's say he gave me the impression that he's a man who likes to be noticed too.'

'Do you think anybody else there recognised him?'

'Hard to say. He didn't advertise his presence, but he did nothing to disguise it either.'

'What do you think he was doing there?'

'Sussing out the enemy? Your guess is as good as mine. I didn't talk to him.'

I looked at Chris, knowing that he would have avoided a known pornographer at a gathering like that. Everybody present would have, that is those who'd recognised him.

'Did he speak to McFadden?'

'Not that I'm aware of.'

'When did you last see Eden Carmichael?'

'It would have been the twenty-first. We put on a bit of a Christmas do.'

'And invited the local pollies. How many turned up?'

'A few.'

'Ken Dollimore?'

'He dropped in.'

'How did he and Carmichael seem? Were they talking to each other?'

'Carmichael was drunk,' Chris said.

'Did Dollimore try and sober him up?'

'Fat chance.'

'You were at that party, weren't you? At the old Parliament House. Where Carmichael had his heart attack.'

Chris's brown eyes became wary. 'Yes,' was all he said.

It had been one of those crowded functions with lots of free booze, guests squashed against pillars and each other, a noise level that made attempting any kind of business hard. Doing business, or trying to, had been the reason I was there. I didn't much enjoy the networking part of my job, and that night it had been a waste of time.

'Did you talk to Carmichael that night?' I asked.

'I bumped into him in the men's. He was pissed.'

'What did you say?'

'I asked him if he was okay. He said, "What's it look like, *mate*." I thought, stuff you then. He wasn't that old, only fifty-seven. If he'd decided to look after himself after that he'd be alive now, wouldn't he?'

'Did you notice Ken Dollimore that night, I mean after Carmichael fell?'

'He was ahead of me on the stairs. There was that doctor too. There were lots of people gawking.'

'Did you notice where Dollimore went?'

'No.'

'How long did you stay?'

'Till the ambulance came. I felt – I don't know – not responsible, but I'd seen the guy in the men's not ten minutes before, and he was obviously out of it. I should have offered to drive him home. It's not as though he was a friend or anything, but I should have offered.'

'Did he say anything else? Did you notice anything else?'

Chris flushed with anger. 'He – he couldn't get his fly done up.'

He looked at his watch, perhaps to avoid meeting my eyes, or to let me know my time was up. I thanked him for talking to me, and agreed to pass on his best wishes to Ivan.

. . .

When I tried to access Stan Walewicz's website and found that it had been taken down, I decided to give him a call. His number was easy to find in both the white and yellow pages. He sounded mildly surprised, but, after a few moments, as interested in meeting me as I was in meeting him. He'd heard of me and knew about our consultancy. When I commiserated with him over the closure of his site, he laughed and told me there were ways around it.

He was heading back to the coast that afternoon. He'd only just popped in to pick up his mail. We arranged a time to meet after his holiday.

I sat back in my chair and stared out the office window at my dying lawn, which summer water restrictions had forbidden me to water. I felt annoyed with Ivan for not referring to the Minister's recommended list in his notes, and even more for his failure to mention that Richard McFadden was well known for his gambling. Surely this was the kind of detail Electronic Freedom had been after when they'd asked him to do some background research on the company. Though Lucy hadn't spelt it out, rumours about McFadden's gambling may have been what had drawn Electronic Freedom's attention to *CleanNet* in the first place. Ivan had barely scratched the surface. To be fair, he'd made the point about being pressed for time himself.

I narrowed my eyes against the glare outside. Since Ivan's report and notes were so lacking in detail, that rather left the field open for me to provide it.

. . .

Over the next couple of days, I contacted all the Canberra companies listed as belonging to the *Herman Marcus* group. Some of the people who spoke to me knew Dollimore, and had known Carmichael reasonably well. They were happy to chat about both men, speculate on the reasons behind their disputes and long-lasting friendship, and help me fill in details of local IT businesses. I learnt, among other things, that Carmichael and Dollimore had gone to school together. But none admitted to knowing of any special connection between Carmichael and *CleanNet*, or was willing to express an opinion about *CleanNet* beyond saying their product was competitive. When I pushed for their views on censorship, the opinion came back to me, blandly expressed, though not without sincerity, that many parents and schools wished to restrict children's access to sites they considered unsuitable. It was a straightforward case of supplying a demand.

I made myself finish the report that I'd been putting off, then wrote an assessment for Lucy, dressing it up a bit and making it seem as though Richard McFadden's love of gambling might be casting a mantle over other vices. I had to be careful, but I needed to whet her appetite as well.

. . .

Ivan had a predilection for gadgets, which I was gradually weaning him off, or so I thought. When I first met him, the main room of his house had been converted into a cross between a computer museum and an inner-north Canberra spy station. He also loved playing around with digital images. A message, any message, was improved by pictures. Ivan's latest, conceived a couple of weeks before he left Australia, was a series of small flags, all variations on the Australian one.

I noticed one of these flags pulsating in the top left-hand corner of my computer screen, and cursed Ivan under my breath. I couldn't remember what each of the flags was for. It was like him not to have taken me through them before he left, or to have provided any kind of key. This one was mainly red. I double clicked it. A xylophone played an arthritic 'Waltzing Matilda'. A message came up on the screen saying that someone had tried to hack into my computer.

I rang Lucy, who sounded more relaxed than she had the last time, and chuckled when I told her about the flags. Like any business with a clientele to protect, the lobby group had ways of guarding sensitive files. She kept me on the line while she checked their log. There was no record of an attempted break-in over the last forty-eight hours.

Had my would-be hacker been after the *CleanNet* material, or was the timing a coincidence? Ivan and I had had our share of snoopers. We were an obvious target. Ivan didn't mind. It was all part of the game to him.

I emailed him to let him know what had happened. Because I wasn't sure what message his notes might contain for a would-be thief, I copied them to a disk which, after thinking about safe places and not-so-safe places, I sticky-taped to the roof of Fred's kennel. Fred sniffed at it, then, realising that it wasn't food, showed no more interest. Then I burnt the hard copy, and deleted the file from my computer, thoroughly deleted it, as Ivan had taught me to do.

Three

In Canberra, prostitution was zoned light industrial, and the zoning system seemed to work. The suburbs of Mitchell, Hume and Fyshwick mixed brothels and X-rated movie rentals with used cars, discounted white goods and shops selling computers. Their streets were deserted after dark, except for a cluster of sex traders, single lines of ant cars heading towards honey, or a corpse.

I stood at the corner of the street that Eden Carmichael had driven to, parked in, habitually crossed, and squinted at the lines of low-slung, cheap, no-nonsense buildings. White wood swelled in the January heat. Grosvenor Street, Mitchell, looked like the main street of a country town, wide as our local rivers never were, a row of parched eucalypts along one side, stamp-sized shadows underneath the awnings. I smelt raw pine furniture, and felt that deep quiet of a country town in the middle of a summer day, when not much can happen out of doors. A timber yard backed onto paddocks, where sheep and cattle rested behind fences, under the little shade that they could find.

Inland homogenising light filled every opening. I shaded my eyes and spotted number 23. It was built on the same model as its neighbours, regular and squat, except for a circular neon sign, unlit now, that said *Margot's* in a curly script.

My phone call to Margot Lancaster had been brief. As soon as I'd introduced myself, she'd asked if I knew any journalists. I'd replied that I did. Margot had asked whether any of them would be interested in telling her side of the story. When I'd said I had a friend who might, Margot immediately wanted a name. Realising I had a bargaining chip, perhaps my only one, I'd persuaded her to talk to me first.

. . .

Margot's close-fitting hair was dyed a deep blue-black. The sleek helmet suited her. She was tall and slim, dressed neatly in a navy pants-suit. Air-conditioning made her club's small foyer a pleasant twenty-two degrees.

I asked her if she'd mind showing me around.

Her nod of agreement was a small, economical, unrevealing gesture. Silently, she led the way to the back of the building, where I heard music and laughter through a door.

Margot opened another door and stood to one side. In the centre of the room was a queen-sized bed, covered by a dark-blue quilt. The walls and ceiling were painted creamy-white, the blinds fully closed. A TV and DVD player stood opposite the bed. Apart from this, a polished pine bedside table with a lamp, and a chair upholstered in heavy cotton were the only furniture.

It was very still, the only sound coming from the air-conditioning. I pictured the room when it was occupied, filling out, becoming a space lit subtly by the lamp, taking on the shape of a couple having sex. Daylight would fade, night bring its own custom. I gazed around the room, knowing, without having to ask, that it was the one Eden Carmichael had died in. Though there were no obvious, outward indications, I sensed that it had become a kind of shrine.

I turned to Margot. There seemed to be a filament of blown glass between us and the world outside, and I felt suddenly close to her, as though, if we remained there a few minutes longer, I would grasp what lay behind her silence and her self-control.

She turned quickly on her heel, and led the way back to the front of the building, where there was a reception desk with a computer, phone and fax machine.

Positioning herself behind the desk, she looked me up and down, noting my bare legs, the awkward repair job I'd done on one of my sandal straps, my plain denim skirt and T-shirt. My hair was almost as short as hers, cropped for the summer, and I wore no make-up. Perhaps I should have felt discomforted by Margot's scrutiny, her hint of disdain for someone who took as little trouble over her appearance as I did, but my aim just then was to give her the impression I was harmless, and I hoped I was doing that.

When she decided to speak, her voice was brisk, with an undertone of contempt. 'I run a good business here. You know reporters, and you're pally with the cops. They kicked me out of my own club for two days while they went over everything with their fingerprint brushes, and took the mattress away for DNA testing. A lot of good that will do them. I can't see them taking samples from half this town's MPs to get a match, can you?'

Knowing I wasn't expected to answer, I asked a question instead. 'How did Eden Carmichael die?'

'He had a heart attack. The autopsy confirmed it.'

I didn't say what was surely obvious to Margot, that the death of a cross-dressing politician was bound to be treated as sensitive. The forensic people were not likely to risk taking short cuts.

'I'm being treated like a suspect,' Margot complained. 'All I want is for someone to give me a fair hearing.'

She'd agreed to my visit because she thought I could help her. But 'pally' was not a word I would have used just then to describe my relationship with the police. I wondered how much she knew about my association with Detective Sergeant Brook, how much she'd made it her business to find out.

'At least the TV cameras have gone,' she said, 'but the phone keeps ringing all the time. If it's not some preacher abusing me, it's a reporter trying to trip me up. "Sixty Minutes" wants to do an interview.'

'Not "Sixty Minutes". Say no.'

'That's what I thought. But who?'

'My friend works for *The Canberra Times*,' I said.

'Them! They published that revolting photograph.'

'They've also published the letters of complaint.'

'Yes. But not one sticking up for me.'

'I'll speak to my friend about it. The editor might be happy to print your side of the story.'

'Would he show the article to me before it was published?'

'She. I believe she would. I'll ask her. Could the photo have been taken on the day Carmichael died?'

'Not from here,' Margot said emphatically. 'I'd never do that to a client. Never. Just because I run a club, people assume that I've got no moral standards.'

'Would you mind telling me what happened that afternoon?'

After giving me another long look, this time accompanied by a wary frown, Margot explained that soon after Denise had gone into the room with Carmichael, there'd been a phone call from the holiday camp where Denise's daughter was staying. The girl, whom Margot referred to as Rebecca, had sprained her wrist. She was upset, and Denise had left Carmichael to speak to her.

'Did he always see Denise?'

'Yes.'

'How long was he on his own?'

'About ten minutes.'

'Did he already have his dress on?'

'Yes, he did.'

'Did Denise shut the door?'

'It was slightly open.'

'Did you hear any noise?'

'No.'

'Where were you?'

'Here at my desk.'

'Where did Denise go to talk on the phone?'

'The room next door.'

'Did anyone come to the front door? Did the phone ring?'

'No.'

'What were you doing during that time?'

Margot flushed and looked embarrassed, as if this small detail was the odd one. 'I was doing the crossword in the newspaper.'

'Who else was here?'

'That's it.'

'Just you and Denise?'

'And Ed, of course.'

'Wasn't it unusual to have just one girl on?'

'January's our quietest time.'

'What time *was* it?'

'When Ed arrived? Around four-thirty. A bit after.'

'Had he made an appointment?'

'No.'

'Was that usual?'
'Sometimes he made appointments, sometimes he just turned up.'
'Did he always wear the dress?'
'It was his dress. He brought it with him.'
'Why didn't he leave it here?'
'He liked to wash it himself.'
'And the wig?'
'That stayed here. It's mine. I mean, it's the club's property.'
'Other clients used it?'
'From time to time.'
'But Carmichael always did?'
'Yes.'
'Where's it kept?'
'In its box. It's a valuable wig. Real hair.'
'Where is it now?'
'The police still have it. And the dress.'
'What happened when Denise went back to Carmichael?'
'She called out. Screamed. I ran in. Ed was lying on the bed. We tried to revive him, but we couldn't. I phoned the ambulance.'
'Had he seemed upset?'
'No.'
'Had he been drinking?'
Margot paused, then said, 'About as much as usual.'
'Apart from his heart, did you know of any other health problems?'
Margot shook her head.
'How long had he been a client?'
'For about three years.'
'Did he visit other clubs as well?'
'No.'
I wondered how she could be so sure.
'What about Ken Dollimore? Has he ever been a customer?'
'I know my local politicians. Clients use false names, but they don't often go to the trouble of disguising themselves.'
'Perhaps not as a client?'
'I have never met Ken Dollimore.'
'But you knew he was Eden Carmichael's close friend.'

Margot studied me before replying. 'You're mistaken,' she said finally, 'if you think a client would discuss politics with any of the girls here.'

I wondered why she felt it necessary to make this disclaimer.

'Has Dollimore phoned you, been in contact with you?'

'Look, I've done you a favour, talking to you like this. I think I've answered enough questions, don't you?'

Margot was expecting a favour in return, but since we both knew that, there didn't seem much point in repeating it. When she shut the door behind me, I could feel her relief.

I ducked involuntarily, meeting with the heat again, a solid wall, white and hard and entirely lacking moisture.

The discount tyre place next door to Margot's club did not go in for air-conditioning. I stood sweating underneath a fan in a small office, while an adolescent boy went to get the manager.

I'd told him I was a private investigator who'd been hired by Eden Carmichael's family. The manager, when he came in, didn't ask to see my ID, which was just as well. He seemed inclined to treat Carmichael's demise as a joke. 'The old fool had it coming to him,' was his first remark. He looked to be in his mid fifties himself, judging by his weathered face, but his body was straight and hard-looking, and his brown eyes bright with the opportunity for a bit of gossip. I would not have been surprised to find that he was one of Margot's customers. Mentally, I filed the question away as one I might ask later. Now I wanted to concentrate on January 4.

'Were you at work?' I asked him.

'Yep. I take my holidays in winter. Head up north. We had Christmas week off and re-opened on the third.'

'Did you see Eden Carmichael arriving?'

'Can't say I did.' The manager looked sorry to be disappointing me. 'Don't notice every punter. Some days it's quiet, some nights the carpark's full, though they've never had a night like that, I must say.'

'You mean so busy?'

'I mean with the police cars and the ambulance.'

'Did you know Carmichael was a regular?'

'Silly old coot. Poncing in there with his shopping bag. He didn't care who saw him.'

'Do you know what was in the bag?'

'Me and the boys speculated. It was one of those fancy ones with handles.'

'But you realised what it was once you saw the photo in *The Canberra Times*.'

The manager laughed.

'Any idea who took the photo?'

'Not a clue.'

'Did you see anyone with a camera hanging round?'

'Negative to that too, I'm afraid.'

'What do you think of the girls?'

'The girls are nice.'

I wondered if he was leaving Margot out, making a distinction. 'Denise?' I asked.

'Denny's gorgeous,' he said without a hint of embarrassment. I thought he might have answered my curiosity on one point.

'When did you first know that something was wrong?'

'When the ambulance came screaming down the road. Thought it was a car smash.'

'What happened then?'

'Paramedics dashed inside. When one of them came out, I asked what was going on, but he wouldn't tell me.'

'Did the police interview you?'

'It was getting close to knock-off time. A guy in uniform came over and asked us to wait. He didn't want us going home until he'd spoken to us.'

'How many of you were there?'

'Just me and Robbie. You met Robbie. There's only three of us. Lex's got a young family. He takes his leave in January. A detective came and asked us questions, like did we see Carmichael? What time? Who else went in and out?'

'Did you see anybody else go in that afternoon?'

'No one. No cars. No taxis. And I can't imagine Johns catching the bus.'

'What time did Denise and Margot arrive?'

'Margot got there first. At lunchtime, around one it would have been. I'd gone round the corner for some sandwiches. Her car was pulling up when I got back.'

'And Denise?'

'That was later.'

'You saw her?'

He coloured slightly. 'Yes.'

'What time?'

'Before four.'

Robbie came in with a question from a customer, and we said goodbye. I didn't think he was holding anything back. On the contrary, he would have enjoyed having more of a story to share.

I wondered what Margot had been doing for three hours on her own, and if it was usual for her to get to work early in the afternoon. Her other neighbouring business, a shop selling reconditioned office equipment, had been closed on January 4, the receptionist told me. She was cold to the point of rudeness, and I knew I'd get very little out of her. She was clearly sick of being asked about Ed Carmichael.

The timber yard opposite covered an area equal to that of *Margot's* and the tyre and furniture places combined. Though it had been open on that Tuesday, neither the receptionist nor any of the workmen had noticed Carmichael arriving. At least that's what the receptionist said. Everyone at work that day had been questioned by the police. She was afraid she had nothing more to tell me.

. . .

The Legislative Assembly building was a modest rectangle, intoned within a city block. I listened to the weather report on my way there. Already thirty-eight degrees.

In the air-conditioned interior, Carmichael's former PA, Laura Scott, lifted curious dark-brown eyes, well prepared to be distracted by my visit.

Before asking me to take a seat, she looked me up and down, as Margot had, giving me the feeling she'd been hoping for somebody more interesting. As for herself, she was dressed and made-up for a date with Brad Pitt. Her perfect tan made me more than ever conscious of my freckles, and the creases in my skirt.

'You wouldn't believe these letters.' Laura sighed. 'I've had people ringing me up and abusing me. Photographs of women tied up. Whips. Gang rapes.'

'Who sends them?'

'Religious nutters. It's as though I've got a direct line to Ed, wherever he's gone. Hell, I'm sure they believe.'

'Have you told the police?'

'That detective's nice.' When I didn't comment on this, Laura said, 'Ed's heart packed up. There's no mystery about it.'

When I'd rung Laura and said I'd like to come and talk to her about Eden Carmichael, she'd sounded curious to meet me. She'd recognised my name from a case I'd been involved with a few years earlier, the same one that had led to my run-in with Ken Dollimore. The publicity that case had gained was opening doors, and I felt grateful for it.

As we continued to size each other up, Laura doing nothing to hide an interest that was tinged with disappointment at my lack of glamour, it occurred to me that she was probably without a job. No one was going to employ her to answer a dead man's hate mail. She didn't seem anxious though. Perhaps she'd already been offered another one.

'What about Ken Dollimore?' I asked.

'What about him?'

'Where does he fit in?'

'He's devastated.'

'But in public he and Carmichael were enemies.'

Laura made a face. 'It suited them. Well, it suited Ken, and Ed had learnt to live with it.'

Her tone was tolerant, even affectionate.

'The feud got pretty nasty, didn't it? Didn't Dollimore once accuse Carmichael of poisoning his dog?'

'That was horrible,' Laura said, with another face, of revulsion this time. 'Max was gorgeous, and he was only three years old. You don't think Ed did it, do you? Ed wouldn't hurt a fly. Besides, their arguments were all noise and no action.'

'You mean a front.'

'If you like.'

'For what?'

'Like I said, it suited them.'

'And in private?'

'They'd known each other forever. They were mates,' Laura added, as though no further explanation was necessary.

I thought that it was time to bring up *CleanNet*. 'I've been told Carmichael was impressed by one of these new filters for blocking out undesirable material on the Internet. Could Dollimore have helped to change his mind?'

Laura gave me a long look. When she spoke, I thought her reply had been rehearsed.

'The censorship legislation's Federal, that's the first point. The states and territories are forced to implement it, or try to. Ed was a practical man. Once he'd accepted that something was a fact of life, he'd find a way to deal with it.'

'What about *CleanNet*?'

'Do you mean the company that put on a show for Senator Bryant last year?'

'What did he say about it?'

'Pretty good, he thought. He thought the guy in charge was interesting. I've forgotten his name. A character, he said.'

'Richard McFadden's his name. Did you ever meet him?'

'No.'

'Do you know if Carmichael bought shares in their company?'

'He would have declared them if he had.' Laura's tone suggested that whatever faults her former boss had had, dishonesty wasn't one of them.

I told her Ken Dollimore had phoned me wanting information about *CleanNet* and asked her what she knew about his interest in the company. She said she hadn't known he *was* interested.

'Ken didn't go to the presentation, I do know that much. Ed told me.'

'What did he say?'

'Just that Ken wasn't there.'

'Do you think they'd discussed going together?'

'I don't know.'

Laura had called Ed Carmichael practical. I wondered how practical accorded with his visits to Margot Lancaster's club, his blue dress and yellow wig, indifference to his heart condition.

'You know what I've just realised?' Laura said, as though my question had been voiced aloud. 'I'm beginning to think I didn't really know Ed at all. I keep on seeing that stupid wig. It's like the joke's on me, like he's having a go at *me*. I know that's crazy, but it's the way everyone around here's been making me feel. I've even started thinking maybe Ed only went into politics as a joke.'

'On whom?'

Laura gave me a sideways, speculative look. 'Himself.'

'Why would he bother?'

'Boredom. To fill in time.'

'What was he waiting for?'

'It's funny you should put it that way. I've never thought of it quite like that, but he *was* waiting.'

'Who for?'

'I don't know.'

'Did he have a girlfriend?'

'No.'

'You're sure?'

'I think I would have known.'

'A boyfriend?'

'I don't think so. Ed wasn't the kind of guy who hid stuff. It wasn't his style.'

'But he was secretive about some things.'

'Why do you say that?'

'How many people knew about his dressing up?'

'Enough, obviously.'

'That was bad,' I said, 'blasting his picture across the paper like that. Do you have any idea who took it?'

'No.'

'Ed never suspected he was being photographed?'

'If he did, he didn't tell me.'

'What about his family?'

'He didn't have any. Not immediate family.'

I recalled seeing a West Australian cousin being interviewed on television, and thinking at the time that he was possibly the closest relative the press had been able to find.

'What about his will?' I asked.

'I don't know anything about that.'

'Would you mind telling me what were you doing on the fourth of January?'

'It might sound callous, but I had a very ordinary day.'

'What about phone calls?'

'This guy I'm seeing – kind of seeing – rang. We chatted for a bit.'

'Anyone else?'

'Ed had an appointment with Senator Bryant. I'd made it for him before Christmas. The fourth was the Senator's first day back at work. But then they rang and cancelled.'

'What time was the appointment?'

'Four o'clock.'

'Do you know what it was for?'

'No.'

'Why was it cancelled?'

'Something came up. That's all I was told.'

'What time did they ring?'

'It was lunchtime, twenty to one. Ed had gone to get some sandwiches.'

'What did he say when he got back?'

'He was annoyed.'

'Upset?'

'Yes, you could say that.'

'Had he been upset before?'

'What do you mean?'

'Earlier that day.'

'He looked tired and worried, exhausted actually, and –'

'And?'

'Hung-over,' Laura said resignedly.

'Did you ask what was worrying him?'

'He wouldn't say.'

'What happened then?'

'I went out to the post office, and to get something to eat myself. When I came back, Ed had left. I never saw him again.'

'Did he have a mobile phone?'

'He refused to get one. He said they fried your brains.'

The phone rang and Laura indicated that it might be time for me to leave. I mouthed thank you and she frowned, not at me, I thought, but at whoever was talking on the other end.

I had a few minutes before my appointment with Ken Dollimore. His office was just along the corridor, but I didn't want to wait there. Dollimore had agreed to meet me when I'd said I wanted to talk to him about Ivan's notes.

I sat outside, in a corner of shade, thinking that Carmichael must have decided to visit Margot's club after learning that his appointment with Senator Bryant had been cancelled. He couldn't have planned to be in two places at once.

I rang Bryant's office to check the time of the appointment and to verify that it had been in fact been cancelled. Malcolm Hewitt answered, a staffer for whom Ivan had once done a favour. He confirmed what Laura had said, but couldn't, or wouldn't, tell me whether Carmichael had rung back. I tried to keep him talking, pump him a bit, but he cut me off.

The square was practically empty. As I watched a child cross it, hurrying to keep up with a determined parent, my memory slipped a cog, and I remembered Laura Scott standing over Carmichael the night he'd had his heart attack at the old Parliament House. I hadn't known who Laura was then, but her expression, as I recalled it, struck me as odd. She'd raised her head and looked up the stairs as men in suits ran down them, her attitude that of a person not shocked, nor even surprised, but one whose expectations had been met. Another memory surfaced. One of the suits rushing down the stairs had belonged to Ken Dollimore.

I'd left a few minutes later. A doctor was looking after Carmichael, an ambulance had just pulled up. The carpark was ahead of me, the lights illuminating the building behind. I'd walked slowly towards the rows of cars, feeling as though what had happened back there, over the staircase, was floating in a giant bubble.

It was then that I saw Laura for the second time. At least, I saw a slim, dark-haired young woman in earnest conversation with a tall, silver-haired man, and it struck me now that the woman had been Laura. Ken Dollimore's head had been bent over hers, and it had been clear, even from a distance and in the semi-darkness, that what they were saying to one another couldn't wait.

There is a kind of sculpted, silver-white hair that, once it attains a certain set, will keep it till the wearer dies. Dollimore's hair was like that. He looked effortlessly the patriarch, and both these effects, the effortlessness and the patrician elder statesman, were present in every photograph I'd seen of him. They were there, as might be expected, when he posed for the camera, but also when he was supposedly caught off guard, in those shots and TV interviews snatched from him in the days after Ed Carmichael died.

He sat upright behind his desk, inviting me to take a seat on the other side. His eyes were blue, opaque, his manner at once condescending and placatory. His office had a January closeness, the quiet, inward closeness of a large building holding its breath between Christmas parties and the return of business. Adjacent were the theatre and museum, the fountain in the middle of the square, shadowless at noon, and between Dollimore and myself the sudden alertness of two people with a score to settle.

'What is it about *CleanNet* that concerns you?' I asked in a respectful tone of voice.

Dollimore leant back in his chair. I thought he was pretending to relax. He eyed me steadily and said, 'I'm sorry about that. It had been a particularly bad day.'

'Do you have a problem with the company?'

'No.'

'Did Eden Carmichael own shares in *CleanNet*?'

'What makes you say that?'

'It would be one reason for your interest.'

Dollimore frowned. 'You said you wanted to talk to me about your partner's notes.' He used the word 'partner' in a way that made it clear he considered me very much the junior one.

'That's right. They refer to a presentation *CleanNet* put on for Senator Bryant last November. I was wondering if you'd been there.'

'I'm afraid not.'

'Did you meet *CleanNet*'s director when he was in Canberra?' I prompted, acting on a hunch.

'We – briefly, yes.'

'I understand Mr Carmichael was impressed by the presentation.'

'Is that what it says in the notes?'

'No. Just that he attended.'

'Then how do you know he was impressed?'

'By talking to people who were there.' Mentally, I crossed my fingers, expanding Chris Laskaris to a range of sources.

Dollimore's face stiffened, becoming sculpted like his hair. 'I'm besieged,' he told me. 'Everyone wants answers – my constituents, the press – they want me to make a definitive statement so *they'll* know what to make of Ed dying in such a dreadful way.'

I saw how a reputation for definitive statements could catch up with a person, just at the moment when he did not want to make one. And how a responsibility towards constituents might weigh heavily on someone who'd built a career on his readiness to speak with moral certainty.

'The good citizens of Canberra are shocked and disgusted, and want you to express shock and disgust on their behalf?'

'They *are* good citizens, Mrs Mahoney. If they weren't, the whole thing would be a lot easier.'

Dollimore's hair curved up off his forehead, in the style of an ageing Elvis Presley, but with none of Presley's extravagance or sensuality. I thought of Carmichael's wig, the way it framed his face in that troubling, enigmatic picture. Dollimore's hair looked solid and reliable, but I guessed that his facial muscles were being held together by considerable effort.

'I guess it's confusing for people when you and Mr Carmichael were opposed to one another publicly, yet close friends in private.'

'They want me to condemn him. The reporters are the worst.'

'Did you share similar views on Canberra's IT industry?'

'Share?' Dollimore echoed, while I wondered about the varied meanings of the word. 'Ed had this idea that if someone came along with a good idea they should be given a chance, encouraged – '

'Financial encouragement?'

'Perhaps. If that was possible.'

'And your view?'

'A lot of people who come to us asking for support are charlatans. There's nothing to them. Nothing worthwhile.'

'Is that what you think of Richard McFadden?'

'I beg your pardon?'

'*CleanNet*'s director, Richard McFadden. Do you think he might be a charlatan?'

'I'm in favour of these filtering devices for the Internet. I think they could be a valuable tool for use in schools and libraries. And in homes, of course. If there's a product available which will protect children from violence and filth on the Internet, then I'm interested in finding out about it.'

'What have you learnt about the company?'

'I'm sure you're aware of my constituency. I receive many letters from parents wanting to know how they and their families can enjoy the educational advantages of the Internet, and at the same time afford themselves some measure of protection. If I am going to recommend a certain course of action to the people who've done me the honour of voting for me, then I need to know what it is I'm recommending.'

'What did you discover about *CleanNet*?'

'As far as filters go, theirs seems to be about average.'

'But you'd heard about McFadden's love of gambling?'

Dollimore hesitated, then nodded sharply. 'Mr McFadden did not impress me as an individual, I have to be honest with you there.'

'What didn't impress you?'

'I asked about his filter. I'd tried using it myself. There were a few problems with it and I asked him about those. He assured me that the problems had been solved.'

'And then?'

'I asked about his gambling.'

'How did Mr McFadden respond to that?'

'He told me it wasn't any of my business.'

'Was Mr Carmichael aware of your discussion?'

'Yes.'

'What was his reaction?'

'He claimed their product was a good one, and that McFadden shouldn't be condemned for enjoying a bet every now and then. Though he knew, as well as I did, that it was more than that. The man used to be a professional card sharp.'

'What about McFadden's relationship with the Minister?'

'What relationship?'

'Did he appear to have Senator Bryant's confidence?'

'I'd say Mr McFadden was rather more sure of that than he had grounds for being.'

'Why do you say that?'

'Just a feeling I had. What do *you* know about Richard McFadden?'

All I had was the information the broker had obtained for me, and what Chris Laskaris had said. I passed this on, while Dollimore nodded again, impatiently, making it clear that I wasn't telling him anything new.

'What about the notes? What's in them?' he asked.

'About McFadden? Nothing we haven't covered.'

Dollimore looked as though he didn't believe me. I decided to change the subject.

'Did you know about Mr Carmichael's visits to Margot Lancaster's club?'

'Yes, I did.'

'What did you think?'

'I thought he was making a fool of himself. Well, there's no originality in that. Ed knew he was making a fool of himself.'

'Did you know about the dressing up?'

'Yes.'

'Carmichael told you himself?'

Dollimore nodded.

'Did you try to stop him?'

'I told him what I thought. We did that, strange as it may seem – told each other what we thought. The way Canberra's gone, with prostitution legal, and pornography – you'll think me a pompous old man for saying it, but it makes me sad. None of the constituents who've written to me in recent weeks, to voice their concerns about the safety of the Internet, are silly enough to believe that censorship is easy or straightforward. They're aware of the many practical difficulties involved. Sex is a great force in people's lives. To trivialise or underestimate that force is a mistake. And to argue that acts of copulation between strangers, photographed and filmed solely so that viewers can use them as a stimulus to masturbation – they have no other merit and I certainly don't consider *that* to be one – to argue that these videos and magazines, and now the swamping of the Internet, are not only legitimate, but even in their own way praiseworthy, is an argument advanced by shallow, venal people, who haven't the imagination to realise what it is they're dealing with.'

When Dollimore stopped to draw breath, I said, 'It's an economic argument when it's advanced by those who make or sell the material, isn't it? Are you pleased with the legislation?'

'It's a brave beginning.'

'Did you know that Carmichael had made an appointment to see Senator Bryant on the fourth of January?'

'Yes, he told me about it.'

'What did he want to talk to the Minister about?'

'He didn't go into details.'

'He was upset when Bryant's office rang and cancelled the appointment.'

'How do you know that?'

'Laura Scott told me. Do you know why the appointment was cancelled?'

'No.'

'Do you know if Carmichael tried to make another one?'

'No.'

Dollimore stared at me. I could see him getting ready to ask why any of this was my business.

'What were you doing on the fourth?' I asked, in order to forestall him.

'I spent Christmas and New Year in Melbourne with my younger daughter.'

'And on the fourth?'

'I came back here that day, as a matter of fact.'

'Did you see Eden Carmichael?'

'No.'

'Speak to him?'

Dollimore shook his head and pressed his lips together.

'When *did* you last see one another?'

'Just before Christmas.'

'How did Mr Carmichael seem?'

'He was –'

'A bit under the weather?'

'Yes.'

'What about the photograph in *The Canberra Times*?'

'Disgusting. Absolutely unforgivable.'

'Do you have any idea who took it?'

'If I had, I'd be finding a way to prosecute them.'

'Do you know if there are any more?'

'Do you?' Dollimore asked, staring at me keenly.

'No,' I said. 'But it wouldn't surprise me.'

Dollimore sighed and said, 'You know, Ed was scared after his first heart attack. He was in intensive care tied up to half-a-dozen machines. He couldn't remember falling over the banisters. He told me I was making that up! To put the fear of God in him, he said. I said any way I could do *that* would be a blessing, but I was telling him the simple truth. You can't save a man who doesn't want to be saved. Especially if circumstances are bent on destroying him. I should have seen – me of all people – that to believe I *could* save him was a matter of sinful pride.'

It was clear that Ken Dollimore's love of talking, of hearing his deep voice resonate around a room, outweighed his caution when answering questions, even when his questioner was someone he mistrusted, like me.

'What will you do now?' I asked.

'You mean this morning, or for the rest of my life? I'll see out the term. I owe my constituents that much. But I won't stand again. I don't want to stay in Canberra. My wife died seven years ago. I have a daughter in Melbourne and another one in Townsville. Even if it hadn't been for – for what happened – I'd been thinking of retiring.'

'One last question – did you try to break into my computer a few nights ago?'

Dollimore laughed with genuine amusement. 'My dear young woman, I wouldn't have a clue how to go about that, even if I wanted to.'

In spite of myself, I felt pleased that he'd called me young.

'Whoever did might have been after information about *CleanNet*.'

'I can assure you that it wasn't me.'

Dollimore half stood up to shake my hand. I left his office reflecting on how he'd survived ten years in the Assembly, while younger men and women had fallen by the wayside. Dollimore was the only politician left from the days when prostitution and marijuana had been decriminalised, and the bill to ban X-rated videos thrown out by one vote, creating a storm which had brought down the fledgling Labor Government and its first female Chief Minister.

Dollimore and Carmichael had been the two survivors. Dependent on each other? And, if so, for what?

The Federal Government had promised its tiny capital territory that it would be allowed to manage its own affairs, and the promise had been honoured up to a point. But the National Capital Authority that had run Canberra before self-government showed its muscle when it felt like it, and the Territory Government had to dance a slippery two-step around them. Dollimore knew Canberra, how to work its double standards, how to ride its waves of prosperity and discontent. I did not think he had been disappointed when sex censorship had riven the scarcely constituted Assembly. When the lights came back on, he and Carmichael had faced each other, two middle-aged men from opposite sides, yet, if I was to believe what I'd been told, with a friendship that ran deeper than any political divisions.

I called in at the library to check on members' assets declarations. Carmichael had declared no personal investments. Dollimore owned a thousand *Telstra* shares, and five hundred in *BHP*.

On my way out of the building, I stopped for a moment and looked back. The Assembly hunched itself, braced against the heat.

Attempting to hack into my computer had been a dodgy thing to do. On the face of it, there was nothing dodgy about Ken Dollimore. Perhaps I'd been wrong to connect him to the break-in. As I retraced my footsteps along the burning footpath to the London Circuit carpark, I realised that what annoyed me about Dollimore was his security. He might be planning to retire, but, for the present, he was secure and consolidated in that air-conditioned office. Canberra might have legal brothels, a legal X-rated video and magazine industry, but the future, as everyone said, was with the Internet, and there an extraordinary victory for censorship had been won by a Federal Independent, a man who shared his views and moral gravity.

. . .

Back home, I moved a second fan into my office, scrambled after a few loose papers, then made myself as comfortable as I could and typed up the morning's notes. With only my own time to organise, I was trying to be more methodical than usual, typing up notes of each meeting or conversation as soon as possible. I added the new ones to a file that contained my interview with Chris Laskaris, making sure they were saved securely, and password protected. I wasn't sure how experienced my hacker was, but if he or she came back, I wanted to make stealing my files something of a challenge. Anybody watching me would know that I was asking questions about Eden Carmichael and *CleanNet*. There didn't seem to be anything startling in the answers so far, but that could be because I did not know how to interpret them.

I mulled over my impressions of Margot Lancaster, trying to recall whether she had answered confidently and immediately my question about whether Carmichael had been anxious or upset.

I sent Lucy an email, saying that I thought the enthusiasm Carmichael had expressed for *CleanNet* was worth looking into, making the point that, if the enthusiasm had been genuine, it represented an interesting shift as far as his beliefs and philosophy were concerned.

I spent the next couple of hours filling in background, contacting anyone I knew who might have an opinion about the friendship between Dollimore and Carmichael. People who'd been around ACT politics since self-government, who were familiar with the two men's histories, recalled them as strong and genuinely independent personalities. Their battles had been fought, as much as anything, over the question of public image – what kind the nation's capital should project.

But the collective memory of those who'd been close to the force of it, at one time or another, was a memory of just that – a force pulling inwards, a fixed and tunnelling intentness.

The Assembly, with its sum total of only fourteen members, operated more like a city council than a legislature with the powers of a state. Within it, there was scope for one man or woman to impose a singular vision on Canberra. It had been that way from the start, first with Burley Griffin, then with the head of the Board of Assessors who had become his enemy.

Canberra had no dirty factories to remodel and clean up, or watch going out of business; no traditional manufacturing concerns. The bland, monochrome surface, the look of easy money, had been tricking people, who were now turning round and asking, what have we got going for us, how will we pay our way? Carmichael had crossed borders, both visible and invisible, behind the city's various facades. It was his death that made the crossing interesting.

I made myself an iced coffee, then phoned Laura Scott.

'What were you and Ken Dollimore talking about the night Carmichael had his heart attack?' I asked.

'What do you mean?' Laura sounded curious, rather than offended by my question.

'I saw you talking to Ken Dollimore in the old Parliament House carpark.'

'Ed, of course,' said Laura. 'We were both worried sick about him.'

We shared our impressions of that night, Laura emphasising the affection and sense of responsibility both she and Dollimore had felt for Carmichael, and how, when their paths had crossed in the carpark and they'd recognised one another, they'd admitted they were both afraid that he would die.

When Laura paused for breath, I asked who Carmichael's solicitor was, and she named a well-known firm.

After she'd brought the conversation to an end, I rang the solicitors, and asked to speak to the partner dealing with Eden Carmichael's estate. When she came on the line, I introduced myself, then asked about his will. She told me it was confidential in the kind of voice that suggested she'd be reluctant to divulge the time of day.

I managed to get in one more question.
'Did he own his flat outright?'
'Yes, he did.'

. . .

I checked my mail. A message from Lucy warned me not to get sidetracked into the shadows surrounding a drunken politician's ignominious end.

Four

I arrived early for Carmichael's funeral at the Norwood crematorium, which was just as well. By the time I got there, the small chapel was practically full. The West Australian cousin had complained in an interview that the police had held onto Carmichael's body for too long. Now he was being cremated on a hot, windy day.

Spotting a spare seat a few rows from the back, and making for it quickly, I did an inventory of who was there. I recognised the tall cousin at one end of the front row. A woman next to him, wearing a pale-grey suit, might have been his wife, or perhaps another cousin. Two adolescent children and three elderly couples made up all there seemed to be of family. Directly behind them were Carmichael's former colleagues in the Assembly, Ken Dollimore prominent among them. The Chief Minister was noticeably absent. Three female members of the Assembly sat side by side, with an air about them of getting through an ordeal together. I wondered what they'd thought of Carmichael. Everyone I'd talked to so far had agreed that Dollimore was the only MLA he'd been close to in the last few years.

There were no Federal politicians. I checked the backs of heads again, then scrutinised the rows behind me to make sure. If the circumstances surrounding Carmichael's death hadn't kept away his immediate associates, they had discouraged those with national agendas.

The chapel was air-conditioned, but the heat outside was making itself felt. A woman at one end of the row in front of me shook out a bamboo fan and began waving it slowly in front of her heavily made-up face. A man padded his white handkerchief fussily into a square and mopped his brow. Extra chairs were lined up along the walls.

I found Laura Scott behind the politicians, in a short-sleeved black dress that set off her tan. Dark hair dove-tailed charmingly against her neck. Two rows back from her, Chris Laskaris took off the jacket of his suit and placed it across his knees, then lifted his head in Laura's direction.

Still mourners kept arriving. The small foyer was full. Others stood outside, along the chapel's glass wall, under dark-green awnings. Whoever had decided on the venue had seriously underestimated how many would turn up.

A woman three seats along from me said, 'Look at that. She's got a hide, I must say.' She'd spoken in the kind of hissing undertone that carries well. Heads turned. Margot Lancaster had joined the congregation at the back.

If she'd heard the insult, then she gave no sign. She kept her head raised, eyes fixed on the coffin. Her skin was paler than the chapel walls, her lips the colour of deeply oxygenated blood. She was dressed entirely in black, her short hair once more resembling a helmet. Whatever else she might be, Margot was a woman who knew how to play a part, and face down the prurient and hostile glances she must have anticipated.

My legs were sweating. I had no one to impress, and was glad I'd had the sense not to get dressed up. Still, Ivan would have laughed if he could have seen me. He didn't understand my interest in Carmichael. In his last email, he'd said he didn't think the pittance Electronic Freedom was paying us was worth the effort.

The service began. The chaplain spoke. A hymn was sung. When Dollimore stood up to give the eulogy, I forgot about the heat.

He began when they were children, boys together, first at primary, then at high school. Chalk and cheese they'd been from the beginning, Carmichael the younger by a few years and always the rebellious one, desperate to buck the system one way or another, while Dollimore had been devout and law-abiding. As adults, they'd gone their different ways, then come together again as political opponents. Ed had done his best for self-government, giving years of his life in service to the Canberra community, both before and after his election to the Assembly. As everybody present knew, they'd had more than their share of teething troubles. It hadn't been an easy time. But Ed had stuck it out. And when his health began to fail – he hadn't given up then, either.

When Dollimore got onto God, my attention began to wander. I supposed it was his day as well as Carmichael's. He was making it his, in any case. As an orator, he wiped the floor with the chaplain, and he knew it. He let his bass voice reverberate just long enough to give each word the right amount of weight. His eyes sought out, and gathered in, now this row, now another. He must have noticed Margot at the back, standing straight and tall. His voice didn't falter at the sight of her, or change its tone. He was too good a performer for that. And his message was not hell and damnation, but forgiveness. He pitied people who condemned themselves to living in a world bereft of faith.

A prayer, another hymn, a few words from the cousin, who wisely kept them short, then condolence messages, including one from the Chief Minister. A Bach concerto accompanied the mechanics of the floor opening up, the coffin disappearing into a human fire.

The moment I stepped outside, I noticed a change in the air. Thunderclouds massed over low hills the other side of Mitchell. The sun shining through them was a rich, pregnant yellow. I looked round for Margot, but she'd already gone, probably to avoid the TV cameras. Local politicians emerged in a clump, then quickly made for their cars, all except for Dollimore.

I realised with a start how close the crematorium was to Margot's club. I pictured her driving with the windows down, letting in thick, sweet air that carried the smell of rain, returning to her club to change. Or perhaps she'd keep her suit on all evening, greet prospective clients in her widow's black.

I spotted Chris Laskaris, jacket slung gracefully over one shoulder, looking down admiringly at Laura Scott. He hadn't wasted time. She seemed suitably impressed.

Dollimore was shaking hands with everyone, towering above them, eclipsing the poor show made by Carmichael's relatives. A journalist stood at his elbow writing in a notebook, and two photographers were busy taking shots.

As I watched, Dollimore lifted his prophet's head and gazed solemnly past them, into the intense colours of the approaching storm. It occurred to me that, retirement plans aside, he possessed the kind of energy that strengthened with age, a resilience that derived, at least in part, from his ability to turn any situation to his own advantage; a swell that ran beneath the wave's head, fluid, willed, long-lasting.

. . .

It began to bucket down as I was driving home, a true summer storm. I let Fred in – he was frightened of the thunder – and made myself a kind of high tea to compensate for not having been invited to the wake. I sat with my bare feet on Fred's back, staring out the window. A branch broke off the crab-apple tree and landed on the porch. I wondered if it was raining at the coast. I wondered if Brook's partner, Sophie, had arrived yet. After Brook had gone off in a huff, I wasn't surprised to learn that Sophie had adjusted her holiday plans to fit in a trip to the coast as well. She was visiting her daughter, but due back any day.

From Brook's point of view, it didn't matter that taking Peter to Tasmania had been Derek's idea. Brook hated being reminded that his role as my children's uncle was voluntary, and that biological parents could usurp it any time they chose. Before Ivan left for Moscow, they'd argued over the wisdom of his taking Katya. Brook was worried about Katya getting sick. Ivan, usually patient, had told him that she was *his* daughter. She was going with him and that was that.

I looked forward to catching up with Brook at the weekend, talking things over – already hearing his dry, laconic voice, his way of cutting through the outer layers of a problem. Brook's bone-marrow transplant had been a success, surpassing the doctors' expectations, but no one who was close to him could forget that a recurrence of leukemia might be just around the corner.

. . .

By dusk, the sky was almost clear. I took Fred for a walk across the road. A last storm cloud rolled its golden underbelly over the O'Connor ridge. The sodden grass, the dark grey and yellow of the cloud, seemed like a fanfare that had missed its cue.

Gold spread through the cloud, touching the spears of poplars that lined Sullivan's Creek, vertical to its high horizontal, the last light massy, indiscriminate and yet precise. I thought of the divisions, within and through my city, small ones, cracks in pavements and in people's minds, that were familiar, nondescript, repeated as often as the scene in front of me was repeated, glowing and then gone. I thought of bigger divisions, moral and political, how Eden Carmichael had moved across them, and how that movement might be felt in the air. Just then, Canberra seemed to be a city struggling to give itself some kind of independent life.

But Carmichael was dead. He'd died dressed in a wig and women's clothes, on a bed paid for by the half-hour. In his speech, Ken Dollimore had not once referred to the circumstances of his friend's last hours. His words had run counter to the image I was sure had been prominent in the minds of every person in that chapel. Heart failure, Dollimore had said. An accident. A good man, a good Canberran, cut down in his prime.

Deliberate actions might be dressed up to look like chance. I wished I knew more about Carmichael's secret, or not so secret, life. It was curious that he'd avoided public condemnation for so long. He'd run the risk of scandal and ridicule for years, hanging onto the support of just enough voters to continue in office. Rather than change his lifestyle, he'd courted a second heart attack. I pictured his trousers with the fly undone, the way Chris Laskaris had described them just before his fall, then his blue dress, gorgeous in the last light, and the yellow, soft enhancement of his wig.

. . .

Too restless to spend the evening shut up in my house, I called on Gail Trembath, who'd just returned to work at *The Canberra Times*.

She met me at the door to her flat with a complaint.

'I'd forgotten Canberra was so bloody *hot*.'

'You wish you'd never left the tropics?'

'Hell I do,' Gail said, leading me down a short corridor to her living room, the floor of which was covered with boxes at various stages of unpacking. A desk lamp sat unplugged beside lengths of silk and embroidered tablecloths, which had to be for presents, since Gail would never use them. Her untidiness reassured me. In one respect, at least, she hadn't changed.

'You should leave this town before it destroys your nasal passages.' Gail made a complicated face, and moved a green case to one side with her foot. 'In fact it probably already has.'

'Good to see you too,' I said.

'I'm serious, Sandy. You're wasting your life here.'

'Thanks for your concern.'

I looked around the room. Gail's new flat was much the same as the one she'd rented before leaving for Vietnam and Thailand. I wondered whether she'd spend as little time living in it as she had in the old one. Inside the case, still half wrapped in bubble plastic, was a small wooden statue of a phoenix standing on a turtle.

Gail nodded at the shoulder bag that held my laptop. 'Thinking of doing some work while you're here?'

'I took it with me to the crematorium, then forgot I'd left it in my car.'

'Well, I suppose thieves are more active in my street than in other parts of town.' Gail's voice held more than an edge of sarcasm. 'You know, Sandy,' she went on, 'ten years ago, I could have got by as a stringer in Bangkok. Now unless you're working for *Time* or CNN – '

There was a sadness in her unfinished sentence. Gail had grown the shell proper to her profession during the time I'd known her. It seemed to have become brittle, thin.

'Have you got anything to drink?' I asked.

She waved her arm towards an open doorway. I headed for the kitchen, knowing better than to expect her to wait on me.

Her fridge was working, and even had some food in it – tomatoes, lettuce, a container of garlic dip. In the door compartment was a litre carton of milk and another of orange juice. I bent down and found what I was looking for on the bottom shelf.

A drawer held a bottle opener. Glasses had already been deposited in an overhead cupboard. I filled two with beer, handed Gail hers, then raised mine towards it.

'Welcome home.'

Gail made another face. I waited for her to explain what was upsetting her, then said, 'I missed you at Eden Carmichael's funeral.'

'What?'

'Your colleagues were there, sucking up to Ken Dollimore. Margot Lancaster turned up too.'

'What's she like?'

'What she'd *like* is a chance to show she runs a decent business.'

Gail frowned, but looked interested.

'Would you do an interview with her?'

'Why me?'

'You're sympathetic. You know how to listen.'

'Yeah?'

'And a good journalist.'

Gail laughed, and said, 'What makes you think she'd talk to me?'

'I'll recommend you. How much did Bob Halford pay for the photo of Carmichael?'

'What makes you think he paid for it?'

Gail put down her glass and began unpacking a box of assorted crockery.

It wasn't all that comfortable standing in the kitchen, but there were no chairs, or furniture of any kind, apart from bookshelves, in the living room. Here at least I had a bench to prop against.

'If I had a hot picture to sell,' I said, 'I'd at least offer it to *The Australian* or *The Sydney Morning Herald*.'

Gail pulled out pieces of broken plate and tossed them into a bin. When she didn't answer, I continued, 'I'm assuming the seller had a personal motive. Revenge comes to mind. Humiliation on home ground. But that's too vague. Something more precise. A personal relationship with Halford maybe. A favour being returned?'

I'd rung the editors of both *The Herald* and *The Australian* and asked them if they'd been offered any pictures of Carmichael in his dress and wig. Both said they hadn't, which was what I'd expected.

'Plus, I'm assuming that there must be others.'

Gail straightened up and turned to face me. 'What's it to you?'

'I have my reasons for wanting to know.'

'Which are?'

'I'll trade them, but at the moment I don't feel like giving them away.'

Gail gave me a long, calculating stare, then picked up a stained and dented saucepan. All her kitchen utensils were of the basic, hard-used kind. She threw the saucepan in a cupboard, then asked, 'How's your little girl?'

'She's fine,' I said, surprised.

'And Peter? And Ivan?'

'They're fine too.'

'You know I had a bloke over there?' Gail said, joining me at the bench and downing half her beer in one go. 'A lovely guy. Vietnamese. Most of his family killed in the war. Smart, great sense of humour. Bit younger than me, but that didn't matter. I met him through the agency. I started thinking about all that stuff. Marriage. Kids.'

'What happened?'

'His name's Tan. He got moved to Hanoi. We kept it up for a while, shuttled back and forth.'

'Did he meet someone else?'

'He says not. I think he has, though. I think he's trying to let me down softly.'

'I'm sorry.'

'And I'm curious. This tough bitch attitude. This shit about trading information. Where's it come from Sandy? Is it the new you?'

Five

I smelt the intruder before I found any evidence of him. Nights on my own had made me sensitive to the sighs and solitary breathing of my house, the leftover smells of my rudimentary cooking. Something else was in the air, a faint, alien, metallic scent.

I let Fred in, and he raced down the corridor, nose to the floor like a dog doing his duty.

All the drawers in my filing cabinet were open. Files and folders lay scattered on the desk and floor, mixed with floppy disks and CDs that looked as though they'd been hurled across the room.

Fred snuffled while I checked the back door. My office window was securely locked, and didn't look as though it had been forced, the living room and kitchen windows the same. But the flyscreen on my bedroom window had been taken out and crookedly replaced. The paint work at one corner of the frame was chipped, as though someone had used a chisel to lever their way in.

I splashed cold water on my face, and sat on the edge of the bath for a few moments, thinking that the intruder must be somebody who knew my habits, had watched me driving off that evening, and knew that Fred was harmless, no sort of guard dog. What if he'd left the house just as I was arriving? What if he'd heard me pulling up, was still out there, deciding to come back and take by force what he hadn't been able to find?

I knelt on the concrete in front of Fred's kennel and felt around the inside of the roof. The disk was still there. Back in my office, I began to gather paper into piles, trying to recreate the intruder's movements. In my mind, he'd already firmed into a 'he', and not a random male either, but one with sculpted silver hair. This break-in and the attempted electronic one could hardly be coincidental. Perhaps Ken Dollimore had lost his temper when he hadn't been able to find what he'd come for, and had trashed my office out of spite.

The filing cabinet had been emptied first. Folders from it were buried under the papers from my desk. Books had been flung at the walls. Pages had come loose, and some had broken spines. I examined book covers, holding them carefully by the corners, to see if they had marks, possibly even a footprint. The ground outside my bedroom window was still soaked from the storm. Still, a footprint was too much to hope for.

I waded through the mess and switched on the only computer in the office, since Ivan had taken his laptop with him to Moscow and I had taken mine with me to Gail's. Our old machine didn't seem to be damaged, but an infuriating red flag was flashing again in the top left-hand corner. The hacker had been back to try again at closer quarters. But was it the same person? Would someone who thought they could steal my files from a safe distance have broken into my house and lost his temper, or did the loss of temper suggest a different personality, a different kind of character?

My palms were sweating. I felt sick, but I made myself keep looking. Nothing seemed to have been altered or deleted.

Fred had learnt all he could from the new smells. He looked at me and wagged his tail, as if to say he was quite happy with this late night activity, but a snack to accompany it would be nice.

'Useless dog,' I told him.

He wagged his tail again, uncertainly this time. I bent to pat him, and exhaustion hit me. Even if I lay in bed without being able to sleep, bed was where I needed to be.

But first, I phoned Ivan. Luckily, I caught him at his sister's flat, though he told me he was just on his way out. He asked questions, made sympathetic noises, told me to go to the police, but his words and voice sounded impossibly remote.

I asked to speak to Katya, but she was on a shopping expedition with her aunt.

I heated some milk, though the night was very warm, and poured some into Fred's bowl as a treat. I stirred a large spoonful of honey into mine and drank it sitting on a kitchen chair with my bare feet scrunched into his fur, realising, with another spike of fear, that I'd have to keep my bedroom window closed.

In spite of thinking I wasn't going to be able to, I slept for a few hours, and woke as the sun began to heat my room at six.

I lay watching a path of light, and thought again about the break-in. Much of the work that Ivan and I were hired to do involved following payments from one company or government department to another. Often we were asked to track, through a maze of numbers, the relationships between suspect individuals and institutions, in order to discover who might be responsible for missing dollars, or the leak of information. Usually, by the time Ivan was called in, the trail had already been stamped on by half-a-dozen others, then abandoned as too messy, or because the security people supposed to be doing the tracking might themselves be implicated.

It had been a change to have a decomposing body and the suggestion of a sex scandal to mull over. In the currents surrounding Carmichael's death, my questions about his connections with *CleanNet* had seemed no more than a ripple. I wasn't about to admit this to Lucy, but I'd begun to wonder who took filters seriously, apart from lobby groups and kindergarten teachers. I had the feeling that everyone else, from Senator Bryant down, with the possible exception of Ken Dollimore, was only pretending to. A professional would not have overturned my office looking for a CD, or a few sheets of paper. Was I barking up the wrong tree? Had the thief been after something else entirely?

I had a quick breakfast, two cups of strong black tea, and went on with my cleaning up. As soon as I thought he'd be awake, I rang Peter at Port Arthur. He was full of excitement, chattering about his plans for the day. They'd been walking in a national park, and now they'd come to the part of the trip that he'd been looking forward to – convict history, the more gruesome the better. I said nothing about the break-in. I hadn't intended to. I just needed to hear his voice. When Derek came on the line, I didn't tell him either, replying to his, 'Is everything okay?' with 'Sure', aware that I could not expect reassurance from my ex-husband.

I phoned Gail Trembath later in the morning. 'Seems I might be dealing with an amateur.'

Gail said, 'If that makes you feel better, dear.'

I thanked her for her sympathy.

Deciding that it was a good opportunity to get rid of a lot of useless junk, and coughing from the huge amount of dust that had settled in amongst it, I carried piles of paper out to the recycling bin, every so often distracted into reading something I'd forgotten about. I pictured Ken Dollimore's silver eyebrows clenched in concentration, his growing fury as he emptied one drawer after another. Whoever he was – whether Dollimore, or a complete stranger – he was out there, on the other side of brick and concrete barriers I had foolishly believed secure. Had he been at the funeral? Had he driven to my house and parked outside? Had any of my neighbours seen or heard him?

I sent Lucy an email, then door-knocked up and down the street. Hardly anyone was home. Both my next-door neighbours had gone to the coast. One elderly man, opening the door after I'd knocked about thirty times, regarded me with undisguised alarm, as though I was telling him that he would be next.

I stood at the counter of the city police station to fill in a report, trying to ignore the young constable whose expression said that I was wasting my time. I knew there were a dozen burglaries in Canberra on any given night, and I couldn't even claim that my belongings had been stolen. I wished Brook was there, upstairs in his office, trading insults with his old friend Bill McCallum. I forgot what I was supposed to be doing for a moment, and stood with my pen in my hand, imagining dinner with Brook in a pub overlooking the ocean, picturing myself swimming in the sea. Brook was a strong, yet cautious swimmer. If there were flags, he'd be between them, yet far enough out to catch the good waves, bodysurfing them to shore with his action of a well-groomed seal.

• • •

Gail turned up in the middle of the afternoon.

'What are you doing here?' I asked her.

She grinned. 'A nice welcome. Come on, show me the damage then.'

My office was pretty much back to normal. Gail looked disappointed at having to settle for a description of chaos in the past tense.

She sniffed the air, as Fred and I had done, but the vagrant chemical smell I'd picked up was gone, destroyed by my vacuuming and dusting.

I couldn't think what had made it. It could have been a male deodorant, or aftershave, but it had smelt too sharply astringent for that.

Gail marched around my house, observing neatness and clean surfaces, rattling off the reasons I should not be on my own. Her eyes flicked back and forth, seeking out reminders of my absent family.

Over iced tea, I asked her if she'd ever seen Ken Dollimore lose his temper.

Gail rubbed her nose with the back of her hand and said, 'I was at the Assembly to interview the Chief Minister. It was at the start of those protests over the Gungahlin Drive Extension. I passed Dollimore in the corridor and with no warning at all he grabbed hold of me.' Gail took hold of imaginary coat lapels and shook them. 'He called me a parasite and a human mosquito.'

'Did you bite him?'

'Yick!' Gail shook her head. 'A guy with such a reputation for standing on his dignity. And I'd done sweet nothing. I hadn't even breathed on his hair.'

I said I didn't think a bit of journalistic harassment would do Dollimore any harm. In particular, I thought Gail might pester him about what he'd been doing on the afternoon Carmichael died. I reminded her about contacting Margot Lancaster, and said I had something she might be able to use in return. Carmichael was supposed to have been in Senator Bryant's office in Parliament House at four o'clock on January 4, not gasping his last in a brothel. The appointment had been made before Christmas, and cancelled at the last minute. I'd confirmed it with one of Bryant's staffers.

Gail nodded, then gave me a smile that was like a handshake, confirming a deal.

Six

It was six o'clock, but already felt like midnight. Because I'd chosen to turn my back on the meat raffle, I found myself sitting with my nose pressed against a penny-farthing bicycle. The raffle that made my stomach turn comprised not one frozen chook, or ten, but floor to ceiling meat – newly dead, red and white and bloody. Close up, it separated into chops, sausages, roasts and steaks in individual packages, gladwrap tight, set artistically like tiles in a wall mosaic.

I asked Denise Travers if it was a weekly thing. She said it was. I asked her how she thought the winner might store his or her prize. She lit a cigarette, looked bored, and said she didn't know.

Denise had long black hair and fingernails to match. Her lips were the colour of an undertaker's shadow. She was above average height and slim, dressed in dark, well-fitting clothes. At a distance, and apart from the length of her hair, she could have stood in for Margot Lancaster. Close up, she looked half Margot's age.

Not wishing to put her off by staring, I turned my gaze back to the largest exhibit in the bicycle museum.

Denise smiled to let me know she was pleased by my discomfort. She'd chosen our table, in an area of the *Tradies* that was reserved for smokers. She told me that when her daughter was little, she and her husband used to go to the *Tradies* every Friday night. She'd have a middy and he'd have two schooners and a plate of chips.

I raised my glass. 'To absent husbands.'

'Yours pissed off as well?' Denise turned her head to blow smoke away from me.

'The first one did.'

'And the second?'

'In Moscow, visiting his sister. You haven't given it a second go?'

'Nah,' Denise said, with a self-deprecating smile. I've had a few nibbles, but.'

'But?'

'Something always puts me off. Margot said you've got a friend who's a reporter.'

'Do you want to talk to her?'

'Maybe.'

'What about your daughter?' There wasn't a polite way to ask, but I was too curious to let it go.

'Rebecca knows what I do for a living.'

That makes you a remarkable mother then, I thought.

I needed to eat before I had any more to drink. Meat was out, but a plate of chips sounded good. I didn't want Denise getting restless though, while I waited in a queue.

'Tell me about Eden Carmichael,' I said.

'Half the clients have got some sort of health problem. I mean, if you start quizzing them.'

'Who knew about his?'

'Whores can read, can't they? I mean, generally speaking.'

I thought about this question, inclining my head away from the huge weight of dead animals at my back, while Denise smoked and regarded them steadily over my left shoulder.

'What was he like?' I asked her.

Denise shifted in her chair. 'Why should I –' she began, then nodded, as though reminding herself of an obligation. She stubbed out her cigarette, and twined her hands around her glass.

'You know, the cops took fingerprints off all the girls? You know how many clients pass through the club in a week?'

'Tell me.'

'Well, not so many now it's summer holidays. But in a good week –'

'How many girls does Margot have working for her?'

'Three.'

'Business has slowed down?'

'It's January.'

'Clients are superstitious?'

Denise made a face, then said, 'We'll see, won't we.'

I knew she was trying to steer the conversation away from Carmichael, and asked again, 'What kind of bloke was he?'

'He made a girl feel special. He was old – well, not as old as some – but he had this – you could have a conversation with him. He made you feel he was interested in you as a person.' She caught my eye. 'I know, I know. But Ed had this warmth. And there was something brave about him. There was his heart, his daggy dress – he was like, I don't know, *courageous*.'

'What happened that day?'

'I helped him put his dress on. He liked me to do that.'

'What about underwear?'

'He brought it with him.'

'You helped him to put that on as well?'

'I – yes.'

'The wig?'

'He had to unwrap it himself. It all had to be done just so.'

'Unwrap?'

'From the tissue paper. In the box.'

'How long has Margot had the wig?'

Denise frowned, as though there was more to my question than met the eye, but all she said was, 'Like forever.'

'What happened then?'

'My phone rang.'

'Do you normally leave it on?'

'I was worried about Rebecca. She was at summer camp. She didn't want to go. She rang because she'd had an accident. I asked Ed to excuse me for a minute.'

'Had you ever left him alone before?'

'Not once he had his dress on.'

'Did he seem upset?'

'He seemed a bit unwell, and – '

'Yes?'

'He'd been drinking.'

'More than usual?'

'When he visited the club, he'd usually had a few.'

'Was he in a hurry?'

'He didn't seem to be – before I left him, that is. He knew it was Rebecca. Take your time, he said.'

'Did he say anything about where he should have been that afternoon?'

'Why? Where was he supposed to be?'

'I was told he had an appointment. It was cancelled.'

'I don't know anything about that.'

'Where did you go to talk to your daughter?'

'Next door.'

'Would you have seen Carmichael if he'd come out of the room, or if somebody else had gone in?'

'I was facing away from the door, and anyway it was only open a few centimetres.'

'Would you have heard the door opening?'

'Beck was crying. She was in a bad way. Have you got kids?'

'Two. My son's thirteen, but my daughter's only little. Did the phone at reception ring while you were talking to Rebecca?'

Denise took a moment to think about it, then she shook her head.

'What about the people at the camp?'

'They were okay. Really, they were fine. But she didn't want to go. School holidays are hard. I talked her into going because it suited me. She knew that.'

'How long did you leave Carmichael on his own?'

'I was back in about ten minutes. Margot says I yelled out, but I don't remember what I said. His face was all purple – and his tongue – it was horrible!'

'Was there anything different about the room when you went back?'

'The police asked me that. I wasn't looking at the room. I don't remember.'

'Think about it. Take your time.'

'Well, the bed was messed up and Ed was sprawled all over it, so that's a difference. The table – there was the lamp, cigarettes, tissues, condoms, clock radio – all the stuff that's usually there.'

'His clothes?'

'Some guys drop their clothes on the floor, but Ed was neat. He always folded his.'

'Where were they?'
'On the chair.'
'The wig box?'
'What about it?'
'Where was that?'
'On the floor.'
Something in her tone made me ask, 'You're sure of that? You saw it?'
'That's where Ed put it. He always put it under the table. It was too big to fit on with the other things.'
'What time did you leave that evening?'
'When the police finished interviewing me. About nine o'clock.'
'Did you notice anybody in the carpark?'
'The police cars. No one else.'
'Did Carmichael have sex with men?'
'I don't think so.'
'Did he talk to you about men friends?'
'He mentioned that religious one.'
'What did he say?'
'That they'd known each other for ages.'
'Was Ken Dollimore ever at the club?'
'I never saw him there.'
'Did Carmichael see other girls?'
'No. Only me.'
'How did the dressing up start?'
'It was way before my time.'

I felt Denise's guard begin to slip, a physical sensation like loosening a tie. She and Margot really did look alike. Both had dark brown eyes. Margot's were bedded in a nest of lines and slackening skin, but their expression was youthful, and Denise looked to me, on balance, as though she would age more quickly.

'What's Margot like to work for?'
'Fine.'
'And the other girls, are they local?'

Denise coloured, then lit another cigarette. 'Margot's got an arrangement with a place in Sydney. They send girls down for three months to try out.'

'Do many of them stay?'

'Some do. If they like it here.'

'I guess Margot has to like them too.'

I waited, but Denise said nothing further.

'Are the Sydney girls experienced?'

'Some are, some aren't.' Denise bit her lip. 'I'd like to stop working.' She flashed me a quick, challenging look. 'But I want to give Beck the things I never had. And you can't do that on eleven bucks an hour.'

This seemed self-evident, and I did not know what to say that would not sound trite.

'What's the place in Sydney called?'

'*Sans Souci.*'

I wondered if Denise knew what it meant. I also wondered what it was about our conversation that was making her uncomfortable.

'What happens if Margot doesn't get on with a girl?' I asked.

'She leaves,' Denise said, standing up.

I told her that I thought it would be all right to get Gail to do an interview – meaning, we both knew, if Margot wanted the interview arranged. It was clearly Margot's idea to try and organise some favourable publicity. But Denise had, commendably I thought, decided to check me out for herself.

I walked home from the *Tradies* thinking about the similarities and differences between the two women. My first impression had been that Denise copied Margot in her style of dress, but now I wasn't sure. I sensed that both had learnt to treat free talk as suspect, synonymous with waste. Say only as much as a client may be entitled to insist on, and no more. Dignity coexisted with a studied reticence. Words failed, or were inadequate, for so much. In a brothel, I suspected, they became a measure of the margins.

But Denise had said she'd enjoyed talking to Carmichael. In spite of her denial, I wondered if he *had* told her about his cancelled appointment with Senator Bryant. The more I thought about it, the less inclined I was to believe that he'd said nothing about where he should have been.

Who had Carmichael most embarrassed by ending his life the way he had? Ken Dollimore? His colleagues in the Legislative Assembly? Margot? His constituents? And whose interests was it in, if anyone's, that he should have done so?

. . .

I wasn't looking forward to spending another night alone, listening for footsteps, or the rasp of a chisel at my bedroom window.

Gail rang. I began to tell her about my conversation with Denise, but sensed she wasn't listening.

'You've heard from him, haven't you?'

Gail said, 'He's getting married.'

'I'm sorry.'

'Don't be. I'm not the marrying kind, am I? Never have been.'

'Come over,' I told her. 'I need company.'

. . .

It was the right kind of night for a long, leisurely walk, clouds engorged and heavy once again, holding the heat close to the earth with a lover's insistence. I thought of my house locked up and empty, of my intruder circling.

Gail kept giving me quick, sideways glances, but said she didn't want to talk about Mr Engagement.

Before we knew it, we'd walked all the way into the city. Landmarks so familiar that, during the day, I scarcely noticed them, appeared to be improved, spruced up. Old buildings, whose paint was worn, shapes tired in the sunlight, looked washed clean, well-proportioned in the darkness. The white arches of Civic seemed part of a forgotten Spanish town.

Gail was walking with exaggerated bow legs, pretending to be drunk.

She rushed ahead, a cowgirl with a posse after her, turning around and shouting, as though I was a mile away, 'Sandy! We're the last two women in the world!'

'Where *is* everybody?' she demanded.

'Down the coast,' I said.

'Oh, Sandy.' Gail's eyes glittered with tears she would never admit to.

'Why didn't you go to Moscow with Ivan and Katya? A person needs to get out of this dump once in a while.'

A car's headlights picked us out. I stopped in the middle of the empty footpath, suddenly afraid. Gail was standing ramrod straight, accusing, as though the harsh, indifferent lights and echoing forlornness were my fault.

'What would we do, if we were the last two women in the world?'

'Well, I wouldn't go to bed with you,' I told her.

'Oh Sandy, what an *awful* thought.'

. . .

That night, I huddled into bed with Fred for company, Fred surprised and delighted to be offered an old blanket on my bedroom floor. I woke to the sound of his toenails clicking in the corridor, as he took himself off for a drink. For the next day and night, I stuck to my small area of habitation, Dickson Pool, the shops, the house, which I greeted after each brief absence as though I had been gone for days. I conducted my business by telephone and email, daring my intruder to pay a return visit, telling myself I was ready for him if he did. Images of the funeral kept coming back to me – thunderclouds shot through with yellow, Ken Dollimore dispensing largesse at the crematorium, Ed Carmichael's last goodbye.

Seven

I'm working on the theory that it was Dollimore looking for your notes on CleanNet, and that he lost his temper when he couldn't find them.

Set down in an email to Ivan, my theory looked pathetic, but I hadn't realised how far Ivan and I had moved apart until I received his reply. It was composed entirely of statistics on break and enters in the part of Moscow where his sister lived.

Staring at the numbers, I wondered if there'd always been this arrogance in Ivan, the assumption that what he was into at any given moment was more important than anything I happened to have taken on.

I found his file on Malcolm Hewitt, now one of Bryant's senior staffers. About a year ago, a leak from the office had been traced to Hewitt's computer. It could have earnt him the sack. Ivan had found a hole in the email system and plugged it. He'd counselled the senator that an outsider could easily have got in. There was no proof that Hewitt was guilty of leaking, or even that he'd been careless. I hoped he would still be feeling grateful.

I rang the office, and, when I was put through to Hewitt, said I'd like to meet. He agreed, but didn't sound too happy about it.

Driving up to Parliament House, I recalled a scene I hadn't thought about for years. One November, Bogong moths, migrating to the Snowy Mountains in high winds, and blown off course in tens of millions, were attracted by the light on the hill. Inside the House, they'd caused havoc with the air-conditioning; outside made a velvet cloak, wingtip to wingtip for warmth. One early morning, I'd watched masses of them lift together, light as air, surprising as an unheralded eclipse.

Hewitt led the way to *Ozzies*, a small coffee shop on the ground floor. He took a long time ordering coffee and waiting at the counter for it, deliberately delaying our conversation. A minute into it, his phone would ring and he'd say he had to go.

'The censorship legislation seems to be settling in okay,' I said, when he joined me at the table.

'I've learnt how to deal with scaremongers,' Hewitt replied. 'How's Ivan getting on?'

'Up to his collar bones in relatives. It's good for him. He's paid them no attention for the past twenty years.'

'When's he due back?'

'Couple of weeks.'

Hewitt smiled and said, 'You know, you and Ivan don't need to worry about the new legislation. If anything, it ought to increase your business.'

I smiled back. If Hewitt thought I wanted to talk to him about my concerns, so much the better. I let him explain, and arranged my features into an expression of grateful interest.

When I felt that he was running out of steam, I asked if he knew why Senator Bryant had cancelled his appointment with Eden Carmichael.

'Something came up,' Hewitt said mildly.

'Do you know what Carmichael wanted?'

'No.'

'Did he try to make another time?'

'Not that I'm aware of.' Hewitt stared at me. 'You're not trying to suggest it had any bearing on his death?'

I waited.

'The old drunk died of a heart attack,' Hewitt said impatiently. 'Everyone knows that.'

I asked when the list of recommended filters was due to be announced.

'How do you know about that?'

'The grapevine. When will it be made public?'

'Soon.'

'There's been a delay?'

'Not at all.'

'Is there a problem with the list?'

'Why would there be a problem?'

'Put it this way – some information has come to light that's caused the Minister to reconsider his recommendations.'

'I don't know what you're talking about,' Hewitt said, glancing at his watch.

'When was the last time Carmichael met Senator Bryant?'

'Last November, so far as I'm aware.'

'At *CleanNet*'s presentation?'

'Yes. You know, Carmichael wasn't as laissez-faire about the Internet as some people claim. He didn't believe such a valuable resource should be hijacked by peddlers of violence and muck.'

'Is that what he told the minister?'

'He supported the bill. Actually, he didn't believe that it went far enough.'

'He made a name for himself in the Assembly by opposing censorship.'

'People can change.'

'Who proposed the *CleanNet* presentation?'

'The company's director, I believe.'

'Did anybody else contact the minister about it?'

'Not through me.'

'Through other staff?'

'I don't know. I'd have to check,' Hewitt said, in a tone of voice that made me sure he wouldn't.

His phone rang, pretty much on cue. I knew I wouldn't get any more out of him that day.

. . .

I phoned Chris Laskaris from the carpark.

'I think there might be a problem with that list of filters you told me about.'

'Really?' Chris asked, curious but wary.

'I've just been talking to one of Bryant's staffers. When I asked him about it, he got twitchy and clammed up.'

Chris said, 'I told you what I think of filters. Technically speaking.'

'I think the problem might be more political than technical.'

'Sorry. Look, I have to go. I've got another call. And Sandra, when you came to see me, maybe I said too much. Ed Carmichael and I were never mates or anything, but he wasn't a bad bloke. I wouldn't want you to get the idea that I was down on him.'

I'd been going to ask Chris what he thought of Laura Scott, but that question could wait for another time.

. . .

I drove home and rang Brook from my office phone, got directions to his beach house, and asked if he could arrange for me to see the police photographs and video of the room where Carmichael had died. Brook clicked his tongue. I was annoying him by reminding him of work when he was on holiday. Then he said, 'Okay, cobra,' in the voice of a middle-aged policeman who has seen it all.

I typed up my conversation with Hewitt, made a note that Chris Laskaris had seemed reluctant to talk, and was back-pedalling for some reason, then wrote a report for Lucy. I told her I suspected that the recommended filters list was being delayed, and I'd do my best to find out why. Carmichael's change of attitude in relation to censorship, and his support for *CleanNet*, were definitely worth pursuing. I looked over this sentence once I'd written it, convinced that it was true. I wasn't just saying it to impress Lucy, and rebut her criticism that I was spending too much time on him.

Deciding I'd done enough for one day, I sat outside and savoured the deep hours of evening solitude, the long warm night, brushing at mosquitos as I pictured myself slipping sideways into people's lives.

The day's hot blue clarity was gone, but the city's grid lines, superimposed on the night, seemed to promise a truth that, if I only reached my hand out, would be within my grasp. I stared until my eyes watered, leaving the skin around them raw.

I was giving Fred his dinner when an idea came to me.

. . .

Hesitating in the narrow hallway of Carmichael's flat, I asked myself how his mind had been working in the days before he died. If he'd wanted to hide something, where would he have hidden it? Should I have enquired about a safe in his office, or a safe-deposit box at his local bank, before forcing the catch on his bathroom window, squeezing myself through it?

Two could play the break and enter game. The fact that I was there, that I'd acted on an impulse, had already done wonders for my morale, but I had no intention of inflicting any damage. I just wanted to see for myself where the man had lived, and, if possible, find out who owned the apartment now.

I flexed my hands in latex gloves and looked around the living room. My first impression was that it was completely empty of personality. I was reminded of the room at Margot's club, its feeling of a shrine.

One shelf held novels and biographies that looked like Christmas and birthday presents. I picked up a few and leafed through them. There was a New English Bible, with Dollimore's signature on the flyleaf. I wondered if Carmichael had kept it to please his friend, or if he'd been in the habit of reading it himself.

A TV stood in one corner, a cheap CD player in another. A couch was covered with ugly synthetic material. Another shelf held a few video and audio tapes, and no more than a dozen CDs. I scanned the titles, tempted for a moment to take them. I could have fitted the lot into my backpack. The tapes might hold anything, despite their labels. There was no computer.

The fridge was empty and switched off. There was no food in the kitchen cupboard next to it, but others contained a small variety of pots and frying pans, and a plain white dinner set. Should I have been surprised by how few possessions Carmichael had accumulated? The bedroom contained a single bed with a new mattress, and a built-in wardrobe where three dark suits and one of pale-grey linen hung against shirts and a couple of tweed jackets, a parka and a raincoat. Shoes were lined up underneath them. I pulled underclothes and handkerchiefs out of a chest of drawers. No women's shoes or dresses, nothing that could remotely have been called lingerie.

Carmichael's suits and jackets were good quality, well made, anonymous. There were no notes in any of his pockets. I checked to see if any of the drawers had false backs or bottoms, suspecting that Ken Dollimore had been there before me, doing what I was doing now. Not climbing through the bathroom window – that was too undignified.

But his ageing masculine righteousness seemed to fill the space left by his friend's death. Maybe he'd hired someone to break in to my house. I wouldn't be surprised to find that his theology left room for accomplices.

The bed base was fitted with two large drawers. I pulled the first one out, unfolding sheets and pillowcases, dark-blue towels. In the second, I found several manilla folders underneath a blanket, and in the top one was a copy of Carmichael's will.

Eight

Margot Lancaster looked tired. She was wearing the same trouser suit I'd seen her in the first time. Her hair was neat. Her make-up looked freshly applied. The morning sun was hard on the lines around her eyes, but she smiled with pleasure at having got her wig back from the police.

I watched her stroking the wig with long polished nails, the weight, shiny slipperiness of thick natural hair, falling from hand to hand. It smelt freshly washed, but there was another smell, faint but recognisable underneath the shampoo.

'It is lovely,' I said.

Margot glanced at me as though she'd forgotten I was there. She bit her lip, leaving a smudge of red lipstick on her front tooth.

'Can I hold it for a moment?' I asked, reaching out.

Margot snatched the wig away from me. I drew back my hand, aware that she would have liked to slap it. We stared at each other for a long, considering moment. It struck me that fatigue was claiming all but her outer edges, and these edges were black against the walls.

'What did you think of the funeral?' I asked.

'What do you mean?'

'Did it do Eden Carmichael justice?'

'Justice,' Margot repeated harshly. 'I had as much right to be there as anyone.'

I agreed that she had, then asked her what she thought of the interview Gail had rung me to say she'd recorded.

'It was okay,' Margot said carefully.

'Someone broke into my house and trashed my office,' I told her. 'They'd already tried hacking into my computer.'

'What were they looking for?'

'I don't know.'

'Maybe it was the challenge. Like breaking into NASA?'

'Only harder,' I said. We laughed. Margot relaxed with a sigh, and replaced her wig carefully in its box.

'Here's the funny thing,' I said. 'I've got my sights on Ken Dollimore.'

Margot's face showed no more than a neutral kind of interest.

'Are you sure he never came to see you?'

'Quite sure.'

I took advantage of her lighter mood to ask, 'Did you and Eden Carmichael have sex?'

'Many times.'

'Here in Canberra?'

'In Sydney.'

'Where did you work in Sydney?'

'It's closed now.'

'Where was it?'

'The building's been pulled down.'

'How did it start, you and Eden?'

'He turned up one day. I got him.'

'How old were you?'

'Nineteen.' Margot's expression hardened, and she stared at me as though I needed to be taught a lesson. 'Men get obsessed,' she explained. 'Men in their fifties. With young women. Girls.'

'Carmichael was obsessed with you?'

Margot narrowed her eyes and looked superior. 'You can make a lot of money out of them. Canberra's perfect for it. Middle-aged men away from home on a regular basis. Three months here, three months gone. They think that going home will cure them.'

'But Carmichael was a local politician.'

'Oh, Ed wasn't like them. He was young when we met. And it wasn't me he asked to see either. It was a blonde with big tits.'

'But he noticed you.'

'We had a line-up.'

'You don't do line-ups here?'

'I always hated them. Most clients accept what they're given.'

'And the ones who don't?'

'Go somewhere else.'
'How did it start?'
'The blonde left. He ended up with me.'
'He wanted to dress up in women's clothes?'
'Oh, no. That came later. Ed was very shy. I tried to remember what I'd been told about – when they were having trouble.' Margot laughed again, recalling her mistakes with something like affection.
'I was hopeless.'
'But he asked for you again.'
'I nearly refused. If I'd been older and surer of myself, I would have.'
'The dress and the wig were – '
Margot interrupted. Again, I felt that she was teaching me a lesson. 'Like most men, Ed didn't want to talk about his problem,' she said briskly. 'He just wanted me to fix it. I was wearing a blue dress one night. It was summer, hot and humid. I tried to put it on him for a joke. Ed had had a few drinks, and so had I by then. I pulled the dress over his head. I couldn't do the buttons up, and the stitching at the waistband broke. He looked ridiculous. We laughed, and couldn't stop. It was so hot, and – ' Margot paused, her expression far away.
'What happened then?'
'Ed had his own dress made. Like mine, only bigger.'
'How long did it go on?'
'Until I left.'
'Where did you go?'
'I'd had enough. I'd saved quite a bit of money.'
'Did you tell him you were leaving?'
'What could I have said?'
'Goodbye comes to mind.'
'I gave Ed a lot, more than any client has a right to ask for.'
'How did you feel when he turned up here?'
'I've been in the business for over thirty years. I've learnt to handle more difficult situations than ex-clients landing on my doorstep.'
'You gave him to Denise.'
'I thought Denise would suit him.'
'You were right?'
'I was.'

'No sign of the old problem?'

'None.'

'But he wanted you.'

'Who told you that?'

'Isn't it obvious?'

'You're married, aren't you?'

'Was,' I said.

'You're living with a man?'

'He's in Moscow.'

'Has he left you?'

'He's visiting his sister.'

'Then forgive me if I state the obvious. You're sentimental about men. I'm not. Ed didn't patronise my club because he wanted to have sex with me. All that was a long time ago. He used my services because I knew his tastes and could accommodate them. He wanted a girl, someone half my age. That's why men go to brothels. They can fuck their middle-aged wives at home.'

Carmichael didn't have a middle-aged wife at home. He didn't have a wife of any age. But it could have happened the way Margot told it.

The hardest thing, it occurred to me, watching Margot watching me, was not to reconstruct a crime scene, or discover why a senator had cancelled an appointment with a local politician. The hardest thing was to return desire to a dead man.

Two girls walked in, arms around each other's shoulders, laughing softly, stopping when they saw us.

They looked like twins at first glance, but I noticed that one was a few years older than the other. Both had short, pale hair and clear, creamy European skin. They wore identical make-up, bright red lips and fingernails, red tube tops and skirts. The older one gave me a quick, appraising glance, but the younger one's eyes stayed glued to Margot's face, her grip tightening around her companion's arm.

They moved on without speaking. A back door closed behind them, while Margot offered me the smile of a hunter certain of its prey. Fatigue seemed to be falling away from her, as though she'd found reserves of energy and determination that had been buried deep.

'Mieke and Kristina. They're very popular,' she told me.

'Did they come down here from *Sans Souci*?'
'Who told you about *Sans Souci*?'
'Who did Carmichael leave his flat to?'
'How should I know?'
'No reason,' I said, 'except I thought it might be you.'

. . .

I left Margot, my thoughts on the wig, and, more particularly, its smell. I couldn't put a name to it, but the metallic, possibly petroleum-based scent, was the same I'd noticed in the corridor leading to my office the night my house was broken into.

I had a nodding acquaintance with Detective Sergeant Saunders, the officer in charge of the investigation into Carmichael's death. He belonged to the generation after Brook's, joining the force with a criminology degree. Though I was beginning to think he might be interested in my information, I didn't feel ready to go knocking on his door. I did wonder, though, what he made of the fact that Margot had inherited Carmichael's apartment.

I rang Canberra's wig manufacturers and suppliers, hoping to find the shop where Margot had bought hers. It was a small job, since there were only two retail outlets listed, one in the foyer of the Canberra hospital. Most of their customers were cancer patients, and they often hired out their wigs, rather than sold them. I was sure it couldn't have been them.

The other supplier responded to my question with a 'you're wasting my time and I don't have time to waste' attitude. Unless I could give her a date for the purchase, she couldn't help me.

'Blonde,' I said. 'Real hair. Exclusive.'
'All our products are exclusive.'

I realised I'd get nowhere on the phone. The yellow pages listed one Sydney outlet as well as the local ones. 'Custom-made. We come to Canberra,' the ad said. I made a note of the address.

I was tired after my excursion of the night before. I sat in front of my computer, typing up my notes and organising them into categories. 'Wig' was my current favourite, but the word swam in front of my eyes, and I knew I was reaching the stage of imagining connections where there might be none at all. I made a note to ask Margot how many wigs she owned, and to ask Denise the same question, assuming I could persuade her to talk to me again.

I did some shopping, then rang Gail, who was too busy to talk for long, but told me her feature on Margot's club would be run early the next week.

We arranged to meet the following morning. The evening was cooler, and I took Fred for a walk to Southwell Park.

. . .

The suburb of Fyshwick, where Gail worked, was similar to Mitchell. Fyshwick was bigger, busier, more of everything, but dominated by the same fast-buck architecture, the same squat, low-slung buildings, brothels sandwiched between discount furniture and white goods.

I waited in the foyer of the *Times* building, surrounded by famous photographs, wondering if Carmichael would end up there one day, tastefully framed, posterity lending dignity to his expression and attire.

Gail was late. When she finally appeared, she looked rushed and dishevelled.

I gave her a quick hug. She returned it with a look that warned against sympathy and said, 'Let's go round the corner. I've only got a minute.'

I remembered one night in Melbourne. We were students. Gail took me to a bar where I quickly got drunk. I was very bad at judging how little alcohol it took for this to happen. A young man I fancied was holding court in the centre of a big group of people. Gail counselled me to compose myself, pick a better time. She held my head under a bathroom tap, bought me coffee, made me drink it.

Gail never needed that kind of help from me. She liked big, quiet men in those days, and attracted enough of them to be able to pick and choose.

'How are you bearing up?' I asked, hurrying after her along the street.

She pushed open the door of a fast-food place. 'How do I look as though I'm bearing up?'

'You look tired.'

'I'm busy,' she said, with a dryness in her voice that reminded me of Brook.

There was a smell of rancid fat. The battered fish looked as though it had been cooked a week ago. Gail bought a bottle of water, and paid no further attention to her surroundings.

'Mike Carnegie wrote up a presentation *CleanNet* did for Senator Bryant last November,' I said. 'I was wondering if he'd talk to me about it.'

'Why don't you ask him?'

Carnegie had been one of Gail closest colleagues before she went away.

'He might be more likely to say yes if you did.'

Gail made a sceptical face. 'Is that why you wanted to see me?'

'Strange as it may seem, I do care how you're feeling.'

'And?'

'And I'd be grateful if you'd smooth the way with Mike Carnegie.'

Gail took a gulp of mineral water. 'I got no joy out of Bryant's office. Yes, there was an appointment made for Carmichael, yes it was cancelled on the fourth. No, they won't say why.'

'Malcolm Hewitt wouldn't tell me either, but he's hiding something.'

'Ministerial staffers are always hiding something.'

I agreed, then asked Gail if she'd heard anything more about the photograph of Carmichael that had appeared in *The Canberra Times*.

'Funny about that.'

'What's funny?'

'Usually rumours fly around.'

'Why not this time?'

'I don't know.'

'It would be odd if the photographer had only taken one shot.'

Gail gave me a swift look.

'It would be odd, too, if he – assuming it was a man – had taken them only in order to offer them to your boss.'

'Well, Halford's said nothing, and he won't. You seem to think I'm up there with the eagles, Sandy.'

After tossing this remark at me, Gail checked her watch and hurried back to work.

I walked to my car thinking about confidences, who shared and who withheld them, and about our staccato, at times combative relationship. I wished that Gail would shout, or cry, or call her ex-lover names. Perhaps, alone at home at night, she threw things at the walls.

. . .

I didn't feel like going home. I was tempted to pay Ken Dollimore another visit, but I didn't want to give him an excuse to complain about me. I decided instead to drop into a few of the bars and cafes I'd noticed driving through Mitchell on the way to Margot's club.

The first cafe was empty. I looked through the door, but didn't go inside. The second was a small corner bar within walking distance of the club. Inside it was dim and cool, and appeared to be empty too. I almost missed a young woman sitting in the shadows by herself.

'Hi,' I said, walking up to her.

She looked at me with the merest hint of recognition.

'I saw you at *Margot's*. Can I buy you a coffee?'

'Why not?' The young woman's raised eyebrow said she wouldn't have picked me for a dyke.

'I'd like to ask you a few questions.'

She looked doubtful then, as though I might turn out to be a freak.

I ordered at the counter and came back with two coffees, a twenty dollar note folded underneath one.

The young woman pocketed the money without comment.

'My name's Sandra Mahoney,' I told her. 'You're Mieke, is that right?'

'Are you police?'

'No, but I'm interested in what happened to Eden Carmichael.'

She grimaced as if to say, not another one.

'Where's your friend?' I asked.

Mieke frowned, and didn't answer. She was dressed, as I was, in well-worn, comfortable clothes. She wore no make-up, and her hair was held back off her face with bobby pins.

'Sorry,' I said. 'You must get sick of that question.'

'I so do.' She had an attractive, singsong voice, with a serviceable European accent.

'How do you like working for Margot?'
Mieke stared at me, her expression hard to read.
'How long have you been at her club?'
'Few months.'
'Did you come down from *Sans Souci*?'
'Why do you want to know?'
'Just curious. Does she pay well?'
'Money is okay.'
'Did any other girls come down with you?'
Mieke looked me in the eye. I took another twenty out of my wallet.
'There was one,' she said carefully.
'What was the problem?'
Mieke pressed her lips together.
'What happened?'
'I don't want to say. Don't tell Denise or Margot I say anything.'
'I won't. How long are you planning to stay?'
'In Canberra?'
'At *Margot's*.'
'She wants to sell up.'
'Has anybody made an offer?'
'There is one guy she talks about, but I don't know if he is buying.'
'Do you know his name?'
'Lawrence something. Or it might be something Lawrence.'
Mieke glanced nervously towards the door, and said she had to go.

I felt a certain satisfaction as I thanked her for talking to me. Having found her so easily made me feel I could do so again. I was moving my investigation forward, however awkwardly and slowly. I'd have to watch the money, though. I needed an alternative employer to Electronic Freedom. A second employer would be better, while managing to hang in there with them.

. . .

An email from Ivan said that everyone, including Katya, had the flu. I rang immediately, forgetting it was 5 am in Moscow. Katya was awake. She sounded congested, but cheerful, when Ivan put her on the phone. He breathed hoarsely in my ear, and told me not to worry. I tried to take his advice, telling myself that worry wouldn't do my daughter any good.

Restless and unable to concentrate, I rang *Sans Souci* in Sydney. I said I was a friend of Mieke's who was looking for a girl who'd come down to Canberra with her and Kristina last year. I thought it unlikely that anyone would be willing to talk to me, but the woman who answered the phone asked me to wait. Another, very softly spoken woman came on the line and asked me what I wanted. I told her a computer software company I was being paid to research had led me to Eden Carmichael, and then Margot Lancaster's club. I said I'd be in Sydney on Friday. After some hesitation, she agreed to meet me at a cafe in Glebe.

Nine

I began the three hour drive to Sydney early on Friday morning, heading first for Richard McFadden's office, in Castlereagh Street, Sydney CBD. After that I'd meet the woman from *Sans Souci*, check out *Julia's* wig shop, whose advertisement I'd noticed in the Canberra yellow pages, then drive south along the coast to Brook.

Sydney heat was different, thick and humid. Summer had a way to go yet, but what I was beginning to think of as my summer would be over as soon as Peter, Ivan and Katya came home – my summer that was long days in a city that the heat beat back to bones, the task I'd set myself of sifting through them.

Ivan had rung to say that Katya was recovering. I'd phoned Peter again too. He'd sounded grown-up, full of self-importance.

· · ·

Richard McFadden's office was in a well-preserved 1930s building. I passed under chandeliers, by polished hat and coat stands, and even more deeply polished hexagonal tables bearing silver urns filled with hydrangeas. The lift was lined with mirrors set into dark-red padded velvet. There was more red velvet in the small waiting area, where I sat in a deep chair with huge armrests.

CleanNet had begun modestly, McFadden told me, with a smile down-turned at the corners, in the days when Internet censorship was just becoming an issue. Until the share float, there'd been no board of directors. After that, the heads of the three major investors sat on a board he chaired.

I couldn't see any resemblance to the Maverick Chris Laskaris had described, though Chris had made it clear as well that McFadden was well on the way to putting his past behind him. His smile was transparent, his rather small teeth the product of expensive dentistry. There was a sprinkling of grey through his short dark hair.

I'd tried my filter for a second time and found that it continued to block the National Party site. I'd brought it with me to show him.

McFadden laughed. 'Oh dear. I'm surprised that one's still in the shops. Where did you buy it?'

I told him and he made a note of the name.

'We've recalled all that batch,' he told me complacently. 'If you'd allow me to offer you a replacement?'

After McFadden had demonstrated the newest version of his filter, I asked about staff, and learnt that they consisted of two programmers and a young woman who doubled as secretary and receptionist.

'Let me tell you the history of my company.'

I thanked him, hoping for something new. When ringing to ask for an appointment, I'd told the secretary I was researching filter software for my master's thesis. But all McFadden did was repeat what he'd already said, plus the few facts I'd learnt from ASIC.

'So you're not a programmer yourself?' I asked.

'No. Or, I should say, an amateur rather than a professional. But the two young men I have working for me are first rate.'

'Glitches not withstanding.'

'Glitches not withstanding,' he repeated with another smile.

'How did you like Canberra?'

'A beautiful city. So much space. Clean air. And the gardens. Beautiful.'

'And the political climate?'

McFadden looked thoughtful. He picked up my superseded filter and turned it round a few times.

'How would you rate the climate for *CleanNet*?' I prompted.

'Favourable, I'd say. Very favourable.'

'Will *CleanNet* be on the recommended list?'

'The minister was kind enough to say he was impressed.'

'How was your presentation arranged?'

McFadden asked why I needed that information for my thesis. I told him I was looking at the social and political aspects of using filters, that I'd prepared school surveys for example, and that kind of thing.

'Did you receive support from Eden Carmichael?' I asked.

'That poor man. He was generous enough to compliment us. I was sad to hear he'd died in such distressing circumstances.'

'What kind of compliment did Mr Carmichael pay you?'

'Very generous. He admitted that he hadn't been in favour of mandatory regulation in the past. But now he was convinced.'

'What happened to change his mind?'

'His constituents did that for him, I believe. Concerned parents. It's shocking what children are exposed to these days. Truly dreadful.'

'I was wondering if Mr Carmichael had assisted you by recommending your filter to any members of the Federal Parliament.'

'I would have been most grateful, but I know of no such recommendation.'

'You never spoke to him about it?'

'Never.'

We talked for a while longer, but no matter how I phrased my questions, McFadden's replies were bland and unrevealing. He got his receptionist to make us coffee, but I felt that I'd learnt all I was going to from him, and was soon on my way.

• • •

I stood outside, looking up and down Castlereagh Street to get my bearings, stepping close to the window of a shoe shop to avoid a group of teenagers. I looked into the window and caught the reflection of a man's face staring back at me. He had dark hair and a strong, inexpertly-shaven jaw. I swung around. The street was crowded with shoppers. The man was already a few metres away, head bobbing above a suit that looked too big for him. He was moving fast, with a peculiar bouncing walk.

I recognised the woman I'd spoken to on the phone before she spotted me. It was her air of expectation, as much as the features she'd described.

'I'm a blonde,' she'd said. 'One of those. And you?'

'Kind of,' I'd replied.

She was sitting inside. I watched her for a moment through the window. Her gaze was locked with that of a young woman standing behind a counter, dressed in a navy singlet, shorts, and tiny apron. Both appeared to be about to say something, and intent on this.

The waitress raised an eyebrow. The other woman eyed me for an instant before she nodded a greeting.

She introduced herself as Rose. The flyer she pulled out of her bag looked professionally done, with some care given to its composition. There was a bunch of red rosebuds in the centre, half open and enticing, and above them a man's dark curly hair, dimpled chin, smiling mouth with a hint of cruelty about it.

Large black letters said 'THIS MAN IS UGLY ON THE INSIDE'. There was a description, brief but telling, of the incident Rose began describing as I studied it.

'Jen said they were nearly finished when he ripped the rubber off and held her face down on the bed. She yelled out and the girl next door rushed in and got him off her. Margot took his side and ticked Jen off for making a fuss.'

'Jen?'

'Jenny Bishop. She's dead. She died just after Christmas.'

'How did she die?'

'The police said it was an overdose, but Jen wasn't using. She stopped using a year ago.'

'What do you think happened?'

Rose said stubbornly, 'She never killed herself.'

Her T-shirt smelt of some backyard clothes line by the sea. Her expression was determined, but she was so nervous she could not keep still. I noticed rows of old needle marks along the insides of her arms. She saw me looking and rested her elbows on the table, making no attempt to hide them.

'Who was the girl who helped Jenny?' I asked.

'I think Jen said her name was Denise.'

'When did Jenny die? What date?'

'December thirtieth. She never made it through the year.'

The waitress came to take our order. She frowned at Rose, and avoided meeting my eyes.

When she'd gone, I glanced at the flyer again. The man's name was

Simon Lawrence and he was described as owning a flower shop in Parramatta Road.

'Did you show this to the police?'

'I gave them one. You can have that one if you like.'

'What did the police say?'

'Nothing. Like nothing to *me*.'

'Do you think they interviewed this Lawrence?'

'I don't know.'

'Where did Jenny live?'

'In Wigram Road.'

'Do you have a photograph of her?'

Rose smiled then, as though I'd passed some kind of test. She pulled a small, wrinkled, dog-eared snap out of her bag. The young woman it showed was fair like Rose. Long, wavy hair blew off her face. She grinned at the camera with a child's enjoyment of life.

I thanked her, then asked, 'When was it taken?'

'On her birthday. September the first.'

'I'd like to help find out what happened.'

Rose nodded. She wrote down Jenny's full address for me on a scrap of paper.

'What did Jenny tell you about Margot Lancaster?'

'That she was a cow to work for.'

'Did she say anything else?'

'Just that she took the side of this pig over her.' Rose tapped the flyer with a pointed nail.

'When did Jenny leave Canberra?'

'At the end of November.'

'Did Margot force her to leave?'

'They had an argument, I know that much.'

'Why did Margot take the client's side?'

'She was sucking up to him because she wanted him to buy her club. That's what Jen said. I don't know.'

I asked Rose if she'd had any contact with Simon Lawrence herself.

'Are you kidding?'

'Did Jenny? After she sent the flyer round?'

'She never told me. I reckon she'd have told me.'

I took out a photograph of Carmichael and asked Rose if she'd ever seen him at *Sans Souci*.

'He's the one who carked it, right? I saw it on TV.'

'Did Jenny ever mention him?'

Rose was about to answer when she ducked her head, hunched her thin shoulders, and whispered hurriedly, 'I gotta go.'

'What's wrong?'

'Some creep who's after me.'

Her head was level with our table and she was moving crabwise, fast. The waitress was walking towards us with our coffees. Rose said something to her, then disappeared through swing doors.

I looked round for whoever had frightened her. I couldn't see any likely candidates in the street, and no one came inside.

Not knowing quite what else to do, I drank my coffee. While I was paying for it, I told the waitress I hoped Rose would be okay. She gave me a hostile stare.

. . .

A block away, at Glebe Post Office, I found a stained copy of the yellow pages and looked up Lawrence's Flowers. I wrote down a phone number and address in Petersham, studied my street directory, then drove straight up Parramatta Road and found a park in a side street.

I walked past the florists on the opposite side. Constant buses and semis, a footpath full of people, gave me the confidence to pass back and forth several times without worrying about being noticed. A young man with long dark hair tied back in a ponytail was preparing a window display – heart-shaped red and pink balloons and a huge mock-up of a Valentine's Day card. He was pretty early, but then people did prepare early for festivals these days.

There was a small cafe not quite opposite, the only window table occupied by a woman with three shopping bags, leaving one spare seat.

The woman barely glanced at me when I took it. She was absorbed in eating a sandwich that seemed to consist entirely of beetroot. I was hungry, but if hers was anything to go by, the sandwiches were to be approached with caution. I ordered a soft drink, keeping my eye on the boy in the florist's window. The shop was narrow, but made good use of the pavement space in front. It was a busy area, but I didn't think the people in the street, the woman with her shopping and her slit-vein sandwich, looked the kind to spend twenty dollars on a bunch of roses.

I finished my drink and ordered another, this time with a bagel.

My thoughts returned to Jenny Bishop, and I asked myself if there was any way of creating an effective blacklist, getting it to work. I thought about Rose, the story she'd told, her sorrow for her friend. Who'd been after her back there? I should have stayed and nagged the waitress. I had a feeling that she knew.

. . .

The roses looked better in reality, close up, and so did Simon Lawrence. He smiled at me from behind the counter as though I was his first customer for the day. The young man had disappeared, and Lawrence seemed to have the shop to himself. His skin was lightly tanned, his curls a boy's. The dimple in his chin was deep.

I smiled in return, and said, 'Roses, I think, red roses. Though it's early for Valentine's, isn't it?'

'Never too early for love.' Lawrence smiled again, crookedly this time, to undercut what he'd said, but not entirely.

The roses that surrounded him, high, mid-summer roses, looked as though they'd just been picked. Their perfume filled the small space. The buds and half-open blooms seemed to expand as I watched them, as though glorying in an unnatural power, demanding that I pay attention, while their maker went on smiling, secure behind his counter.

'They're beautiful. A small bunch will be fine.'

'Thank you. I haven't seen you around before. Are you new to the area?'

'Just visiting.'

I watched the florist walk slowly from behind the counter to the buckets at the front of the shop.

Carefully, he chose half-a-dozen blooms and wrapped them, aware, all the time, of my eyes on him.

'Be sure to get them into water as soon as you can. They won't last long on a day like this.'

I nodded, paid the rather high price, took my change and left.

From half a block away, I turned and looked back down the footpath. The crowd of shoppers had thinned, and I chanced to see a tall young man in a baggy suit, with an ungainly bouncing walk, turn into Lawrence's doorway. His head was down, but I knew that, if I'd been able to take a closer look, I would have seen that his jaw was badly shaven, or perhaps that he was starting to grow a beard. It was the man whose reflection I'd caught in a shop window in Castlereagh Street.

. . .

Julia's wig shop was also in Parramatta Road, about five kilometres closer to the city. I found the number on a dark-green door, opened it and climbed some stairs. A faded sign told me that what had once been a ballroom had been divided into shops and offices. *Julia's* was one.

Wigs were displayed on the heads of mannequins. Some had faces and some didn't, which created an unsettling impression. The old-fashioned showroom was somewhere between respectable and down at heel. I guessed that *Julia's* must do practically all of its business by mail order.

A young woman behind a counter was plaiting yellow ribbon into long brown hair. She looked up and asked if she could help.

I sniffed a familiar smell in the air, then smiled and complimented her on the wigs. I'd seen a beautiful ash-blonde one, I told her, on a Canberra woman whom I knew by sight. I wanted one just like it.

The young woman showed me several wigs, none as striking or so finely made as Margot Lancaster's. I described the one I wanted, and asked how much it would cost. My eyes widened involuntarily at the answer.

Perhaps they kept photographs of the wigs they sold?

The sales assistant asked me to wait a moment, and disappeared through a door behind a counter. I heard her voice, but would have sworn that nobody else was in the shop, and assumed that she was talking on a phone.

When she came back, she was polite, but apologetic. She had no photographs of a wig such as the one I'd described. It would be possible to make it though. She offered to email me a quote. I said I'd think about it and thanked her for her time.

Descending the stairs with a backward glance, I felt that Margot might well have bought her wig from *Julia's*, but that didn't bring me much closer to identifying my intruder. I admitted to myself that the smell, which I'd now noted three times, could easily be a common one used in the cleaning and maintenance of wigs, and that it might have other uses too.

As I joined the long snake of traffic heading back out along Parramatta Road, I wondered if it was a coincidence that *Julia's* and Lawrence's shop were both in the same street. I did not think a firm offer had been made for Margot's club. If it had, she would not have kept the good news to herself, or cared about using me to arrange a favourable interview. On the other hand, assuming she *was* keen to sell, where were the For Sale signs and advertisements? Perhaps Margot was avoiding drawing attention to her wish, because it might lead reporters to speculate, and bring more bad publicity.

My thoughts returned to Simon Lawrence. Yes, I could see him smiling, being charming, then holding Jenny Bishop down, face squashed into the pillow, frightening and humiliating her.

I parked and walked down Wigram Road towards Harold Park, keeping in the shade as much as possible. The roots of large trees had buckled and tipped the footpath, which sloped steeply down. I made for each one's shadow, the illusion of cool air closest to the trunk, where the smell of earth was concentrated, and eucalyptus resin rose from huge, ant-filled cracks in the asphalt, heady as a cough inhalant.

Double- and triple-storey terraces lined both sides of the street. Their owners' cars did too, which was why I'd parked further up the hill. The houses were all renovated, with front doors painted sophisticated shades of green. The one belonging to the house where Jenny Bishop had lived boasted an outsize knocker. Its shape was suggestive. I considered it, then knocked with my fist.

I introduced myself to a tall, thin, fair-haired man, and told him the same story I'd told Rose, adding that Jenny's name had come up in connection with Margot Lancaster's club, and I wondered if he'd mind answering a few questions. He looked doubtful, but didn't refuse outright. After a moment's hesitation, he invited me inside.

I followed him down a passageway of polished pine, past a row of hooks where last winter's coats and scarves hung waiting for the next, to a kitchen that smelt of summer fruit. He motioned me to sit down at a wooden table, and told me his name was Ian. He was very skinny indeed, with the long, transparent thinness that seems to have trouble remaining upright.

The kitchen was cool, the walls of the old house thick and well-shaded by trees surrounding a courtyard at the back. Windows with white frames and old-fashioned metal catches were closed against the heat.

'Did you know Jenny well?' I asked.

Ian leant against a bench. I noticed that his hands shook slightly, but his voice was steady enough. 'We met when she was in first year,' he said, then, in a different, agitated voice, 'Jen had been giving death the finger for years.'

'This time she succeeded in killing herself – is that what you think?'

'That's what it looks like. I really don't know what to think.'

'Why would she start using again?'

Instead of answering me, Ian said, 'What about this club you mentioned?'

'It's called *Margot's*. Jenny worked there for a while last year.'

Ian nodded in recognition.

I took out the flyer with the photograph of Simon Lawrence and asked him if he'd seen it.

'She did show me. Us. Yes.'

'Us?'

'Me and Francesca. My girlfriend.'

'Francesca lives here?'

Ian nodded.

'What did you think when Jenny showed it to you?'

'If it made her feel better – why not? The guy was an arsehole. It was her way of letting off steam.'

'But –'

'These things can backfire,' Ian said impatiently. 'Jen knew that. She wasn't dumb.'

'Did it backfire?'

'She never said anything about the guy finding out. But she wouldn't have minded if she'd pissed him off. That was her intention.'

'Would you mind telling me what happened the night Jenny died?'
'We came home from a friend's going-away party and went straight to bed.'
'We?'
'Fran and me.'
'Did you assume that Jenny was at home?'
'I guess so. I wasn't thinking about it.'
'What time would this have been?'
'Around two.'
'Did you leave any lights on while you were out?'
'The porch light. At the front. We always do that.'
'Was it on when you got back?'
'Yes.'
'Did you switch it off?'
'Fran did.'
'What about the back of the house? Is there a light there?'
'The globe went and we didn't get around to replacing it. Our back gate's padlocked. We hardly ever use it. And the fence is quite high.'
'Did you go straight to sleep?'
'More or less.'
'Did you wake up at all during the remainder of the night?'
'I'm actually a very sound sleeper. It takes a lot to wake me.'
'How did Jenny intend to spend the evening?'
'As far as I knew she wasn't going out.'
'Was there anything to indicate she *was* home?'
'What do you mean?'
'Glasses on the bench, dishes in the sink?'
'There was a glass and an empty bottle of Fosters. The police took them.'
'What time did you wake up?'
'Fran woke around nine-thirty. She got up and had a shower. I stayed in bed for another half an hour. Someone rang for Jenny.'
'Who?'
'Rose, a friend from work. Fran went up and knocked on her door. You know, all of this is in Fran's statement. And mine. The police made us go over every step.'

'If you wouldn't mind repeating it for me?'

Ian studied me with an exasperated expression, then he said, 'Fran knocked. When there was no answer, she opened Jenny's door. Jenny was just lying there. Fran went over to her. She screamed. I woke up and ran upstairs. Jenny was lying on her back. I – I had to stop Fran from trying to revive her. I could see that she was dead.'

'Where was the syringe?'

'Beside the bed. I made Fran come back downstairs, and rang the police.'

'Do you know Jenny's dealer?'

'If you mean personally, no. I've taken calls, but that was a long time ago.'

'What about alcohol?'

'What about it?'

'What did Jenny like to drink?'

'Beer. Spirits. Whatever.'

'She kept a good supply?'

Ian shrugged.

'The Fosters. Do you know when she bought it?'

'I bought that, as a matter of fact. Look, Jenny was a grown woman, and I was not her keeper.'

'What about the garbage? Were there any bottles in it?'

'The police took the bin. It's not as though me and Fran had the chance to become little amateur detectives. We were shoved out very unceremoniously.'

'What about Jenny's family?'

'What family?'

'You mean she was an orphan?'

'I mean her parents disowned her. That's a good word, isn't it? Disown. Implies that they owned her to begin with, which I guess they thought they did. Anyhow, clear enough in the circumstances. When they found out she was using heroin, they refused to have any more to do with her.'

I wondered if Jenny's body was still lying in the morgue.

'What about brothers and sisters?'

'There's a boy and girl. Much younger. Jen's mum had her when she was very young, then married again. After Jen left home, she tried to keep in touch with her half-brother and sister, but her parents wouldn't have a bar of it. Particularly her stepfather.'

'But surely, once she stopped using – '

'We'll never know what *might* have happened, will we?'

'Where did Jenny come from?'

'She went to college in Canberra. Before that, she lived in Orange. That's where she was born. Just outside it, actually. Her real father was a market gardener. He died a few years ago.'

'Did Jenny talk about her clients?'

'If something unusual happened, she might tell us. But she liked to keep work and home separate.'

'What about an ACT politician called Eden Carmichael?'

'He's the one who just died? Of a heart attack?'

'He died at Margot Lancaster's club. I was wondering if Jenny ever spoke about him.'

'Not that I recall.'

'Did she ever mention a computer company called *CleanNet*?'

'I don't think so, no.'

'Could I see her room?'

'You can look through the door. There's not much to see.'

I followed Ian up the stairs. It seemed to get a degree hotter every step. The whole top of the house appeared open to the sun.

'How many bedrooms are there?'

Ian answered me over his shoulder. 'Three. Fran and I share a bedroom and a study.'

He opened the door to the room that had been Jenny's, and stepped to one side. I stood in the doorway.

Bands of heat and light followed one another in regular pulsations, reflecting off pine floors stained a darker colour than the ones downstairs. White curtains were pulled back. There was the feel of summer in a humid place. The end of life in Jenny Bishop's room smelt soft, rotting, sweet. There were a million ways for life to leave a body, a million small ways every second, so common as not to be remarked on, as unworthy of comment as masturbating in a handkerchief.

A low table held a lamp, cigarettes, a box of tissues. A bookshelf along one wall was practically empty. Three books stood in a pile on the floor, the top one open and face down, a paperback copy of Toni Morrison's *Beloved*. There was a wooden bed base underneath the window.

Ian followed my line of sight and said, 'The police took the mattress for tests. They took the syringe as well, and DNA samples from Fran and me. And our fingerprints.'

'Was there blood? Or any sign that there'd been a struggle?'

'No. Fran thought Jenny was asleep, but then she saw the syringe –'

Ian's voice caught. I waited before asking, 'Did Jenny own a computer?'

'She used mine.'

'For email?'

'Yes.'

Jenny's room was at the head of the stairs. Three other doors led off a narrow landing. I peered into the bathroom. It was the same age as the rest of the house. Nothing had been done to modernise it, to replace the bath in one corner, or the shower recess with its wide, old-fashioned nozzle. Blue and white tiles were chipped in places. The floor was tiled as well, the tiles cut and angled carefully for drainage. Like the kitchen and every other part of the house I'd seen, it was clean and well-kept. A window to the left of a deep handbasin was wide open. Hot, thick Sydney air poured in.

I walked over to the window and looked out. The view was of the racetrack: huge arc lights, grandstands, horses' stalls. Sprinklers were swinging, dampening the dust. I noted that some of the terrace houses still had outside lavatories. Others had garden sheds. The laneway behind them was too narrow for cars.

I pulled the window in towards me. It had an old-fashioned catch like the ones in the kitchen, no more than one bit of metal fitting behind another. A flyscreen was coming apart from its wooden frame at the bottom. A narrow strip was missing.

'Did Jenny ever bring customers home?' I asked as we headed back downstairs.

'She wouldn't have wanted to.' Ian sounded tired. 'Jen wasn't – she wasn't careless about what she did, you know.'

'Would you mind showing me around outside? I promise I'll be quick.'

Ian said something under his breath that sounded like, 'For God's sake'.

He took me out the back door, through the kitchen. I noted that this door was fitted with a simple lock, and had neither chain nor deadlock. The wood was old, paint peeling here and there.

Someone had put a fair amount of work into a vegetable garden. Healthy, thick-leaved tomatoes climbed their stakes. Other beds held zucchinis, lettuce, capsicum. I asked to see the back gate first. It looked solid enough, but was fitted with an ordinary chain and padlock, the kind you could buy at any hardware shop. I scanned the rest of the yard and fences.

The flowerbed was moist underneath the kitchen windows, and the bathroom one above it. A pipe ran up the brick wall, vertically at first, then at an angle. Standing underneath and looking up, the damage to the bathroom flyscreen was obvious. A kitchen knife slid under in the right place could have levered it out. But the pipe did not look climbable.

'Where do you keep your ladder?'

'In the shed.'

'Is it locked?'

'Yes. We keep our bikes in there as well.'

'Did you notice if anything in the shed had been moved?'

'The police moved stuff around. I don't know.'

An intruder, if there had been one, would have been working in the dark. He or she would not have risked a torch. But there was no back light to worry about, and any slight noise would not be likely to carry to the neighbours.

Ian opened a side gate and led me to the front of the house.

He turned without warning, and said in a hard voice, 'Jen was a dangerous person to be around. To herself, and to anyone who was fond of her as well.'

'How was she dangerous to you?'

'She could be charming. Fun.'

'But?'

'She let herself down. That's what hurts the most.'

. . .

I knocked on doors up and down the street, but found only one woman at home. She looked to be in her early seventies, and was wearing an old checked shirt over olive-coloured cargo pants.

I repeated my story, now sounding a bit stale, about how Jenny Bishop's name had come up in connection with an investigation I was working on in Canberra.

The woman stared at me, unsmiling, and asked if I had a business card, or other ID.

She studied the card I gave her for some time, then looked up, a glitter of curiosity at the backs of her hazel eyes.

'Did you see anyone coming or going from Jenny's house on the night she died?' I asked.

'I saw that tall one and his girlfriend leaving.'

'When would that have been?'

'Around eight-thirty. What is it you're investigating?'

'To begin with, a computer software company. I'm trying to find out if there's a link between the company and an ACT politician who died recently.'

'That one who dressed up in women's clothes?'

I nodded. 'He died in a brothel where Jenny Bishop worked for a while last year. I'm guessing you know what Jenny did for a living.'

The woman nodded economically, and then, apparently deciding I was harmless, she observed, 'You're hot. Come in out of the sun for a few minutes.'

I followed her down a corridor very similar to the one across the road, except that, instead of polished wood, the floor was carpeted in dark blue. A row of hooks held sunhats, a raincoat, gardening gloves.

She poured lemon cordial for me, and nothing for herself, remarking as she did so, 'Canberra's a lovely place. My brother and sister-in-law live there. Mason is their name. Colin and Vera Mason.'

I said I was afraid I didn't know them. 'Across the road – do they have many visitors?'

'Not many.'

'Did Jenny have her own?'

'Single men, you mean? No, Jenny kept her work and home lives separate, so far as I could see. She was a friendly girl. She'd often stop for a chat if she saw me in the garden.'

I glanced down at the woman's hands. They were callused, with enlarged, roughened knuckles.

'What did you and Jenny talk about?'

'Plants. She loved my garden. She used to ask me the names of things. And she remembered them too. She used to say that when she went back to university she was going to get into some serious gardening for relaxation.'

The woman smiled. For someone who spent a lot of time outside, her face was pale, no pink in her cheeks, careful with her sunhat.

'Did Jenny have women friends who came to visit?'

'There was one lass. A fair-haired lass. Jenny was fair as well. And such a little thing –'

'When did you last see her friend?'

'About a month ago, it would have been.'

'Did you see or hear anything unusual on December thirtieth?'

'Nothing you could really call unusual.'

'Tell me about the usual things, if you wouldn't mind.'

'Well, I went to bed at around ten. I'm not up much after ten. Sometimes I read in bed. I didn't that night, though. The heat makes me tired.'

'Where's your bedroom, at the front or back?'

'The back. I wouldn't like to sleep close to the street.'

'Did you hear anything during the night?'

'The possum. I heard the possum. He clatters on the roof. He's out foraging till twelve or thereabouts, then he clatters on the roof. He made a lot of noise. Hissing and, that kind of screech, you know. I took my torch and opened the door. He doesn't like the torch. Then I heard a car start up.'

'Where?'

'Up the street.'

'On your side?'

'No, the other.'

'Did it pass your house?'

'It kept on going up the hill.'

'What time was this?'

'Around midnight. Actually, it was ten past twelve when I went back inside. I checked the kitchen clock while I was getting myself a glass of milk. I was wide awake by then. I thought a glass of milk might help me to get back to sleep.'

'Have you any idea whose car it was?'

'I didn't see it. I just heard the engine starting up.'

'Who are your neighbours on that side?'

'There's Mr and Mrs Horowitz. It wasn't their car. It was further up, and anyway, they wouldn't be going anywhere so late. Then there's a young couple. He's a lawyer, I think. Leastways, he looks like a lawyer. He's hardly ever home. His wife has two little kiddies. One's starting school this year. It might have been him coming home, but not going out at that hour, unless of course they'd had a fight –'

She stopped and looked at me, head on one side, lips pursed, to see if I might be interested in speculating about this. Seeing that I wasn't, she went on, 'Next there's a young man. I don't know his name. He has a very nice garden. He's just that bit further up the hill, you see, and the soil's less clayey.'

'Have you told the police about the car?'

'No.'

'Has anybody been to question you?'

'I've been away visiting my son and his family. I left on New Year's Eve.'

'Ring Glebe Police Station and tell them about the car. Will you do that?'

The woman said she'd think about it. I thanked her for the cool drink, told her she could keep my card and asked her to contact me if she thought of anything else about that night.

...

Sans Souci the suburb stretched along one side of Botany Bay. From an esplanade of multi-coloured cement, a metre or so above the sand, I looked out at twin headlands, Cook's landing place on one side, La Perouse the other. From where I was standing, the cliffs appeared to be so close together that no *Endeavour* could have made it through.

I thought of the Pacific pushing from the other side, squeezing bits of itself between the heads twice a day.

Other aspects of the bay seemed likewise set in balance, the jumbos taking off and landing at the airport, two oil tankers lined up at Kurnell. The afternoon had become overcast, the sea grey and choppy, smell of the tankers so close I felt that I was sitting on them. Botany Bay – funny how your mind scrabbled round for things to rhyme with it – breathed out, with a tired, congested sigh.

In the middle of the beachfront was a huge Novotel, complete with shopping mall and flyover, so hotel guests didn't have to bother with the traffic on La Grande Parade. I found the brothel without any trouble in a side street three blocks back from the sea. It was a white, double-storey terrace. Everything was white, including the iron lace around an upstairs balcony.

Sans Souci, I repeated to myself, glancing up and down the street. Cars passed at regular speeds. All the pedestrians seemed to be minding their own business. *Not a care in the world.*

I stood watching for a few more minutes. Nobody went out or in. Cars were parked bumper to bumper on both sides of the street, but they were parked that way on every street I'd walked along. How much custom should I expect late on a Friday afternoon? I felt quite comfortable standing there with the sea at my back – oil tankers and pier, commerce of a nation bending, as the sun was, towards a quiet horizon. But after a while I felt I ought to move, and began circling the block. From a distance, I watched two men in suits leave by the front door, making for their cars. A couple of minutes later, a young woman emerged, shutting the door behind her. The men hadn't done this. The door had been shut for them. The woman was carrying a large shoulder bag. She was tallish, with an athletic walk. Dark hair swung around her shoulders and partly hid her face. She turned away from me along the street, then round the first corner. I thought of Denise Travers, and what she'd said to me about providing for her daughter.

I lifted my head and smelt the wind. Botany Bay smelt like St Kilda and I was reminded of Port Phillip Bay, where I'd grown up – those fists of southern headland, rush of water at the ebb tide. I used to love swimming off St Kilda pier at the end of the day.

It was too late to drive all the way down the coast to Broulee. I didn't want to knock on Brook's door at ten o'clock at night. I had the number of a motel in Elizabeth Bay where I'd stayed before. It was pleasant, inexpensive, a short walk to the harbour. I rang them, sitting in my car with the door open, then drove back towards the city centre against the peak hour traffic.

My room had a stove and a selection of saucepans in a cupboard. I could have set up house. I almost threw the roses in the bin, then changed my mind and stuck them in a drinking glass.

The bed was big enough to lose yourself in, then spend a lifetime looking.

I rang Brook to let him know I'd be arriving the next morning, then plugged in my computer.

Simon Lawrence's website seemed, at first glance, to be boring. Flowers and more flowers. He specialised in roses. There were links with growers' clubs, prizes won at the Easter Show. I scrolled back to the beginning of the site. The business was a lot larger than I'd guessed from the shop in Parramatta Road.

You could click various blooms to move to different parts of the site. Their composition reminded me of something, though I couldn't put my finger on exactly what. I clicked a white rosebud. Photographs of a nursery came up, a terraced hill with rows of plants. A gardener's shed at the bottom looked incongruous. I clicked it and found myself looking at a close-up of a woman's exceptionally large breasts. I tried the backspace. It didn't work. I moved over the woman's body. A border of rosebuds ran down the left hand side of the screen. I clicked one and was rewarded by a smorgasbord of couples having sex. I tried the backspace, got the breasts again. What I couldn't do was go back to the beginning.

I switched off my computer, which was the only way I could exit the sequence. Then I began again. Exactly the same thing happened. Once I'd passed the shed, I could not return or exit without shutting down. I'd heard of mousetraps, or webjacks, but this was my first experience of one.

That Lawrence was into net pornography should not have surprised me. It seemed he'd turned his interest into a joke against the censors. It required a bit of ingenuity, yet the ruse was simple, not something he could expect to get away with for long. But the site was still there. I wondered if he'd been ordered to take it down.

I cut the power, then began again for a third time. A single line at the bottom of the nursery's home page said 'Web Design by Stan Walewicz'. Below the name was an email address and post-office box number.

I double clicked the word Walewicz, and my screen filled with a list of magazines and videos. I scrolled down. There were extracts from latest issues, new releases in bold type, discount prices, what looked to be a straightforward ordering system, and another feast of pictures. Stan Walewicz's website was neatly hidden inside Simon Lawrence's.

I recalled Walewicz's comment that there were ways around the new law. The trick increased my surprise that Lawrence's site was still up, and I wondered why his friend or business partner – for surely Walewicz had to be one or the other – would bother playing it. Not many new customers were going to find him by this circuitous route. Walewicz had his mail-order business, with its established customer base. No one was threatening to shut that down. The net was useful for attracting new customers, which brought me back to the question of how potential ones would find him. Unless he'd simply done it as a way of giving the authorities the finger. Perhaps he planned to advertise Lawrence's web address all over the place, as though it was his own.

I got myself a drink, then wrote to Ivan, including a summary of what I'd learnt in Sydney and my conclusions to date. I thought the rosebuds should be worth a laugh, but Ivan seemed so far away that I no longer felt confident of his sense of humour.

On impulse, I visited the *CleanNet* site again and found the balloons. I double clicked one. Nothing happened. I tried each one. The same. It seemed that there was nothing hidden under the striped beach balls either.

We had a couple of contacts in ASIC who'd been helpful in the past. I pulled one off my address book, and sent an email to a guy called Andrew Glover, asking if he'd do a complete archive search for

CleanNet, looking for any mention of Carmichael, Dollimore, Margot Lancaster, Simon Lawrence and Stan Walewicz.

I spent some time typing up that day's conversations and sent a report to Lucy, thinking that her group could well get some mileage out of a porn merchant distributing his pictures and thumbing his nose at the censors, apparently with ease.

Next, I checked out *Julia's* custom-made wigs. Their site was simple. Good quality graphics. Good-looking models, rather than faceless shop dummies. None wore Margot's wig though, or anything resembling it. I mulled over the smell, and made a note to visit the two shops that sold wigs in Canberra, to see if I could identify it.

I made sure the glass door leading to my room's small balcony was locked, and locked the main door behind me, then walked down the hill towards Rushcutters Bay.

The sun was setting over the city, turning the seawater pink. I stared straight down over a stone wall. Viscous water, blackened with oil, moved slowly up the rocks. I could stay and watch the tide come in, at least until it got too dark. I decided that I liked the way the oil sat on the water, playing with it. Herds of pleasure craft grazed quietly in the dusk. Golden-pink and mauve light caught a mast here, a railing there. I pictured Lawrence's clientele, amateur growers logging onto his site, reacting with shocked amazement. Surely at least one of them would have complained. Was it a signal, a message to someone in particular? But why? Roses had thorns. You could breed them out, or try to. Were thorns part of the message the florist was sending?

I turned my back on the sea and began climbing the hill towards Kings Cross. Interesting to think of Margot in her early days, and Margot now. Interesting to speculate about what Carmichael had felt for her. And where would Denise Travers be, what kind of person, in ten, fifteen years' time?

The lights over Rushcutters Bay gathered in behind me. I ordered a bowl of Thai soup from a small cafe, and sat down at an outside table. When the soup arrived, I held my face right over the bowl, breathing in the chilli, the night air thick around me – not that immense relief of heat lifting off dry land I'd left behind in Canberra.

I watched the street girls for a while, then walked slowly back down McLeay and Greenough streets to my hotel. As I climbed the stairs to the first floor, I thought with pleasure of my outsize bed.

I checked my mail. There wasn't any. I hoped Ivan and Katya were better. I settled down with that sense of luxury it always gave me to sleep between sheets that someone else had washed.

Ten

The green hill with the sun shining on it looked serene – top-knot of hill, beneath it a wealth of flowers in the early sun.

Again, I recalled the small, single-fronted shop in Parramatta Road. If Simon Lawrence owned all this, he ought to be master of an emporium in Pitt or George Street, all glass and mirrors to magnify the blooms. Or a chain of shops from Hornsby to Cronulla. How much was his business worth? How many shops, across Sydney and beyond, bought plants from this spacious, well-tended nursery?

It was scarcely eight o'clock, and there didn't seem to be anyone about.

I got out of my car and walked up to the gates, which were large and made of black wrought iron, fitted with a heavy padlock. A sign said 'Simon Lawrence, Retail and Wholesale Supplier of Quality Floral Produce'. Beneath it were the opening hours, 9 to 6 six days a week, 9 to 9 on Thursdays.

Now that I was closer, the area the nursery covered didn't seem quite so extensive. Clever terracing had made the most of the available space. I wondered what the land had been used for before Lawrence took it over. Perhaps, from the early days of European settlement, it had been one type of market garden or another.

A man startled me, appearing from behind a shed that might have been a model for the one on the website. I hoped he hadn't seen me. Though my car was parked back along the road, I didn't want anybody noticing that either. The man wasn't looking in my direction, but up the hill, where sprinklers suddenly came on. One second the air was clear, the next filled with water.

He was wearing khaki overalls and gumboots, and too far away for me to see his face, which in any case was hidden under a broad-brimmed hat. Though it was hard to be certain, I didn't think I'd seen him before. I began to walk away, turning for a last look over my shoulder. The man was heading for what I took to be the main office and sales building. As I turned, he did too.

. . .

Tall gum trees with salmon-coloured trunks framed the cedar house, a house for families, for summer letting, too large for one man on his own.

But Brook was not alone, as I discovered seconds after I knocked on the front door. I heard my name spoken from the other side, in his voice, then a female one, further away and indistinct, floating down the stairs.

Brook smiled, kissed me on the cheek and said, 'Sophie's just arrived.'

Sophie descended the last two steps like a movie actress mindful of her cue, holding a hat and sunglasses in one hand. She smiled hello, waving them casually in my direction. I smiled back, thinking of my overnight bag in the car, thinking of the surf, white water breaking on my shoulders. I knew Sophie could see the disappointment on my face.

She exchanged with Brook the glance of a man and woman who have just got out of bed, touching his arm just above the elbow as she asked, 'Is there anything you want me to pick up from the shops?'

'Not right now, I don't think.' Brook's voice was reassuring.

The whole ground floor of the house was open plan. I pictured the two of them laying claim to corners.

'Coffee?' Brook asked, leading the way towards the kitchen end. 'Then you can tell me your news.'

'How long will Sophie be?'

'As long as she considers necessary.'

I let myself fall into a cane chair, while Brook made coffee and toasted raisin bread. I began at the beginning – not rushing, but not lingering over details either, now that I knew our time together was rationed. I mentioned Ken Dollimore's phone call, Eden's Carmichael's aborted appointment with Senator Bryant, what I'd learnt about *CleanNet*, my conversations with Margot Lancaster and the women who worked for her, the break-ins to my computer and my house.

Staring out at the trees – the pink trunks looked soft – I was aware of Brook listening with his familiar slow consideration, and felt doubly certain that I had interrupted love-making.

I said my office had been trashed, but nothing stolen. 'It seems we might be dealing with an amateur.'

'We?'

'You'll get stuck into all of this when you come back to Canberra.'

Brook laughed. 'Don't you ever have a holiday?'

His laughter seemed a continuation of his morning's occupation in the cedar house, and I felt that he was moving even further away from me. There was surprise in it as well. There'd always been something in Brook that greeted physical pleasure as an unexpected guest.

I sniffed. The beach house smelt of salt, sea air. I showed him Jenny Bishop's flyer, and told him what Rose had said, that she didn't believe Jenny had died of an overdose.

'Lawrence, the guy who ripped the condom off, his website's a front for porn. I'm wondering if he's been reported to the Broadcasting Authority and if so what they've done about it.'

Brook handed me a plate of toast, then settled himself comfortably in a wicker chair.

In my mind's eye, I saw Sophie returning, arms laden with provisions, edging the door shut behind her with one foot. She would smile. She would not need to say, 'I'm glad Sandra's gone.'

Facts tasted dry in my mouth. I couldn't see the point in pulling more out. Eucalypt trunks through the window were orange-pink, robust, mildly obscene. The garden had the look of a stage set, though it should have been the other way around – audience out there, and on the stage two people sitting opposite in matching chairs, one relaxed, the other nervous – two people who knew each other well, yet suddenly, without warning, strangers.

Brook crossed his sleek legs in their cotton pants. He was proud of the weight he'd put on and managed to keep.

'Why are you doing this?' he asked me.

I'd told him over the phone, but I repeated it. 'My time's currently being paid for by Electronic Freedom. Not at a massively generous rate, but what else is a girl supposed to do in Canberra, in January?'

Brook did not say, you could have come down here. We both knew that, without Peter as a chaperone, it would have been impossible.

I remembered the bunch of roses and fetched them from my car. I'd sprinkled them with water before I left the hotel, and they'd survived the coast road pretty well. I handed them to Brook with a flourish, a matador with a living cape.

'Tell Sophie where they came from,' I said.

The flowers got us to the kitchen, where we made a small ceremony of looking for a vase. We found one eventually, in a top cupboard. Ugly, but it would do.

'What's he like then, this florist chappy?' Brook asked mildly.

'Attractive in a dark way. Heathcliffian. Dimple in his chin.'

I looked up from arranging the roses. They seemed meagre somehow, not enough to fill the vase, and artificial in the beach house setting.

'I have a feeling Simon Lawrence doesn't forget a face,' I said, 'not even one belonging to the most casual of customers.'

. . .

During the long drive back to Canberra, I was overcome by a drenching tiredness and emptiness. I'd walked into a trap at Broulee. On the snake road up the Clyde, I thought about the roses, pictured Sophie throwing them away, saying, with a short, careless laugh, that they were already dead. I realised how much I'd been looking forward to the weekend, the treat of spending time with Brook. Now it was over prematurely, and had left me feeling bad.

. . .

I woke to a mist slipping down Black Mountain's hips, dry eucalypt smells, clean air of the hinterland. Not wanting to face the hot idleness of a Sunday on my own, I phoned Gail as soon as I thought there was a chance she'd be awake.

Gail chuckled at my description of the rosebuds. Perhaps, being more used to the solitary life than I was, she understood the mood swings it induced – pleasure in solitude one minute, fear of it the next. I told her about Jenny Bishop, Lawrence and the flyer. In return, she said that Mike Carnegie, the journalist who'd written up *CleanNet*'s presentation for the minister, would be happy to chat with me. I felt comforted by the thought of Gail just a few kilometres away, in her echoing, half-unpacked, single woman's house.

I rang Laura Scott and suggested an afternoon swim at Civic Pool. Somewhat to my surprise, she agreed.

Then I drove by *Margot's*, thinking it would probably be closed.

Two cars were parked next to each other in the carpark. When my knock on the door was met by silence, I knocked louder.

Margot opened the door, a crack at first, then a fraction wider.

'What do you want?' she asked.

'Can I come in for a minute?'

'Why?'

I peered round Margot's shoulder, catching a glimpse of Denise standing in the shadows. She plucked at her eyes with a tissue, a hasty, almost cruel movement, then turned her back on me.

'Jenny Bishop's dead,' I told them, thinking that it was unlikely to be news.

I stared at Margot as I spoke, but it was impossible to tell whether she already knew. I wondered why she'd answered the door at all, and why Denise had stayed in the foyer, rather than disappear into one of the rooms. Was it possible that Margot had ordered her to stay where she was? There was something vindictive in her manner.

'The blonde wig, do you wear it yourself?' I asked.

'What are you talking about? Why would I?'

Margot pushed the door shut. I backed away, not wanting to cause any more trouble for Denise.

Driving home, I asked myself if Margot and Denise were lovers. Perhaps I'd interrupted a lovers' quarrel.

. . .

I looked up Ken Dollimore's phone number.

'Good morning,' I said when he came on the line.

'Good morning, Mrs Mahoney.' Dollimore sounded as if he'd just got back from church.

'Did Eden Carmichael ever mention a young woman called Jenny Bishop?'

'I don't think so,' Dollimore replied smoothly and politely. 'I don't recall the name.'

'She worked at Margot Lancaster's club for a while last year.'

'I don't think Ed mentioned names, apart from Madam's. He never criticised or slighted any of the girls, if that's a help to you.'

'Why did he leave his flat to Margot?'

There was a silence, then Dollimore said, 'Because he was a sentimental fool.'

'Do you know what she plans to do with it?'

'No,' he said. 'Do you?'

'I might be able to find out. If I can, I'll trade you.'

'What for?'

'I'll make a list.'

Dollimore laughed. He had a nice laugh, melodious and warm.

. . .

Next, I phoned Chris Laskaris. He sounded friendlier than when I'd last spoken to him, and didn't seem put out that I was ringing him on Sunday. He laughed when I told him about the rosebud trail, then reminded me that it wasn't his group's job to act as censor. Since our initial conversation, he'd heard that Stan Walewicz had been ordered to take down his website.

I asked if he'd heard anything on the grapevine about a meeting between Ken Dollimore and Richard McFadden, when McFadden was in Canberra. Chris said no, but he'd make a few enquiries if I liked.

. . .

Laura's sleek physical assurance reminded me of Brook, a reminder that I didn't want just then. She turned out to be surprisingly athletic. In her office, and at the funeral, she'd seemed so much a mistress of the tight skirt and stiletto heels. She dived off the springboard as though she'd been doing nothing else all summer, and came up laughing, her short dark hair plastered flat against her head. I wondered what had happened to put her in a playful mood.

'How's Ken Dollimore bearing up?' I asked, when she'd pulled a T-shirt over her bathers and sat down on her towel.

'Who can figure these guys out? Hey, you want an ice-cream?'

'What would you like? I'll get them.'

I came back with two Cornettos, already melting in the heat.

Laura polished hers off with a few quick bites, then said, 'Ken kept on trying to get Ed to reform. He never gave up. He was determined to rescue the poor sod.'

'Who from?'

'Himself, I guess. Ed got sick of being lectured, but he put up with it. He told me once that if he was going to die before he reached sixty, it was his business, not anybody else's.'

'What were Dollimore's main worries?'

'Booze.' Laura licked her fingers, then began counting on them. 'Dicky heart. Bad women. Ken needs to save someone. It's his religion. Ed used to say it was a pity the old patriarch's daughters were such good girls. In his secret heart, he would have loved one of them to be a junkie so he could devote himself to rescuing her.'

'That's a bit hard.'

'Hard? Ed loved the silly old goat. But that didn't stop him taking the piss occasionally. And he was shaken up after his first heart attack. He did take more notice of Ken after that.'

'But not enough to give up booze or bad women.'

'No.' Laura sighed. 'Not enough for that.'

'Who was he afraid of?'

Laura gave me a sharp look. 'I don't know who you've been talking to, but I've been thinking about that. Somebody was pressuring him. Underneath, you know, Ed was very much his own person, an independent thinker. In spite of everything, his constituents recognised and appreciated that. They trusted him not simply to go along with a party line.'

'Ken Dollimore must have shared your concerns.'

'That night in the carpark, we were trying to work out what to do when – if – '

Laura's voice faltered.

I waited a moment, then said softly, 'But he did recover. He came back to work.'

'He was determined to see out his term. It was a matter of pride with him to finish what he'd started.'

'Did you and Dollimore keep in touch, compare notes?'

'I tried for a while. But Ken retreated behind that holier-than-thou manner of his. And he'd never thought much of me to begin with.'

'Why not?'

'A pretty face is all,' said Laura philosophically.

'Do you recall anything else about the *CleanNet* presentation? Any little detail?'

Laura thought for a while, then said, 'Not really.'

'Do you know if Carmichael met Richard McFadden privately?'

'I made all Ed's appointments for him.'

'None with McFadden?'

'No.'

Laura's phone rang. From the way she answered, it sounded as though she'd been waiting for the call. She laughed and tossed her head as though the person she was talking to could see her.

She was still smiling when she said goodbye, thanked me for the ice-cream, and told me she was off to meet a friend in Civic.

. . .

Back home once more, I checked my email. Ivan had replied to the one I'd sent from Sydney.

'*A fuck's a fuck Sandy. Poor old Carmichael died of a heart attack. I think you'll find that's all there is to it.*'

Up yours too, I said to the computer. At the same time, I was reminded that it was a trap to categorise, abstract, and then ignore whatever details didn't fit. There was the added impulse to solve a mystery on my own, and double-quick, to present Ivan with it at the airport, all tied up in a wig box, finished, done.

Eleven

Next morning, I called in to Canberra's wig shop, not the one at the hospital, but where the snooty woman had answered my enquiry by insisting that all her products were exclusive. I discovered that they didn't sell women's wigs at all, but turned out to be a hairdresser with a side business supplying wiglets for men. There was no hint of the smell.

Gail rang with a piece of news. She'd happened to mention Jenny Bishop's name to Mike Carnegie, and it had rung a bell. Jenny had made the news a few years earlier when, as a Year 12 student at Dickson College, she'd starred in a porn movie made by a local producer.

'It was one of the first stories Mike wrote.'

'Who was the filmmaker?'

'Something Serbian. Or Polish, could be.'

'Walewicz?'

'Sounds right.'

I congratulated Gail on her interviews with Margot and Denise, which had been in that morning's paper. They'd both come across as intelligent and careful women, as professional in their dealings with their clientele as anyone who ran a successful business.

Gail said she'd already had complaints from the religious right.

'Ken Dollimore?'

'Not yet.'

We talked for a few more minutes, until she said she had to go.

Lucy's reply to my email said she'd found the rosebuds and enjoyed the joke. It proved their claim that the new legislation wouldn't stop pornographers. In the meantime, it was causing a major headache for everybody else. I emailed back saying I was working on a suspicion that someone had complained to the minister about *CleanNet*, and that I hoped to have some details for her soon. My suspicions hardened up,

I realised, when I was composing my emails to Lucy. If I'd been truthful, I would have admitted that what I'd just written was no more than a guess, but it was useful, voicing my opinions to someone who was paying me, not just to speculate, but to get results. I was daring to put my hunches into words, and this was leading me to take them seriously, and to try and test them out.

. . .

The adult video place smelt of old cigarettes. I lingered at the sex aids counter for a while, indulging fantasies I would never have imagined if I hadn't been alone, then made my way to the back of the shop, and began going through the videos. Asking for Jenny Bishop by name would be embarrassing, and I thought it unlikely that she would have used her own name anyway.

I spent twenty minutes reading credits and staring at close-ups of giant dripping cocks. I was beginning to think I was wasting my time when I came across a girl with Jenny's face, dressed in a black G-string and waist-length, wavy chestnut hair.

The credits gave her name as Jane. The movie's title was 'Jane Springs the Trap'.

In order to borrow it, I had to join the library. The young woman at the counter explained tactfully, after she'd asked for some ID, that my borrower's card would be blank apart from the barcode. I bit my tongue to avoid the urge to explain what I was doing.

Back home, I switched on the VCR, then decided I didn't feel like watching it yet. Instead, I did a google search for Jenny Bishop, and came up with hundreds of sites featuring Jennys and Bishops of the ecclesiastical and faux-ecclesiastical variety.

I made myself some lunch, then settled down to see what Rose's friend Jenny had to offer, realising that the reason I'd put it off was that I was no longer sure it was her after all. I don't know what I'd been expecting, apart from disappointment, but I felt surprisingly protective towards 'Jane' when she came on the screen, and relieved when the action switched to someone else. Jane gave a credible performance of pretending to enjoy sex with one man after another, or perhaps she really had enjoyed it. I was beginning to feel I'd seen enough, when a door opened and another man appeared. The camera lingered on his pelvic area, then moved up to his face. Dark, wavy hair. Dimple in his chin. Smile that promised a better time than anybody else could offer. It was a younger, sweeter Simon Lawrence. I checked the credits again. He'd called himself Trenchant. I looked it up in the dictionary, which defined the word as 'keen and effective, vigorous, penetrating and incisive'.

. . .

I rang *Sans Souci* and asked to speak to Rose. The woman who answered said she wasn't there. Something in her voice warned me against questioning her further.

Then I phoned Mike Carnegie at *The Canberra Times*.

'The presentation *CleanNet* put on for Senator Bryant last November,' I said, once we'd exchanged pleasantries. 'How did it come about?'

Carnegie turned the question back on me. 'Favouritism, you reckon? It's not as though the government's about to buy the filters themselves. Nor the ABA. The legislation leaves that up to the service providers.'

'Who aren't going to be impressed by *CleanNet* sucking up to the minister.'

'Not in general. No.'

'And in particular?'

'I don't know of anyone who'd be all that impressed. Given that most of them are against the legislation anyway.'

'Has anyone complained?'

'Not that I know of. Not directly.'

'Indirectly?'

'The guy heading them up – Richard McFadden – he's incredibly gung-ho.'

'And?'

'Guys like that are good at making enemies.'

McFadden's propensity for making enemies hadn't stopped a number of local companies investing in *CleanNet*. I wondered if Carnegie knew this. It might be something I could trade.

'What about the list of recommended filters. Do you know if *CleanNet*'s on it?'

'Do you?'

I bit my tongue to stop myself from pointing out that I wouldn't have asked him if I already knew.

'Afraid not,' I said. 'Did you notice Carmichael and McFadden together at the presentation? How did they seem?'

'They looked to be on good terms. But everyone was sucking up to McFadden that night.'

'Did you talk to Carmichael?'

'Briefly. He gave me the usual bullshit about having to keep up with the latest developments.'

Since I didn't seem to be making much headway with this line of questioning, I changed the subject, and asked about Jenny Bishop.

'Did you know that she was dead?'

'No. I – that's a pity. I heard she'd become an addict, and turned hooker to support her habit. She seemed a nice girl.'

Carnegie had assumed, without a word of explanation from me, that Jenny had died of an overdose. It would be the common assumption, as Rose understood very well.

'Did you know that Jenny was back in Canberra last year, working at Margot Lancaster's club?'

'No, I didn't.'

'What about that porn movie?'

Carnegie coughed. 'I wanted to do a story about her,' he said, then cleared his throat. 'She'd just turned eighteen. My impression was she'd done it for a laugh. It wasn't so much the money, and anyway I don't think the guy running the show would have paid her much.'

I asked him the date his story had appeared, and wrote it down.

'Did you talk to the guys who were in the movie with her?'

'No.'

'Trenchant – does that name ring a bell?'

'That's a name? No, not off hand.'

'What about Simon Lawrence?'

'Negative to that as well.'

I asked Carnegie if he'd followed Stan Walewicz's career.

'I know him as a local character.' Carnegie made the word sound oddly prim.

'Did you know he'd been ordered to take down his website? He's lost the opportunity for advertising on the net.'

'Won't he just go offshore? Isn't that what they're all doing?'

'He was at the *CleanNet* presentation.'

'Yeah?' Carnegie seemed to be trying to remember. 'I didn't see him there.'

We talked about the presentation for a while longer, but Carnegie had nothing new to add.

. . .

With a cup of tea in hand, I rang Brook to tell him about the movie, Jenny Bishop's starring role, Lawrence's cameo appearance. He clicked his tongue disapprovingly, while I listened for Sophie in the background.

'There's a logic to it,' I said, feeling a mixture of pleasure and frustration at keeping him on the phone for a few more seconds. 'These porn companies have had a dream run up till now. Canberra's been a good home to them. But the climate's changed and they're looking to diversify.'

'A good thing too,' Brook said.

'Carmichael was sympathetic. At least he didn't try and shut them down. Then last year it seemed that he was moving over to the other side.'

'The guy had a heart attack. It's hardly unprecedented. Remember Billy Sneddon?'

'Of course I remember Billy Sneddon.'

I could feel Brook smile at last. 'I have to go,' he said.

The phone rang as soon as I'd put it down.

Peter's voice was excited, with a new and charming confidence.

'Is Fred okay? What have you been doing, Mum?'

'Fred's fine. I went to Sydney for a day or two.'

'You're not forgetting to feed him?'

'Would Fred let me do that?'

Peter laughed. I thought of the brown hair beginning on his upper lip, the way he'd turned aside when I kissed him goodbye. His voice, soon to break perhaps, shattered the line between Launceston and Canberra.

I felt restless, jittery, after he'd hung up. It was overcast and hot. I thought about going for a swim, but I wanted the astringency of salt water, water with a bite in it, not the tepid chlorine of Dickson Pool.

. . .

I decided to drop by the club unannounced, but Margot looked as though she'd been expecting me. This time, she let me in.

I was struck by how quiet it was. Once inside, the Mitchell traffic shut out, there wasn't even the noise of a clock ticking, no sign of customers, no sound of the radio or voices from a back room.

The *Times* crossword was open on her desk. Margot fiddled with the page, curling then uncurling it.

'Are you happy with Gail Trembath's piece?' I asked, nodding at the newspaper.

'It's okay,' was all Margot said.

'I hope it helps you find a buyer for the club.'

Margot raised her eyes and studied me.

'A privileged customer should be grateful,' I said. 'And gratitude should breed consideration.'

'What are you talking about?' Margot smiled faintly, as though she expected the riddle to be simple, once I had explained it.

'Was it Jenny Bishop in particular, or does Simon Lawrence make a habit of breaking the law?'

Margot's lips became a thin, hard line. 'I threw him out,' she said.

'You threw Jenny out as well.'

'She wanted to go back to Sydney.'

'You didn't like Jenny.'

'She was a –'

'A what?'

'An addict.'

'I heard she'd given up.'

'Who told you that?'

'Her friends. What did you have against her?'

'I never said I had anything against her.'

'Did Jenny contact you after she left here?'

'No.'

'Why was Denise crying the other day?'

'A personal matter. None of your business.'

'Who was here the afternoon Carmichael died?'

'Me and Denise. I've already told you that.'

'What were you doing for three hours by yourself?'

'The crossword. I don't have to answer any of your questions.'

'That's right,' I said, 'but if I don't get answers from you, I'll take my questions elsewhere, and you might like that even less.'

Margot went on staring at me.

I chanced one last enquiry. 'What are you going to do with the money from Carmichael's flat?'

'What do you think?'

'Sell this place for whatever you can get, and kiss Canberra goodbye.'

Margot laughed. It seemed the prospect made her happier than she'd been in a long time.

I drove home from Mitchell thinking about the words people chose, or rejected, a chance phrase that could catch and hold – but was it chance, then? Margot impressed me as a woman who could turn a lie to suit her purposes better than most. I was pretty sure she'd lied about Jenny Bishop.

But I couldn't help respecting Margot for choosing her words carefully, even for the lies she told. Eden Carmichael had been rushing full tilt towards a burning windmill, though whether he'd lit the fire himself was still an open question. I wished I'd asked her to let me see the room again, the space that I sensed meant a good deal more to her than she was willing to admit. It was too late now. If I went back and asked her, she'd refuse.

I left Grosvenor Street feeling that the brothel resisted, as a sphere will resist from the inside, the denting pressure that is other people's judgements. The past was a treasure which could be visited and looked at, but never removed from its hiding place, and never spent. Something told me that, in spite of Margot's brusqueness with me, and her contempt for sentimentality, the past she'd shared with Eden Carmichael was a place she often visited.

What if a core of carefully constructed lies was at the base of her personality? And what if this base was threatened suddenly? What might she do then, a woman who had lived with, habitually negotiated, the deep contradictions of sex work, within and outside herself, for most of her life?

Twelve

I spent forty minutes in the National Library the next morning, looking up Mike Carnegie's story. In the accompanying photos, dressed in jeans and T-shirt, and without the russet wig, Jenny Bishop looked younger than ever.

There was a voyeuristic tone to the piece that I didn't like. When asked about the men she'd worked with on the movie, 'Jane' had said one was a novice like herself, a guy who'd 'done it for a laugh'.

I was still thinking about this as I drove to Fyshwick to meet Stan Walewicz in his studio.

As I pulled up, a white Hyundai with NSW plates was backing out of the small carpark. Morning light made the driver's cleft chin more acute. His eyes widened in recognition, then he smiled. I smiled back, memorising the rego number.

· · ·

Walewicz's handshake was brisk. His hands were square cut, his nails a manicurist's pride. He was about five foot seven or eight, with very broad shoulders for his height, gym muscles and thin hips, no bum at all. His face was square to match his hands. His eyes and the ends of his fingers flashed hello.

'How's the censorship legislation affecting your business?' I asked him. 'Has it made a difference?'

'That bunch of God botherers in their committee rooms think they can control the Internet? What a joke.'

'They shut down your site.'

Walewicz laughed. It seemed he found the setback amusing. He asked me what I'd like to drink.

'Tea would be nice.'

I sat down in a padded leather chair, in an alcove at one end of a compact film studio. Two cameras on tripods stared at me from the other end. The air-conditioning was quiet and efficient. Dark curtains blocked out the hard tracks of the sun. Wall lamps were easy on the eyes, but powerful lights stood next to the cameras, ready to accentuate every swelling curve. Through an open doorway, I could see a small office with bookshelves, a desk, computer equipment. Two more doors leading off the studio were closed.

Walewicz poured tea from a jug in a bar fridge, while I asked, 'Has it cramped your style?'

He said over his shoulder, 'Depends on what you mean by style,' and repeated what he'd told me over the phone, that there were ways around it.

'What's your way?'

Walewicz handed me my tea. 'To tell you the truth, I'm thinking of getting out. It bores me. No challenge any longer.'

'Diversify, you mean?'

'Like really out. You work in security. I'd like to hear about your side of things.'

'That's rather a back flip, wouldn't you say?'

'I know the sex business, know the guys who run it, but net security's not just about your fifteen-year-old wanking to pictures of Tom and Pammy Lee.' Walewicz looked at me quizzically, and smiled again. 'Why am I telling you this? You know what I'm saying. It's all the company time getting wasted, spamming, invasion of privacy, industrial sabotage, stalking, all that other shit flying round out there.'

'Set a thief to catch a thief?'

'Consumers want security.' Walewicz nodded sagely, refusing to bite. 'It's the old supply and demand. I love the Internet. I love the freedom of it, but it's got its down side. Anybody who denies that is either a liar or a fool.'

My eye grazed a bookshelf in the office. A box had *CleanNet* written on the spine.

Walewicz followed my line of sight. He frowned, and I wondered if he regretted having left the door open.

'If you're thinking of getting into security,' I said. 'They're the ones to beat.'

He thanked me for my advice with a small, polite inclination of the head.

'Their website's well designed,' I prompted.

Walewicz raised an expressive eyebrow. 'That so?'

'I thought you might thank me for the compliment.'

'Excuse me?'

'It's your work, isn't it?'

Walewicz raised both eyebrows this time. 'What makes you think that?'

'Certain stylistic features.'

'I'd like to take the credit, but I'm afraid I can't.'

'You went to *CleanNet*'s presentation though.'

Walewicz nodded thoughtfully.

'And were so impressed you bought their filter.'

'I'm educating myself in the area, like I told you Mrs Mahoney, or do you prefer Ms?'

'I'm not particular. What did you think of Richard McFadden?'

'He's their head honcho, right?' Walewicz made another face, half curious, half envious perhaps. 'I liked his style.'

'He has a sense of humour too, I hear.'

'The security market's expanding. Should be room for all of us to make a buck.'

'Do you employ a programmer?'

'Not at the moment.'

'So your work's all your own.'

Walewicz drank his tea and waited for me to come to the point of my visit, letting me know, by the way he rounded his lips to take in the refreshing liquid, that he was a patient man, but patience had its limits.

'I found one of your old movies,' I told him.

He looked pleased, as though they were collectors' items.

'"Jane Springs the Trap." What was it?'

'Excuse me?'

'The trap.'

'You know, I don't remember.'

'What got you started in the movie business?'

'What gets anyone? Want to watch a shoot? I can arrange it.'

'Thanks. I'll think about it.'

Could I picture myself sprawled naked on the couch, one of his studs going to work on me? I found that yes, I could.

We were alone in the studio. The office was empty too. I gave my denim skirt a tug. Walewicz wasn't looking. I was too old, for one thing.

'Your young stars,' I said, 'have you followed any of their careers?'

Walewicz shook his head.

'What about Jenny Bishop?'

'Can't say I kept in touch with her.'

'She wasn't to your liking?'

'She was okay.'

I watched him carefully, but he gave no sign of knowing Jenny was dead. I decided to leave this for the moment and asked, 'Simon Lawrence?'

'I've known Simon like forever. We went to school together.'

'Have you seen him lately?'

'I don't often get to see Simon. He's a busy man.'

'What about today?'

'He did drop in, as a matter of fact. A coincidence that you should mention it.'

'What about last November?'

'What about it?'

'He was here, in Canberra.'

'Was he?'

'I heard he was thinking of buying Margot Lancaster's club.'

'That's news to me.'

'Do you know if he kept in touch with Jenny Bishop, after they'd been in your movie?'

'Simon likes to play the field. He keeps in touch with a lot of girls.'

'Did you hear they'd had an argument?'

'Who?'

'Lawrence and Bishop.'

'What about?'

'Unprotected sex.'

'That doesn't sound like Simon. He's careful. He wouldn't risk getting a disease.'

Walewicz's expression was both fastidious and scornful. What about the risk to Jenny, I felt like asking him. I sniffed. Somewhere in the studio there was a faint, familiar scent.

'Do you keep costumes here?'

Walewicz's answer was to extend his hand, and, with a slight bow, invite me to follow him.

He opened one of the doors leading off the studio. A small room held a rack of costumes – schoolgirls' dresses, nurses' uniforms. They seemed, at a glance, to be the standard fare, and not, in any case, what I was looking for. Whips hung from hooks on the wall opposite them. A large variety of lingerie occupied one shelf. Above it, another shelf held half-a-dozen wigs, including a shiny chestnut mane.

'Great wigs,' I said. 'Do you get them custom-made?'

'I do.'

'That must be expensive.'

'I don't believe in paying good money for trash.'

'I can see that. Could I hold one for a moment, do you think? That one,' I said, pointing.

I let the red-brown hair slither between my hands, and sniffed again.

'How do you clean them?'

'I send them back to the manufacturer every six months for a bit of re-conditioning. They're too valuable not to take good care of. Look after them, they'll last a lifetime.'

'Who's your supplier?'

'I get them made in Sydney. Want to try it on?'

'Not today, thanks. What's in the other room?'

Walewicz opened the door. It was full of cameras, and sound and lighting equipment.

We went back to the front of the studio. I thanked him for talking to me. I never thought I'd go for muscles, but he made his subject interesting. What more could an investigator ask for, in Canberra, in January?

'Is your old school friend staying in town?' I asked.

'Excuse me?'

'Simon Lawrence. Will he be here for a few days?'

'Why do you want to know?'

'I thought I might bump into him.'

Walewicz rounded his eyes at this, but made no comment. He shook my hand again and said he'd enjoyed meeting me.

. . .

As I drove from Fyshwick towards the city, I pictured the nursery's website, with Walewicz's neatly tucked inside. I thought about secrecy, deception, and what a person might reasonably expect to get away with. It was time to revise my theory concerning the identity of my intruder. I'd already replaced one suspect with another. If the smell was anything to go by, here was number three. I couldn't imagine what motive Walewicz might have for turning my office upside down. But that wig had had the smell, no doubt about it.

I imagined his studio full of sweating bodies, surrounded by cameramen, sound and lighting technicians, a director. Privacy was a commodity for sale, like any other. Carmichael had paid for his at Margot's club, but I suspected that he'd been cheated in more ways than one.

. . .

'Margot doesn't care,' Mieke told me. 'She never gives a shit.'

We were in the same small corner bar, where I'd found Mieke alone again. She'd given me a wary look when I sat down at her table, but had not got up to leave. Instead, she'd started complaining about Margot.

'What doesn't Margot give a shit about?' I asked.

'That story in the paper saying she's a good businesswoman. What a load of crap.'

'What did Margot do to Jenny Bishop?'

Mieke stared at me. I took out a twenty dollar note and she put it in her bag.

'They get into a fight,' she said without expression.

'What about?'

'Don't tell her. You say anything to her about me, I'm history.'

'I won't.'

Mieke licked her lips. 'I was at the front when this customer comes in with Margot. He ask for Jenny. I hear him say her name. Kris tell me later that Jenny don't want to do him, but Margot say she has to. He is bastard, a real prick. I found out later what he did.'

'Was his name Simon Lawrence?'

Mieke nodded.

'Where were you while Jenny was with him?'

'I am answering the phone till Margot gets back, then I am in another room with Kris.'

'Where did Margot go while Lawrence was with Jenny?'

'I don't know.'

'Did you and Kris hear Jenny calling out?'

'Denise did.'

'Did Jenny threaten to go to the police?'

'Margot give her money to keep quiet and leave.'

'Did Denise and Margot argue over Jenny? Denise took Jenny's side, and Margot didn't, is that right?'

'Side, side,' Mieke said, flipping her left hand over and back again. 'Denise and Margot, they don't argue. They always work it out.'

'Did you talk to Denise about what happened?'

'Denise doesn't want to talk.'

'Why not?'

Mieke shrugged.

'How does Margot treat you and Kris?'

'She like us to dress up.'

'In what?'

'Outfits.' Mieke's tone managed to make the word obscene.

'You mean, like schoolgirls?'

Mieke nodded.

'Does Kristina mind?'

'Not so much as me.'

'What about wigs? Does Margot make you wear them, too?'

'She just about go crazy when the police take that one away.'

'Have you ever worn it?'

'No.'

'Others?'

'Sometimes.'

'Did you ever see Eden Carmichael?'

Mieke responded to my change of subject by narrowing her already narrow nostrils, as though she'd just smelt something bad. 'He give me the creeps, that one. Once, when Denise is sick, Margot tell me to do him, but I say no.'

'Who took Denise's place?'

'Jenny. She laugh about it. She don't care.'

'Was that the only time Jenny saw Carmichael?'

'I don't know.'

'When was the time you remember?'

'Not long before she leaves. I think, early in November.'

'How did you find out Jenny was dead?'

'Kris told me.'

'What do you think happened?'

'Jenny never overdosed. That's bullshit. She'd stopped using.'

I put another twenty on the table and asked Mieke for her mobile number. She scribbled a number on the back of her hand, and held it out to me. Her hand was shaking badly.

On the way home, I stopped off at an ATM. Most of the money the lobby group had paid me would be gone before I knew it. But I was supposed to be on holiday, not earning anything for these two weeks, lounging around in a beach house instead. Time to worry about the budget when my family came home. If Electronic Freedom covered my expenses, then I figured that I wasn't doing badly.

. . .

I was writing up my meetings with Stan Walewicz and Mieke when my phone rang. Simon Lawrence sounded the same as he had in the flower shop – charming, with an edge of parody. I asked him how he'd found me and he replied with a slightly sharper edge that he'd used the phone book. We agreed to meet that night. I felt excited to think the nights were mine, to spend any way I liked. Never since Peter was born had it been that way.

I smiled, recalling Walewicz's acknowledgment of the play within the play, as I brought up the list of *CleanNet*'s shareholders I'd obtained from ASIC. I double-checked to make sure Walewicz wasn't on it, mulling over why he'd had their software sitting in his office, thinking about his reaction when I'd remarked that they were the ones to beat.

I'd noted the name on the front of the studio – *Zabawka Entertainment*. I searched ASIC's website again, and came up with a private company. The registration date was 1996.

I fetched the video I'd borrowed, remembering another name at the bottom of the list of credits. *Artysta Limited*. I did a search for that one too. It drew a blank under registered companies, but I found it when I tried the deregistered list. Begun 1991, ended 1996.

I emailed Andrew Glover to ask how his archive search was progressing. Next I rang *Julia's* in Parramatta Road and asked if they supplied wigs to a Mr Stan Walewicz in Canberra. The woman who answered the phone had a smoker's voice, and sounded much older than the one who'd been plaiting yellow ribbon when I'd visited the shop.

She asked why I wanted to know. I said I'd seen Walewicz's wigs and they'd really impressed me. I was looking to buy something similar. She asked me to hold and came back after a few minutes to say that yes, Mr Walewicz was a customer of theirs.

'Would you like to place an order?' she asked.

I said I'd call her back.

I looked up Travers in the phone book, half expecting Denise to have a silent number, but she answered on the second ring.

'Are you okay?' I asked. 'You seemed upset the other day.'

'I'm fine.'

I tried to think of something sympathetic to say, about her daughter, her responsibilities, but anything that came to mind seemed condescending.

'What did you think of Gail's piece in *The Canberra Times*?'

'Not bad.'

'Are things okay between you and Margot?'

'They're fine.'

I'd meant to lead up slowly to my next question, but I was annoyed by Denise's bland and, it seemed to me, false replies.

'How did you feel when you found out Jenny Bishop was dead?'

There was a long silence on Denise's end, so long I thought she'd hung up. Finally, she said, 'Jenny overdosed.'

'Who told you that?'

'She hadn't been using for a while. She gave herself too much. I have to go now.'

'Just a couple more questions. I promise I won't keep you long.'

I asked about clients who patronised Margot's club in order to cross-dress. I sensed that Denise's first impulse was to tell me that there weren't any apart from Carmichael, but she said cautiously that she'd had a few over the years.

'Does Margot encourage them?'

'If a punter's clean, and pays well, what difference does it make?'

'Do you end up with them – since you don't mind so much?'

'It depends who else is working.'

'What about dressing up yourself?'

'I'm not into that.'

'Who else saw Eden Carmichael?'

'Excuse me?'

'Who did Carmichael see at Margot's club besides yourself?'

'Ed only saw me.'

'What about Jenny Bishop?'

'No. I have to go now,' Denise said.

I put the phone down, wondering if Margot was aware how bad a liar her employee was, and whether this could have been the subject of their dispute. Margot gave the orders on her piece of turf. She made the rules. Her girls kept them, or they left. But rules were different to laws, which clients like Lawrence could break, and get away with breaking. I wondered if Jenny might have had other reasons for leaving the club, besides the incident with Lawrence.

Once again, I recalled the pale, practically translucent hair slipping through Margot's fingers, seeing it this time as a demonstration of her wish to control every aspect of her business, her expert fingers saying, 'This belongs to me'.

I remembered what Denise had told me about Carmichael the first time we'd spoken, how she'd praised him and said that he was different from other clients. I hadn't been able to detect anything in her voice that I would call sadness. Regret perhaps, but, in recollection, Denise's expression of regret seemed slippery and ambiguous. Who was genuinely sorry? Of all the people I'd spoken to so far, only Ken Dollimore. And, just possibly, Margot.

My last task for the afternoon was to answer a curt email from Lucy. She was sorry, but the committee had instructed her to tell me that I should come up with something substantial on *CleanNet*, or give up and stop wasting their money. I put a bit of effort into my reply, hoping to convince the committee that there was a story worth waiting for, but it required careful untangling, and could not be rushed.

. . .

I'd arranged to meet Simon Lawrence at a bar in Civic. I deliberately got there a few minutes early and chose a table at the back, after looking around to see if I recognised any of the other customers.

Lawrence was on time. I sensed he always was.

'Well now,' he said, walking towards me with his hand extended. 'This is an unexpected pleasure.'

'Likewise. You must have an extraordinary memory for faces.'

Lawrence smiled. 'And the roses, they were appreciated?'

'Thank you. Yes.'

'What can I get you to drink?'

I thought of insisting on paying for myself, then thought again. 'A beer would be nice. Light. Coopers if they have it.'

Lawrence ordered at the counter.

'Who were the roses for?' he asked when he came back with our drinks.

'A friend.'

'Correct me if I'm wrong, but I sense a complication there.'

'Aren't there always complications?'

Lawrence acknowledged the breadth of my reply with a sideways inclination of his curly head, then busied himself wiping up an invisible spill of beer with his forefinger.

'Why did you want to meet?' I asked.

'You're curious about me. I'm repaying the compliment.'

I smiled at his choice of words and said, 'I'm interested in your website.'

'From what point of view?'

'It's well designed.'

'Thank you.'
'You must be very much against net censorship.'
'Oh, dead against it.'
'I'm surprised your site's still up there. Have you had any complaints?'
'From other florists?'
'From anyone.'
'Not yet.'
'Do you often visit Canberra?'
'Quite often. It's easy now the highway's been improved.'
'Would you say the place has a nostalgic value?'
'I suppose so,' said Lawrence mildly. 'Drink up.'
I took a few sips of beer. It tasted stronger than the light I'd ordered.
'I understand that you have business interests here.'
'What would they be?'
'Margot Lancaster's club. I heard you were thinking of buying it.'
Lawrence sat back in his chair and raised his glass. 'Where would life be without a multiplicity of interests?' he asked, studying me over the top of it.
'Have you seen Margot recently?'
'No.'
'When was the last time you saw her?'
'A while back.'
'Before Christmas?'
'Oh, long before.'
'What about Stan Walewicz?'
'What about him?'
'He told me he was thinking of moving into Internet security.'
Lawrence looked annoyed, but said calmly, 'It's an expanding field.'
'Have you heard of a company called *CleanNet*?'
'I don't think so. Should I have?'
'They're marketing a filter that blocks sites like your embellished one. They put on a presentation for the Communications Minister last year. Stan Walewicz was there.'
'Stan and I went to school together, and we've kept in touch, but I don't keep tabs on all his business interests.'
Suddenly, I'd had enough.

'Jenny Bishop's dead,' I said. 'You forced her to have unprotected sex.'

Lawrence sat up straight. 'That's nonsense. The girl was a hooker and a drug addict.'

'Jenny called for help. Denise Travers pulled you off her. Do you deny that happened?'

'You're making a mountain out of a molehill. I might have got a bit carried away. What of it? She knew the risks.'

'And you knew you were breaking the law.'

'Oh, come off it, Ms Mahoney.'

'Have you seen this?' I asked, pulling the flyer out of my bag.

Lawrence turned it over, frowning, lips pursed.

He looked at me and forced himself to smile, saying, 'Quite a work of art.'

'Did Jenny send one to you?'

'No.'

'I imagine it would have made you angry if you'd got to hear of it – such a crude attempt at revenge.'

'Crude, but ineffective. I'd be a fool if I let a little thing like this bother me.'

'Were you sorry to hear that Jenny was dead?'

'Of course. It's tragic what these girls do to themselves.'

'How did she die?'

'An overdose.' Lawrence's voice betrayed only mild surprise that I should have to ask. 'I admire you,' he said, with another smile that accentuated the dimple in his chin. 'It's not many young women who'd be as persistent.'

'I'm not that young.'

'Yet you have a three-year-old daughter.'

My throat constricted to a small, narrow pipe, but I forced out another question. 'What did you have against Jenny?'

Lawrence leant back in his chair again. 'I like women. I make no secret of that fact. And I like variety. Why not?' His voice was mild, but serious, as though he believed convincing me was a realistic option. 'Jenny and I went back a long way. We met when she was just out of school.'

'When you starred in a porn movie together?'

'That's right.'

'How many movies have you been in?'

'You flatter me. I'm not an exhibitionist. It was fun, but once was enough for me.'

'After the incident at *Margot's* – did you see Jenny again?'

'You're kidding.'

'Did Jenny threaten to get even?'

'She threatened all sorts of things. A proper little wildcat. I had scratch marks for weeks.'

'How did you know that she used heroin?'

'I saw the needle marks.'

'What about when you made the movie?'

'She wasn't using then.'

'When did she start?'

'I don't know.'

'When you saw her in November, did the marks look recent?'

'It was hard to tell.'

'What were you doing on December thirtieth?'

'The thirtieth? What day of the week was that?'

'A Thursday.'

'Then I was working, I expect.'

Lawrence's phone rang. After replying to the caller in monosyllables, he told me he was sorry but he'd have to go. I was used to this excuse, and merely nodded. Perhaps Lawrence had learnt all he'd wanted to from my questions. Perhaps the flyer had made him angrier than he was willing to admit.

I gave him ten minutes, then drove by *Margot's*, but didn't see his car. Just to be sure, I parked at the corner and walked back. It wasn't there.

Thirteen

It was Brook's first day back at work. He rang at lunchtime to say a quick hello. I asked if he could bring round a copy of Carmichael's postmortem after he'd finished for the day.

Brook laughed and said, 'When I was a kid, I had a fox terrier who was just like you.'

At six, I had a shower, then sat on my front step waiting for him, my bare feet resting on Fred's hot fur.

The house behind me was used to my solitary habits now, to the closed daylight cosseting of shade; dry, quickened breathing towards that moment when I threw open doors and windows to invite the cooler air inside, suffering a moment's nerves as I recalled my ransacked office, but unable to bear the prospect of keeping the house shut up all night.

Brook waved as he got out of his car.

I smiled and stood up, wanting to run, to throw my arms around him.

He was dressed in his summer work clothes, lightweight trousers and short-sleeved white shirt. He kissed my cheek, patted Fred, then followed me inside, saying, 'Bloody Canberra. Why do we put up with it?'

'Place has its moments.' I hoped I wasn't in for a lecture on the pleasures of the coast.

Brook glanced round approvingly, and deposited a fat envelope on my clean kitchen table.

'Brought some photos and a couple of statements too.'

I thanked him, touched, then asked, 'Have you had time to check out those rosebuds?'

'Will the sky fall if I don't?'

'It's an experience,' I said. 'On the other hand, big tits aren't everything. What about closing down the site?'

Brook looked surprised, as though, whatever he'd expected me to talk about, it wasn't this. 'Someone has to file a complaint first.'

'I will. It will be a pleasure. But—'

'But what?'

'If we leave it there, it might tell us something.'

'About?'

'About what Walewicz and Lawrence might do next.'

'A couple now? Why should they do anything?'

'A number of reasons. One, money. Two, they won't like the authorities having the last word, if Lawrence *is* ordered to take his site down. Three, there's more to it than tits and fannies.'

Slow down, I told myself, but couldn't. There was so much I had to get through before Brook's mobile rang, or he looked at his watch and said he had to go.

Brook pulled a chair out and sat down at the table. He looked up at me to ask, 'What makes you think Walewicz and Lawrence are connected?'

'Apart from the website? They went to school together. Plus, Lawrence was pulling out of Walewicz's carpark when I turned up there. We had a drink last night.'

'You and Lawrence?'

I nodded. 'It's my impression that he and Walewicz meet quite often. And not for old times' sake.'

'Hardly an incriminating detail, Sandra. You know that filter you were telling me about? Bill McCallum bought one.'

'Tell him to steer clear of the National Party site.'

'What's wrong with it?'

'Never mind. It doesn't look as though Lawrence even made Margot Lancaster an offer for her club.'

'So?'

'So maybe Jenny Bishop was abused for nothing.'

'Sandra.'

'Her friends say there was no way she would have started using heroin again.'

I was thinking of Mieke and Rose, but reminded myself that Denise had said the opposite.

Brook sighed and said, 'I can't get into that. It's not my patch, and I don't know any of the details.'

I bit my lip, then asked him if he'd like something to drink.

'A beer wouldn't go astray.'

I poured Coopers Light for both of us.

'How was work?'

'First day back, and my fingertips are already bruised up to the elbow. I don't want to talk about it. Cheers.'

Brook raised his glass, and I clinked mine against it.

We chatted about Ivan and Katya for a few minutes, and Peter, whose postcard from Port Arthur had arrived that morning. Brook smiled at Peter's description of the jail as 'awesome', with three exclamation marks. I was conscious, as I had been often in the past, of his estrangement from his own children, how this surfaced without warning, and drew a shadow over him.

'Go on, take a look,' he said, nodding at the envelope. 'I know you're itching to.'

I opened it and began reading the first page of the post-mortem, noting that Carmichael's blood alcohol level had been .05.

The top few photographs were close-ups of the body. I stared at Carmichael's face. The wig had fallen across it, covering one eye and part of his left cheek. His eyes were half open, his mouth grotesquely twisted. His dress had been ripped and the upper part of his chest was bare. It seemed he wasn't wearing women's underwear.

Beneath these close-ups were a dozen pictures of the body and the room, taken from different angles. I studied them while Brook drank his beer.

Something bothered me about the photo showing the table and its contents.

I puzzled over it for a few more moments. 'There's no wig box.'

'What?'

'Denise Travers described the ritual for me. She had to dress Carmichael in a certain way. The wig was carried into the room in its box, which was then put under the table. It's not here.'

I passed the photograph across. Brook looked at it, frowning. 'Maybe you misunderstood her. Maybe she made a mistake.'

'If one of them took the box out after he was dead, then yes, Denise did make a mistake. She told me the routine, but not what must have happened that day.'

'A slip of the tongue,' Brook said, but his frown deepened, and I felt that my focus on the wig was justified.

'He hasn't got any underwear on either, and the dress is torn.'

'He could have torn it himself, struggling for air.'

'He could have. But where's the lingerie?'

It was on the tip of my tongue to tell Brook I hadn't found any in his flat either, but I decided to keep quiet about it.

I put aside the photos, and we stared at each other for what seemed like a long time. We might have left that scrubbed table and walked to any other part of the house, finding, when we arrived, that what had seemed a destination carried a further destination still; carried doubts and questions, made uncertain both our stated and unstated aims. We could walk into a bedroom. There was a bedroom waiting for us. We both knew it, as we had before. It was dangerous, being alone together in my house, yet Brook had come to that danger calmly, invited himself into it, offering what I'd asked for, and a little more.

He was the first to look away. I pushed back my chair and said, 'There's something I forgot to tell you. I think I was followed in Sydney. A young guy, scarecrow suit. Needed a shave. I saw him going into Lawrence's shop.'

'Email me a description. Have you spoken to Kevin Saunders?'

I opened my mouth to make excuses.

Brook's mobile rang. 'Okay,' he said, then, 'about half an hour.' He returned the phone to its holder on his belt, his expression resigned.

'It was great down there, you know? I didn't miss work or Canberra for a single minute. It made me think I ought to retire, buy a place at the coast, enjoy it while I can.'

I swallowed, too proud to let him see my hurt.

Brook kissed me on the forehead, and I walked him to his car.

After I'd watched him drive away, I sat on the front porch with Fred curled up at my feet. My stomach was empty, but I couldn't think of anything I felt like eating. The house behind me was drenched with

Brook's good smell, mixed with memories of the ocean, and a woman's voice calling down the stairs.

. . .

There were some surprises in the statements, which I decided to sleep on, and work out what to do with in the morning.

Brook had left me a video as well. It was strange, watching the camera pan across that room at Margot's club. I felt the closed-up stillness of a shrine already in the making, with Carmichael at the centre, in his torn blue dress. I knew that the task of whoever had been filming was to scan the room, providing the connections and overall impression that still photographs might not, yet the focus returned again and again, as though the person holding the camera had been fascinated by them, to the bed and figure on it, the evidence that Carmichael had fought for his last breaths.

I felt a surge of excitement when I noted that the space underneath the bedside table was empty. I stopped the tape, rewound and played it again. I replayed the whole tape from the beginning, looking for small, elusive items.

Fourteen

Gail rang as I was washing up my breakfast dishes.
'I called round to Ken Dollimore's office,' she told me. 'He wouldn't let me in the door.'
'Maybe he's sick of reporters.'
'Bullshit. Publicity's his meat and drink. I went to see his neighbours, asked if anyone saw him on the fourth of January.'
'I don't –' I began, but Gail went on impatiently. She hated being interrupted. 'His neighbours on one side were away. I've checked back with them since. But the other side *was* home – a couple with two kids. They had a wading pool set up and their kids spent the afternoon in –'
'I don't think –'
'What's with you, Sandra? I'm doing you a favour here. Plus, someone told silver hair I've been up and down the street and now he won't talk to me.'
'But –'
'Here's the interesting bit. These neighbours were surprised at me asking if they'd seen Dollimore that afternoon, because they were expecting him to be in Melbourne. He'd told them he'd be away till the ninth.'
'I've got his statement. Brook brought it round last night.'
'Why didn't you say so?'
'If you'd let me get a word in.'
'I'm coming over,' Gail said.
'I'm not supposed to show it to anyone.'
'Tough,' she said. 'You owe me.'

. . .

Ken Dollimore's statement began with the early evening of January 3. I read it through again, looking over Gail's shoulder.

Dollimore had been staying with his daughter in Melbourne, and Carmichael had rung at about ten o'clock that night. He described the phone call as alarming. Carmichael had been drunk and emotional, and had said that he'd promised to help a friend, but realised he wasn't going to be able to keep his promise. Dollimore had asked what the promise was, but Carmichael had digressed, and begun carrying on about this girl he'd had sex with at *Margot's*, not the one he usually saw. When Dollimore had tried to get the details, he'd said the girl was dead, then suddenly changed tack and complained that she'd got him to tell tales. Dollimore had tried to find out what these were, without success.

. . .

I told him to go to bed and sleep it off. Whatever it was, he shouldn't try to do anything that night. But my advice only made him worse. He kept repeating that he'd made a promise, but wouldn't tell me who to, or what the promise was. He was crying with self-pity and remorse. I said I'd phone him in the morning. I rang his flat about eight, hoping he'd done what I said. There was no answer. Of course, he could have been there, sleeping through the phone. That's what I hoped, but I rang his office anyway, though I knew it was too early. All I got was a machine. When I rang his flat back, and still couldn't rouse him, I felt worried. I changed my flight and returned to Canberra. My flight got in just before one. I dropped my luggage, then drove round to Ed's. He wasn't home, or wasn't answering the door. I tried calling out, then I checked the garage and found his car was gone. I drove over to the Assembly. The office was locked. I rang the number and got a machine again. The building was practically empty, but the security guard told me Ed had been in that morning, and so had Laura Scott. I walked around the block, checking out the coffee lounges, then decided to ring the club. That Madam answered. She said she hadn't seen or heard from Ed since before Christmas. I drove by, just in case, but Ed's car wasn't there. I tried some bars. I felt sure he'd be drinking somewhere, but I kept on ringing his flat in case he'd gone back there. I began to feel tired and hungry, so I went home, had a bite to eat, a shower, then drove back to Ed's. That's when I saw the police cars and found out he was dead.

'Where do you think he was between lunchtime and four in the afternoon?' Gail asked.

'Drinking somewhere, like Dollimore said.'

I showed Gail the post-mortem, then indicated the statement.

'Keep reading. The most interesting bit is at the end.'

I wish to add certain facts which I believe have a bearing on the present case. There was an earlier death implicating the Madam at the club my deceased friend was so unfortunately involved with. I believe the police should know about it. Ed told me the story one night when he'd been drinking, but he regretted it afterwards, saying he'd broken a confidence, and I could never get him to talk about it again. Now my friend has also died in suspicious circumstances.

I kept on reading over Gail's shoulder, though most of the statement had lodged itself in my memory.

Ed made me promise not to speak to anyone, and I've honoured that promise to the present day. He said that Madam was ashamed and wished never to be reminded of the episode. She was young and inexperienced. It happened in Sydney, at the house of ill repute where he first met her. Even though the coroner exonerated her, concluding, beyond reasonable doubt, that the man had died of heart failure, she claimed she'd been treated as though she was guilty of murder.

I feel it incumbent upon me, now my friend is dead, to alert the police to this earlier crime. It occurred in Darlinghurst, in a building that has since been demolished. The date was March 13, 1973. I applied for a copy of the coroner's report, but unfortunately my application was denied. The victim's name was John Penshurst. Madam disappeared after the inquiry was over, or Ed believed she disappeared. He spent years looking for her.

'Nineteen seventy-three,' Gail said thoughtfully. 'The Sydney papers would have covered it, maybe ours as well.' She looked at her watch. 'I'd better go. I'm already late for work.'

...

I rang Margot. 'What did Ken Dollimore want when he phoned you on January four?'

There was a silence, then Margot said flatly, 'He was looking for Ed.'

'What did you tell him?'

'I didn't know where Ed was. I hadn't heard from him since before Christmas.'

'What time did he ring?'

'About two-thirty.'

'But he rang back after that, didn't he?'

'No, he – '

'He rang to talk to you about John Penshurst.'

'How do you know about that?'

'What did Dollimore say?'

'The coroner found that I was *not* to blame,' said Margot fiercely. 'It was almost thirty years ago. I shouldn't have to put up with having false accusations dragged up and thrown in my face.'

. . .

Next I phoned Ken Dollimore at the Assembly.

'You don't believe the police are as tough on Margot Lancaster as they ought to be,' I said.

I could feel Dollimore's alert attention on the other end.

'You took it upon yourself to remind Margot about John Penshurst. You remember John Penshurst? He died of a heart attack too, according to the coroner.'

There was a tense silence, then Dollimore said, 'That woman killed him, just like she killed Ed.'

'How?'

'She trapped him, then she killed him. Ed was a fool when it came to women.'

'How did Margot trap him?'

'She drove him to the brink. Plenty of men our age have heart problems. They adjust, learn to live with them. Diet, exercise, a change of lifestyle.'

'Is that all?'

'I don't know how you found out about Penshurst, but you obviously did. I don't know all the details. I wrote to the coroner requesting a copy of the report, but I was refused. Ed told me about it one time when again, I have to admit, he'd had too much to drink. He made me promise to keep it to myself, and I kept my word until he died. That woman got away with murder once, and she's about to do so again. It's her secret, or she thinks it ought to be. She doesn't want any of it made public, and she'll go a long way to prevent that happening. It was the reason Ed lost contact with her. He blamed himself for not being there when she needed him. She changed her name. He spent months looking for her. In England. All over the place. And what did he get for his pains? To end up the same way. Dead of heart failure in a house of sin.'

'Do you think Margot might have confessed to Carmichael details that weren't publicly known?'

'Confession's not her style. She knew how to make Ed feel guilty, make sure he stayed on her side. Whatever he did, he did because she forced him to.'

'How?'

'What about that photograph in *The Canberra Times*? Maybe she took others. It would be just like her. If Ed came across information that wasn't publicly known, it wouldn't have made him suspicious, or put him on his guard. He felt sorry for her. He blamed himself for the life she chose to live. I can't tell you what she did to other men, what she had them doing. I can guess though, and it makes me sick.'

'Did Carmichael keep documents relating to Penshurst's death? Newspaper clippings? Letters perhaps?'

'If he did, he never showed them to me. He was hopeless.' Dollimore's voice cracked. 'He was a silly old goat. A *fool* of a man.'

'Was he being blackmailed?'

'That's what I'm trying to find out.'

I noted down our conversation while it was fresh in my mind, then checked my mail. Lucy's reply to my last message was short and to the point. The committee would give me one more week.

. . .

I phoned Brook, who wasn't all that impressed by the Penshurst story.

'Not much in it, I don't think.'

'What? Ken Dollimore made it up?'

'Oh no, the guy definitely died. Pretty clear it wasn't anybody's fault, that's all.'

I asked Brook whether he thought Carmichael might have been being blackmailed.

'Blackmail victims kill their tormentors,' he told me. 'Not the other way around.'

'Carmichael freaked out. He became a danger.'

Brook made noncommittal noises.

. . .

I asked the NSW Coronial Office to send me an application form for the coronial report on John Penshurst's death, then tracked down Laura Scott at home. When I asked her how she was, she gave me an update on the hate mail.

'Do you think Ed Carmichael was being blackmailed?' I asked.

'What?'

I repeated the word, though I was sure Laura had heard me perfectly.

'What for?'

'I was wondering if you had any ideas about that.'

'Ed didn't have a lot of money. I believe his only asset was his flat.'

'Did you and Ken Dollimore discuss the possibility?'

'Not in so many words. I told you Ken doesn't have a very high opinion of me. We never talked again like that night in the carpark. He saw himself as saving Ed, and I – well, I think he saw me as pretty useless and –'

'Yes?'

'Ed wasn't the type to be intimidated.'

'Could the blackmail have involved a threat to someone else?'

'I suppose so. But who?'

I asked Laura to get in touch with me if she thought of anyone.

I stared out the window, her last question echoing off my back fence, curling round my empty clothes line. I heard a sound and looked round, for one forgetful moment expecting Pete or Katya. No one was there.

The mystery of the wig box niggled at me, the way small mysteries surrounded by large ones do. There were too many threads that I didn't have the resources, or the authority to follow. If the coroner's verdict went as predicted, concluding that Carmichael had died of a heart attack, my questions would become irrelevant. To discover what had happened to a cardboard box ought surely to be within my grasp.

That night, I went through my notes, made summaries, and began a report for Lucy. I was short on proof, but hoped to have more by the end of the week.

Fifteen

I dreamt of Jenny Bishop being chased away from a cafe by Ken Dollimore, woke up knowing Rose had more to tell me, packed an overnight bag, arranged with my neighbour to feed Fred again, and made a detour to the highway via Mitchell.

Margot Lancaster was sitting in her car outside the club. I pulled up and wound down my window.

Margot stared at me. There was sweat along her upper lip and hairline. Grey was showing through the black, pronounced in the carpark's bald surroundings. She'd lost her appearance of being expertly put together, and looked as though she needed to lie down for a long time in a cool, dark place.

'What happened to the wig box?' I asked.

'I don't know what you mean.'

'I think you do.'

Margot switched on the ignition, turned quickly and efficiently, and drove away, early light bouncing off the duco of her well-maintained black Nissan.

. . .

I made my way to the cafe in Glebe Point Road, hoping the same waitress would be there.

She was, but disappeared through swing doors behind the counter the moment she spotted me. I ran after her. By the time I got to the back door, she was halfway down an alley. It was as well for me that she was wearing high black platforms. I caught up and grabbed her by the arm. I was panting, but what I had to say was simple.

'Who was Rose running away from?'

'Ow, you're hurting me. Let go!'

'What's his name? Where can I find him?'

'How should I know?'
'Did he know Jenny Bishop too?'
'Let me go! Get *away* from me!'

The waitress yanked her arm free and ran back in the direction of the cafe.

I bought a felafel roll and a bottle of water at a Lebanese takeaway and sat down at a white plastic table on the footpath. My hands were shaking and I felt far too hot. I shouldn't have taken my frustration out on the waitress. That had been dumb. I hadn't realised how tense and anxious I'd been, but that was no excuse. Any hope I'd had of getting useful information out of her was gone.

. . .

I left my car parked where it was, and approached the Wigram Road house by a series of back streets.

From the nearest corner, where I stood indecisively, I watched a car accelerating up the hill with Ian in the driver's seat. Beside him was a dark-haired young woman whom I took to be Francesca.

It was broad daylight, but that couldn't be helped. I'd just have to hope their neighbours were at work, or away on holiday.

I could have broken the lock on the back gate, but climbed the fence instead. The kitchen door and windows were securely fastened. I didn't want to force an entry. I tried the shed. That was padlocked too. But the bathroom window that I'd noticed on my first visit was slightly open, and the fly screen had not been mended or replaced.

I struggled up the pipe, thinking that if an athletic dunce like me could manage it, then anybody could.

I landed in the basin with a great deal less elegance than I would have liked, and wiped away my footprints with a wad of tissues. With no idea how much time I had, I gave Jenny's room a quick once-over. Nothing appeared to have changed. I went in search of Ian's computer, which was in the room he'd described as a study. I switched it on, and began checking emails.

There were hundreds of them, and none appeared to have anything to do with Jenny.

Thinking I heard someone at the front door, I ran to the top of the stairs and stood listening for a moment, but the door stayed firmly closed.

Ian used an old version of Outlook Express for his mail, and he hadn't bothered with a password. I was almost at the end before I found two that looked as though they could have been for Jenny. The first seemed to be offering its recipient some kind of explanation. *'We were just having a drink together'*, it began. *'We didn't even know he drank there. We met up by accident. Nothing to get your knickers in a twist over'*. The message did not begin with a salutation, nor was the sender's name included. But I knew the sender's address. I'd seen it on Simon Lawrence's website. It was Stan Walewicz.

The second was very simple. *'I warned you to stay out of it'*, was all it said.

Both emails were replies, dated December 19th and 21st. The originals had not been saved, or not on Ian's computer. I quickly printed them, using paper I'd brought with me.

Getting down the pipe was easier than climbing up it, though I scraped my hands and landed with a bump.

I was returning the way I'd come, along the back alley behind the houses, when I heard a click and a rumbling sound behind me. I swung round. A young man was wheeling a rubbish bin. It caught on a stone and he wriggled it, then looked up at me curiously.

. . .

I checked in to my favourite hotel, grabbed a bite to eat, then drove to Sans Souci.

Seven-five-sevens dived for land across Botany Bay. La Grande Parade was thick with traffic. The brothel's street was less busy than the main ones, but still parked out. I left my car behind a bottle shop on the main street, then walked back and stood opposite the house like last time, watching to see who went in and out. Curious about a back entrance, I found a laneway connected to the row of houses. Each had a high fence and a solid gate.

I returned to the street, where I was less conspicuous, and rang the brothel's number. A recorded voice told me they were open from four every afternoon till late, and that there were six lovely ladies waiting to satisfy my every wish.

A man dressed in a dark suit and lemon-coloured shirt came out the front door. He crossed the street, got into a Holden Commodore, and drove towards the sea. I noted down the registration number, just for something to do. A second man followed him a few minutes later. He was younger, wearing jeans, a T-shirt, running shoes. He turned right at the gate, away from me. I watched him till he turned a corner. Other pedestrians were minding their own business. I thought it better not to hang around there any longer.

The sun was starting to going down. I stood looking out over the sea for a few minutes, then back towards the Novotel, which, with all its lights on, resembled a huge berthed ship. The ground floor bar was full of people. Loudspeakers sent *Savage Garden*'s latest hit out across the esplanade.

Drinkers were standing three deep at the bar. A young bartender with lip rings had his work cut out. The front of the bar was brightly lit, but the corners of the room were dim.

Rose was sitting at a small round table by herself, facing the room with her back to the wall.

I walked across and said hello.

Rose looked up at me and frowned.

'Have you found out who was following you?' I asked.

She shook her head.

From the corner of my eye, I saw the barman lift his chin in my direction.

'I can't talk here,' Rose said. 'There's too many people who know me.'

'Right. I'll leave you to it then.'

I crossed the road to the esplanade. Lights every twenty metres or so broke up the darkening walkway.

Rose had looked pale and scared. There'd been no impression of resilience or elasticity about her. I wondered if she'd been waiting for someone. I'd made another mistake by going up to her. I should have bought a drink, sat in a corner, and watched. I wasn't thinking straight.

I walked to the edge of the esplanade, breathing in salt air and the strong smell of seaweed.

A tall man in dark clothes ran out of some bushes at me, with a peculiar, bouncing gait.

I turned and sprinted back the way I'd come, luckily catching a break in the traffic on La Grande Parade. Once in my car, I accelerated as fast as I dared to, heading straight for my hotel.

I parked at the back of the building, and climbed the stairs to my room two at a time. Footsteps echoed on the concrete walk outside. I grabbed my overnight bag, pleased I hadn't bothered to unpack. The glass doors leading to my first-floor balcony were fastened with a simple catch. A black iron railing ran around the balcony at knee level. I balanced on top of the railing and aimed for the centre of a small patch of lawn, trying to remember not to lock my knees.

Leaves and damp grass rose to meet me. I felt my shoulder crunch as I rolled. Shadows took the shapes of young men in need of a shave. Fear entered through the gap between a car door and its frame.

Out in the traffic, heading south-west, I checked my rear-view mirror every few seconds. The man could have followed me and be sitting two or three cars behind. Once on the highway, if he stuck with me, he'd have a range of options. Would he be on his own?

I continued on through Liverpool to the highway. Nothing happened. Slowly, I began to relax. Near the Berrima turn-off, I stopped at a service station, not having a choice, since my tank was empty. There were three other customers in the cafeteria section, a couple and a single, grey-haired man. I chose a seat facing the entrance, ate a sandwich and gulped down two cups of strong tea. No one else came in.

My spirits lifted, and I settled into a pleasant feeling brought on by a full stomach topped with caffeine. I was more than halfway home. I began to enjoy the black and purple of the surrounding bush, when there were no cars coming the other way, no lights to block it out.

I crested a long hill, dipped slightly, climbed again. Headlights expanded from points of light, to beams, to arcs, before the driver dimmed them, and I dimmed mine as well. I counted the gaps in time between passing cars. One minute, three. I got up to seven.

Suddenly, from nowhere, there was a car right behind me.

We were on a divided, two-lane stretch with concrete barriers on either side. Lights on high beam filled my whole car, flashing off my mirrors, blinding me. I accelerated, so did the driver on my tail, trying to push me into the concrete barrier. I tasted blood, and knew my teeth had bitten through my lip. I was going to hit the concrete, but then I realised that, somehow, I hadn't. I was rushing alongside, closer than a lover's breath.

I tried to read his rego number in the rear-view mirror, and cursed myself for not being able to. My speedo was on 220. I could not go any faster. I forced myself to move my hands a fraction.

Three cars in quick succession loomed up on the opposite side, further blinding and disorienting me. I thought of police, and as quickly grasped that it couldn't be. The third seemed to swerve, as though beginning to cross the median strip that divided my lane from his, but it must have been a trick of the lights because all three cars passed, and disappeared.

My pursuer's lights had fallen back a little. I didn't slacken my pace, and a few moments later I had the lane to myself.

I slowly released the pressure of my foot on the accelerator, and thought about what to do. I wondered if I should detour off the highway into Goulburn, find a police station. But I had no idea if the officer on duty would be sympathetic, or even believe me.

I decided to keep going. On the last stretch of the Federal Highway, I fancied I saw a pre-dawn inkling ahead – though it would not be dawn for hours yet – that look of surprise across flat paddocks that here was yet another day.

. . .

Brook responded to my furious knocking, and I half fell through his door.

My mouth wouldn't work. I tasted blood again. I had too many teeth. I thought of my mobile sitting on the car seat, all the times I could have rung him from the highway. I'd been scared to – scared he wouldn't be at home, or that Sophie would pick up the phone.

Brook brought me tea so full of sugar it was almost tart. I gulped it down. He undressed me and put me to bed.

When I woke a few hours later, he was calm, professional. I responded to his manner, watching myself doing so. I looked down at my body, the lines where my swimsuit ended in the unforgiving light. Brook opened the curtains, those thick, invalid curtains Sophie had made for him after his bone-marrow transplant. He plumped up the pillows, brought more tea and toast. I thanked him, waiting for my pulse to slow, body to settle, knowing that it wouldn't. He had told me once, when I'd asked him why he wanted to keep on working, that it was a private test. He'd said this with a dry smile, making light of the challenge.

We met each other's eyes, and I understood that he was not going to reprimand me. If I wanted to, I could recall other reprimands and fit them in, slots in a venetian blind.

Brook sat down beside me. I squeezed his hand, and he returned the pressure. My fingers ached to trace the line from collar bone to shoulder. I thought a grasp at life could be exactly that, knuckle and hunch of muscle – the promise, the capacity, then the falling back.

I wasn't ready to return to my empty house, listen to it creaking as the new day's heat began. My lip, where I'd bitten it, was sore and swollen. Brook brought me some cream to put on it. I asked him if I could stay for a few more hours. He left me, and I fell asleep again, thinking of Jenny Bishop, and the shadow Ed Carmichael had inhabited, in his blue dress and lopsided halo.

. . .

Brook filled his bedroom doorway like some hero from a TV Western, turning away from the hot noon outside. Groggy, hauling myself out of a dream, I imagined a saloon bar's doors swinging shut behind him, that second's squint as the sheriff adjusted from one set of dangers to another.

I'd been dreaming of Peter's first summer, when he was three months old and one heatwave had followed another. In my dream, I'd been angling damp towels around his basinet, layer after layer, till he was in danger of being smothered by them.

I began to talk. Brook listened. I couldn't bear to think that he was humouring me, but I didn't want him to interrupt, or cut my story short. I described again the lanky, dark-haired man and his peculiar walk, the way I'd seen his reflection, then later watched him going into Simon Lawrence's shop. On the Sans Souci Esplanade, he'd run out of the bushes straight towards me.

I showed Brook the emails I'd printed. He didn't ask me how I'd come by them.

He shook his head and said, 'A girl like that.'

'Like what? A girl *like what?*'

When Brook didn't answer, I said, 'Maybe Jenny Bishop knew something about Lawrence that he couldn't afford for her to know.'

'That flyer?'

'Wouldn't have mattered so much on its own, I don't think. But because Jenny was so keen to get even, she nosed around and picked up something else.'

'The weight of opinion will be on the side that she overdosed.'

'Do a bit of leaning,' I said. 'Change the weight.'

'It's not our jurisdiction. You know that.'

'Try and get someone from Glebe to follow up the Canberra connection. At least make sure they know about it. Something might have happened while Jenny was here. Something *did* happen.'

'It's a weak connection.'

'That can be my job then, to make it stronger.'

When Brook didn't reply to this, I said, 'Jenny doesn't strike me as the type who'd sit home drinking on her own. Especially while her housemates were at a party.'

'So?'

'So someone may have kept her company. Her neighbour across the road heard a car start up just after midnight. I told her to get in touch with the police. Somebody should interview her.'

Instead of responding to any of this, Brook asked me if I was all right to drive home, and I said I was.

In the car, which felt like an old friend, I asked myself what prejudice had to do with love. I'd once put Brook in a box labelled sick and middle-aged, and he'd let me know how much that had hurt him. Yet I couldn't bear to think of him labelling Jenny Bishop and dismissing her, couldn't bear to think of him using phrases such as 'girls like that'.

I recalled the Hansel and Gretel story, how the bread trail hadn't worked, but lifeless pebbles had. Pebbles couldn't be eaten, were no good to the birds, and so were left there to be followed. I thought of blood, and its absence from two violent deaths, how Jenny *should* have bled. It was an affront to the logic of death, of life abandoning a young body, that she hadn't.

Sixteen

Margot tried to slam the door in my face. She was a good deal taller than I was, and probably ten kilos heavier, but anger gave me strength. For a few minutes, we pushed against each other, balanced in a way that might have been funny in another context.

Margot was panting, her breath coming in gasps. She heaved the door shut.

· · ·

I rang Gail and told her about being chased down the highway. She made sympathetic noises.

'I could hide out at your place,' I suggested. 'I could make a tent under your kitchen table and move in.'

'Right,' said Gail. 'Good thinking. That way, no one would ever find you.'

'I'd disappear for good.'

'What about that copper who's a mate of yours?'

'I can't stay with him.'

'I see. I found some clippings of that Sydney business – the other guy whose heart stopped.'

'Yes?'

'There's some pretty savage stuff. The press went after Margot, decided that she let him die. She was only twenty-one. Her name wasn't Margot then, by the way. It was Evelyn. Her working name was Eve.'

I told Gail I'd like to see the clippings and she said she'd bring them round the next day.

· · ·

Brook rang to announce, 'That Lancaster woman's threatening to charge you with harassment. Did you force your way into her club?'

'I wouldn't say *into*, not exactly.'

'Go and see Kevin Saunders. Now. Today.'

'Right.'

'It *is* right. And long overdue. Make a full statement, then leave it up to us.'

'What will you do?'

'For God's sake, Sandra. You could have been killed on that highway.'

'What can you or Saunders do about that? I might be able to guess, but I don't know who it was. Anyone I point at will deny it.'

Brook spent a few more minutes lecturing me about the correct way to proceed, then we both hung up.

I sat outside. Layers of the hot day were beginning to peel off. Later, they would reveal a core of twilight. It seemed right just then that the approaching dusk should have a core, and that it should be hard.

I could still feel Brook's arms around me from the early morning, how he'd held me when I fell into his house. There was nothing I would have liked better than to sit beside him on my front porch, while the sun disappeared behind Black Mountain.

The phone rang again as I was getting into bed.

'Hello,' I said.

Silence on the other end.

'Who's there?'

Still no answer, then a woman's voice. 'I saw Simon Lawrence with Jenny. A week before she died.'

'Where?'

'On the esplanade.'

The woman's voice was soft, and getting softer.

'Did you ask Jenny about it?'

'I was going to, but she – she was acting weird.'

'How weird?'

'Kind of obsessed.'

'Who gave Jenny the heroin?'

'Jen was clean. She planned to stay clean.'

'Thank you for talking to me,' I said, and a few seconds later heard a click.

Had it been Rose? I couldn't be sure, but I was sure enough.

. . .

When I introduced myself to Detective Sergeant Kevin Saunders the next morning, he looked me up and down dismissively, though I'd made more effort than usual to dress for the occasion. His expression summarised his low opinion of security consultants in general, and the kind that hung around the edges of the police force in particular.

I swallowed an impulse to defend myself. After Saunders had switched on a tape and recorded our names, the date and time, I began going over the points I'd prepared. I'd rehearsed my statement, guessing that the detective might interpret hesitation as a form of weakness.

I started with the time Jenny Bishop had spent at Margot Lancaster's club, and pointed out that someone had to be lying over whether or not she'd had sex with Eden Carmichael. I mentioned the missing wig box, but didn't linger over it, aware that Brook thought I was making too much of a minor detail. As I spoke, it became clearer to me that those few weeks, from Lawrence's visit to the club, through to the end of December, had been crucial. I said I'd been told that Lawrence had been seen with Jenny on the Sans Souci esplanade about a week before her death and that I believed she'd been corresponding with Stan Walewicz by email.

Saunders listened without interrupting. His gaze was direct, intelligent and disconcerting. His tanned skin was marked by adolescent acne. He looked fit and gave the impression, deliberately I thought, that all his reflexes were super quick.

I summarised what I'd learnt about *CleanNet*, and everything Ken Dollimore, Chris Laskaris, Stan Walewicz and Laura had told me. Saunders continued to fix me with a stare that made me feel as though I was a junior player who'd stumbled onto a field reserved for the major league, and was too dumb to know it.

After I'd finished, he asked a few questions, though not nearly as many as I thought my information warranted.

I left with a feeling of defeat and anticlimax. The detective's manner was so effortlessly superior, it was impossible to guess what was going on behind it. I'd asked about the coroner's report into John Penshurst's death, and he'd told me he'd written to the court requesting a copy, and was waiting on an answer. He hadn't asked me how I'd learnt about Penshurst's death, for which I was relieved. I could not have referred to Ken Dollimore's statement without causing trouble for Brook.

. . .

Gail's appearance was a welcome break from thoughts that circled without moving forward. Neither of us felt hungry. It was too hot to cook. We drank draught beer instead. Gail wandered restlessly about while I read her clippings, struck first, then moved, by images of twenty-one-year-old Margot/Evelyn/Eve. The photographs were old, of course, and the reproductions grainy, but her long dark hair framed a pale, sad face. No matter what the camera angle, or caption underneath – and many of them were snide, or downright nasty – there was a dignity about her, and a youthful clarity of feeling.

Gail stopped her pacing, and sat down next to me.

She fingered the top photograph and said, 'There's something about her that makes you want to respect her.'

I agreed. 'I wonder if that's what the coroner felt, too.'

Gail made a face, meaning that it was possible, but just as possible he'd regarded Margot as a fallen woman, an unrepentant sinner, even if innocent of murder.

Gail got up to fetch more beer, while I went on reading. The articles displayed none of the superficial acceptance of sex work that the last thirty years had brought. Raw prejudice coloured every paragraph. The police doctor, and the coroner, both concluded that John Penshurst had died of heart failure, but there was no way the journalists were going to let a young prostitute off so easily. I found I couldn't think of her as Evelyn, much less Eve. To me, she would always be Margot.

'Darlinghurst whore stops heart of family man', was one heading. 'Panic in massage parlour. Police called. Victim pronounced dead on arrival at St Vincent's Hospital.'

Much seemed to have been made of Penshurst's credentials as a good family man, as though Eve had first of all lured him to pay for sex against his honourable inclinations, and then killed him. The name was turned against her. Comparisons with the original were full of righteous condemnation.

'It's no wonder she mistrusts the press,' I said. 'But she needed someone to write a favourable piece about her club, or convinced herself she did.'

'Because she's trying to sell it?'

'Yes.'

'What about that Lawrence guy?'

'I think he's probably broken off the deal. If there was a deal to break off.'

'So Margot fed him Jenny Bishop for nothing.'

'Maybe. Don't you think it's odd,' I went on after a moment, 'that no one's brought this up? It obviously made quite a splash at the time. There must be plenty of people around who remember.'

'She's changed her name,' Gail pointed out.

'I doubt if that would be enough. And Dollimore's so down on her, why hasn't he been on to the newspapers and TV? He said he promised Carmichael, but he's already broken that promise by alerting the police.'

'It's an important distinction though, isn't it?'

'Maybe,' I said again, 'but he must be sorely tempted.'

We talked around the issue for a few more minutes. I photocopied the clippings. Another headline caught my eye. 'Darlinghurst prostitute accused of callousness. Why did Eve wait before sounding the alarm?' Even the suburb seemed to be condemning her.

. . .

I wondered why it hadn't occurred to me to try and discover the name of the young man with the designer stubble I'd first seen reflected in a Castlereagh Street shop window. I thought of ringing Lawrence's shop in Parramatta Road, but decided that I'd first better give myself a reason.

Who did I know in Sydney who'd appreciate a bunch of flowers?

After deciding that the most likely candidate was an elderly aunt who lived in Strathfield, and whose only contact with me was an exchange of cards at Christmas, I looked up the shop's number, hoping Lawrence wouldn't answer the phone.

A stranger's voice answered. After placing my order, I said I was wondering if he was the same young man who'd served me a couple of weeks ago when I'd bought some beautiful red roses, a tall young man, dark-eyed, growing a beard, as I recalled.

'No,' the voice said, 'that would be Brian. But Brian doesn't work here. He's based at the nursery.'

My call to the nursery was answered by a man with a strong German accent, who told me it was Brian's day off. Crossing my fingers, I asked if there was a mobile number for him. I wished there was somebody to clap me on the back and say well done when the German voice repeated it twice to make sure I got it, and I wrote it down.

Dialling the number, I realised I was sitting forward on the edge of my chair, experiencing again – they'd never been far from the surface of my mind – those moments on the highway, my hands locked on the steering wheel, foot jammed on the accelerator.

I'd planned who I could pretend to be, but at the last minute changed my mind and introduced myself as Sandra Mahoney.

A sharp intake of breath told me that I'd found my man, but Brian Picoult – he revealed his surname after only a second's hesitation – denied that he'd been on the Canberra-Sydney Highway. He'd been organising deliveries that night, and nowhere near Sans Souci.

'How did you get my number?'

'I rang the nursery and they gave it to me. What's Mr Lawrence like to work for?'

After a slight hesitation, Picoult said, 'He's a good employer.'

I went on asking questions about Lawrence, the nursery, and Picoult's whereabouts at the times I believed I'd seen him in Sydney. His replies became progressively more guarded.

I made notes while the sound of his voice was fresh in my mind, thinking again of the highway, headlights speeding up behind me, those few centimetres between me and the concrete wall.

······
Seventeen

As a piece of scenery, Lake Burley Griffin was undemanding. Tourists' eyes passed over it, looking for distinction, perhaps lighting on the Parliament House flagmast, close as the crow flies, yet by road circuitous. The flooding of the valley floor had taken months, and still seemed incomplete.

I felt this incompleteness most at nightfall in the summer, after a day's intense evaporation, the water flat and weak against a fresh-baked band of soil, a sense of urgency and resignation at the same time. Rain would come, a thunderstorm, or at any rate the autumn, but until then the artificial lake would continue to recede, leaving more of its bed uncovered at the end of each hot day.

The lake foreshore was an uncomfortable place for a meeting, yet I'd suggested it to Denise, knowing she would need to be somewhere she could smoke, and realising that she would not agree to meet me again if she thought there was a chance that she'd be recognised.

I'd wasted the afternoon, chasing after details no one I spoke to would, or could supply. I was glad to be driving to the lake at dusk a clear night it would be – heat leaving the ground in gulps, while pelicans folded their wings and settled on an offshore roundabout.

Denise was there before me. She stepped out of a red Valiant as I pulled up. I locked my car, and we walked towards the water.

In the small light from her cigarette, her eyes were tired and wary. She flicked ash on the ground. A spark flared and died.

But then she looked straight at me and spoke in a decisive voice. 'Ed never saw Jenny Bishop. He only saw me.'

'What happened between Jenny and Simon Lawrence?' I asked.

'Lawrence is a pig.'

In the near darkness, I could feel Denise reacting against this now she'd said it, wishing she could take it back.

'I heard you helped Jenny, got him off her.'
'What else was I supposed to do?'
'Did Lawrence threaten her?'
'Why would he do that? What that bastard wants, he takes.'
'What did he take from you?'
'I never let him near me.'
'Margot?'
'You've got the wrong idea. It was just – what he did to Jen.'
'Do you know about the flyer she had made?'
'What flyer?'
I described it, while Denise shook her head.
'Did Jenny get into a fight with Margot?'
'No.'
'Did they argue over money?'
'There wasn't any argument.'
'How was Jenny paid?'
'By cheque.'
'All that she was owed?'
'Margot may be hard sometimes, but she's not stingy, or a cheat.'
'Even when she doesn't like a girl?'

Denise began to protest, but I persisted. 'She didn't like Jenny. Even before the incident with Lawrence.'

'Who told you that?'

'I worked it out. Did Margot ever tell you about some trouble she got into when she was young?'

Denise's cigarette made fireworks. 'What trouble?' she asked with a catch in her voice.

'With a client. He died while she was with him. The coroner's verdict was a heart attack, but she got done over by the press.'

Denise didn't answer straight away. She smoked and stared out over the lake. Finally she said, 'The guy died of a heart attack. It wasn't anybody's fault.'

'Is that what Margot told you?'
'It's what happened.'
'What about Stan Walewicz?'
'What about him?'

'Did Jenny ever talk to you about a movie he made? She and Lawrence were in it.'

'No.'

'But you know who Walewicz is.'

'I'm not stupid.'

'I'm sorry if I gave the wrong impression,' I said. 'I think you're far from stupid.'

The night was stripping layers of heat off itself, flinging them up and outwards, with a carelessness that made me want to shout. Denise strode forward, then stopped, her stillness more impatient than her movements.

I caught up to her and asked, 'Have you ever been to Jenny's house in Sydney?'

'Why would I? We weren't friends. We never saw each other outside work.'

'Where were you on December the thirtieth?'

'At the club.'

'Who with?'

'Margot.'

'Just the two of you?'

'Yes.'

'What time did you start?'

'Round eight.'

'And leave?'

Denise hesitated, then said, 'Shortly after two.' I could feel rather than see her shrug. 'I know what your game is,' she told me. 'It won't work.'

'I don't have a game. I just want to find out what happened to Jenny.'

We started walking back towards the cars.

'Did Margot ever say anything to you about a company called *CleanNet*?'

'Who?'

'A computer company. They make filters for blocking out stuff on the Internet.'

'No.'

'That afternoon Carmichael turned up – did he tell you where he'd been?'

'At work, wasn't he?'

'Is that what he said?'

'I don't remember what he said exactly.'

I felt sorry for Denise. I liked her, and she was doing her best.

We were almost at the cars. 'One last thing,' I said, 'if you could please tell me again what was in the room when you came back and found him?'

Denise sighed, getting out her keys. 'There was the bed, the side table, the chair.'

'What was on the table?'

'What's usually there.'

'The wig box?'

'That was on the floor.'

'Under the table?'

'Yes.'

'What happened before you and Carmichael went into the room?'

'Nothing,' Denise said. 'I mean nothing special.'

'Did he bring his dress in as usual?'

'Yes.'

'What about his underwear?'

'It was in the bag.'

'Did you help him put it on?'

'I – yes.'

'Margot handed him the wig in its box and he brought that in too?'

'I don't remember every single detail.'

'People don't, when things are where they expect them to be. Did you help him to get dressed?'

'I started to.'

'How far did you get?'

'Rebecca rang,' Denise said, unlocking her car.

She got into the driver's seat and said emphatically, 'Jenny Bishop overdosed.'

She started the engine before I could say anything more.

. . .

Walls mocked me – the relentless heat that the house had absorbed all day, and was now throwing back. I saw car headlights where there couldn't possibly be any. In shadowy corners, I caught glimpses of a badly shaven jaw. Hostile brown eyes looked back at me, reflected in my windows when I threw them open to let in the cooler air.

I filled Fred's water bowl, and he lapped and lapped. We sat side by side on the front step. There was hardly any traffic. A few cars passed at an ordinary pace. The sky was clear, and the stars were the best that you could hope for in a small inland city.

I hoped Denise would be all right. I shouldn't have pestered her to meet me. The best thing for Denise would be to report back to Margot that I'd swallowed her lies about Jenny Bishop, and have nothing more to do with me. But Jenny was dead, and so was Eden Carmichael. A person couldn't walk away from that.

The blue of the upper air was the same colour as Carmichael's dress. It seemed that Jenny's death had left a space in the sky for his dress to slide into, a garment empty of its wearer. His death lay next to hers, but so much more public and flamboyant. A politician's death made waves, while Jenny's, if a certain logic, already set in place, was allowed to take its course, would sink without a ripple. Carmichael's heart would have got him eventually, but the embarrassment could have been avoided – this was emerging as the consensus. And Jenny's death – predictable for different reasons, in a different way? A dead man could be pulled in many directions, and a dead woman too. Undertows and currents kept on moving round them. Everyone seemed confident that they could explain one or the other.

. . .

I made myself a late meal of hard-boiled eggs and salad, then sat in front of my office windows, opened as wide as they would go, and typed up my conversation with Denise. I was washing my plate and drinking glass when there was a knock on the front door.

Ken Dollimore stared at me with the demeanour of a man who'd set out with a clear purpose in mind, but had lost his way. His eyes were bloodshot and unfocussed. His hair was less than perfect. I invited him in.

Dollimore blinked, getting his bearings, glancing round my house. It was very late to be paying a social call, but this was a man more capable of surprising behaviour than I'd given him credit for.

He swayed back and forth on the balls of his feet, and licked his lips, which looked slightly swollen. I asked him to sit down, and offered to make coffee. He shook his head at the latter, but lowered himself awkwardly into a chair.

I sat down opposite him and leant forward. 'One night, Ed Carmichael saw a different girl at the club,' I said. 'Not the one he usually saw. Do you know her name?'

'Ed did whatever Madam told him to.'

Dollimore's speech was slurred, but I could smell no alcohol.

'I'm trying to find out what your friend told this girl that turned out to be dangerous. I think I know who she was, but I need confirmation.'

'Ed betrayed a confidence,' Dollimore said, reaching his tongue around the syllables with difficulty. 'A promise he'd made to that woman. I made a promise to Ed and I broke it.'

'You told the police about John Penshurst.'

'The police had better do their job.'

'You reminded Margot Lancaster about Penshurst too.'

'No one else was going to. She got away with murder.'

'How did she do that?'

'Don't tell me it's not easy enough to take a man whose health is failing, and to harass, or frighten him to death, then dress it up to look like a heart attack.'

'What was Carmichael's promise to Margot Lancaster?'

'He wouldn't tell me.'

'But you guessed that it had to do with *CleanNet*.'

'Why else would Ed suddenly turn round and start promoting the company?'

'You told me all he did was attend the presentation.'

Dollimore glanced at me the way a tiger might consider a mouse, too small to be a meal unless he was desperate.

He swallowed as though the movement hurt and said, 'There's all those missing years, you see, years when Ed and I lost touch. Madam disappeared after that business in Sydney, or Ed believed she'd disappeared.

He couldn't get anyone to tell him where she was, except that she was supposed to have gone overseas after the coroner's inquest. He tried to find out where. And then he went himself.'

'Where?'

'Wherever he thought she might turn up. Europe, anyway, I found out later. She hadn't left Australia at all, as it turned out, but she'd changed her name, and her appearance. Become a blonde. She'd told him she was going to Europe before it all happened. Perhaps she was intending to. He used up his savings searching for her.'

Dollimore swallowed again, then winced.

I brought him a glass of water, asking, as I handed it to him, 'Why would Margot want to kill Eden Carmichael?'

'Money. I'm sure he told her he was leaving her his flat.'

'Do you have a key?'

'What makes you think that? No, Ed had areas of his life that were completely private. His flat was one. In all the years I've known him, I could count the times I've been there on one hand.'

Dollimore read my expression and went on, 'Ed knew his days on earth were numbered. If he kept newspaper clippings, letters, anything like that – I'm not saying she did write to him, but I've wondered – I think he probably burnt them after his first heart attack. However much Ed might have acted as though he didn't care, he was afraid of dying.'

'What about his office? Could he have kept letters there?'

'Too public.'

'A safe-deposit box?'

'There'd have to be a key. I asked the police about it when they interviewed me. They wouldn't say, but I doubt it somehow. I think if the police had found papers, letters, that threw some light on what had happened, then they'd have asked me about them.'

I agreed that it was likely, then pointed out, 'Margot must have known Carmichael was in Canberra when she bought the club. Do you think that's why she moved here?'

'I don't know, but once she *was* here, she set out to trap him.'

'She wouldn't have sex with him.'

'That could have been Ed's salvation.'

'How?'

'It could have been the moment when the spell was broken.'

'Is that what he told you?'

'It's what I believe.'

'My problem is that I can't connect Margot Lancaster to *CleanNet*,' I said. 'Can you?'

Dollimore stared at me without replying.

'That's what you were looking for when you rang me the first time, wasn't it?'

Dollimore still didn't reply, but I knew that I was right.

'The other girl Carmichael saw, was her name Jenny Bishop?'

'Ed never told me. I wouldn't have forgotten if he had.'

I pictured Dollimore going from one bar to another on that Tuesday, searching for his friend. I felt that I'd misjudged this proud, censorious man, and underestimated the lengths he might go to once his natural inclination to obey the law had loosened, or a hole had been gnawed in it wide enough for another Ken Dollimore, a more impulsive, less predictable version, to slip through.

'It was you who warned Senator Bryant's office that something was wrong, wasn't it? You phoned and said you thought it might be better if the meeting with Carmichael was postponed.'

Dollimore looked about to deny this, then said, 'I – all right, yes, it was. I was trying to protect him,' he continued woodenly. 'I suspected the appointment had something to do with the promise he'd made. I had to get to him first and find out what it was.'

'Why didn't you tell the police?'

'I should have, I know. I was going to, then I felt ashamed. If I hadn't rung the senator's office, Ed would have kept the appointment. He wouldn't have gone to that club. He'd still be alive.'

'It would be easy enough for the police to find out.'

'I thought they would. I keep wondering why they haven't asked me.'

'Perhaps because they're satisfied that your friend's heart would have got him sooner, rather than later,' I said gently. 'Was Carmichael going to recommend that Senator Bryant include *CleanNet* on his department's list?'

Dollimore's shrug said that this was a possibility he'd thought of and discarded.

'You're thinking that alone wouldn't have accounted for Carmichael's distress.'

'And McFadden didn't need it. He was doing a perfectly good job of lobbying on his own.'

'Could someone have given Margot Lancaster some shares? If they were a gift, they wouldn't show up on ASIC's records.'

'Yes, but who?'

We exchanged another glance. It was possible that Margot had been given shares by a grateful client, but the chances of either of us tracing such an individual were slight. And from what I'd seen of Margot, it seemed unlikely that she would have involved Eden Carmichael for such an indirect, elusive gain. Margot wanted to sell her club, and she might need extra money for some reason as yet unknown to me. But still.

'All I can do is keep on looking,' Dollimore said in a voice that was suddenly exhausted.

A few minutes later, I showed him to the door and watched him walk away, hunched and slow, with none of his confidence or style.

I longed to get into my car, not stop or slow down, until I reached the sea. I went back to my office and typed up our conversation. I did not switch on any lights. The computer gave off just enough, and it was a story suited to the darkness.

Eighteen

I checked my email first thing the next morning, hoping for one from Ivan. Instead, there was a message from Andrew Glover, my contact at the Australian Securities and Investment Commission. He apologised for taking so long to get back to me, and for not being able to answer all my questions.

My eyes took in the two short paragraphs at once. Stan Walewicz had begun his movie business in 1991, taking advantage of the repeal of laws against the production and distribution of X-rated material in the ACT. *Artysta Limited* had operated until 1996, when he'd expanded, launched a website and a monthly magazine, and registered the new company under the name *Zabawka Entertainment*. The largest investment to *Artysta Limited* had been made through a trust fund in the name of Emily Purvis, Richard McFadden's wife.

I emailed Andrew back to thank him, and asked if anyone else had requested similar information from ASIC in the past few weeks. I also asked if he could find out what had happened to the trust fund.

When I phoned Lucy and told her the news, she said with satisfaction, 'Got him!'

I asked her to keep McFadden's investment to herself for the time being. She argued with me; it wasn't my job to tell her what to do. I interrupted to say that I was building up a picture of connections between Walewicz, McFadden, and Simon Lawrence. It would make more impact once the full story was known, and if the lobby group accused McFadden publicly and prematurely, then they might lose the opportunity to get it.

Lucy wasn't happy, but I got her to agree to wait at least a few more days. I didn't think I'd been exaggerating, but it was possible that I'd learnt as much about the three men as I was going to, that there was no 'full story'.

. . .

Brook dropped by at lunchtime, bringing a transcript of the inquiry into the death of John Edward Penshurst, who'd breathed his last in a Sydney brothel called *Full House*. My personal request to the NSW coronial office had been refused.

I was touched that, in spite of our differences, Brook was still taking the trouble to bring me material that I would not otherwise have access to.

He gave me a crooked smile and said that if I stayed home reading, I was less likely to get caught up in a car chase.

'That reminds me,' I said, and told him about my conversation with Brian Picoult.

Brook asked me to put it in an email. I brought him up-to-date on what Ken Dollimore had told me, and the investment made in McFadden's wife's name, while he gulped down a sandwich and three cups of tea.

. . .

I read until my eyes crossed. The coroner had been tough on Evelyn Burns, alias Eve, alias Margot Lancaster, but a strength and steeliness came through her testimony, and the way that she presented it. I picked up more than a hint of pride in her professional abilities, in spite of the fact that she'd been having sex with a client when his heart had stopped.

John Penshurst had been forty-eight years old. Eve had not been aware that he suffered from any health problems. He'd been a heavy smoker. But so many people smoked in the early 1970s that this point, though mentioned, was not dwelt on by the coroner.

The post-mortem had revealed arteries so clogged with cholesterol that it was a wonder his heart had lasted as long as it had.

There was some dispute as to the time of death. Penshurst's sister claimed that Eve had waited too long before calling for help. It seemed the sister had conducted her own investigation. She'd spoken to the ambulance people, and the doctor who'd pronounced her brother dead on arrival at St Vincent's hospital. She'd questioned a girl who'd worked with Eve, who'd been at the reception desk when Eve had walked out and said she needed to call an ambulance. Eve hadn't run, nor had she seemed distressed.

Eve didn't come across as someone who was liked by her co-workers. Reading their testimony, and their answers to the coroner's questions, I was struck by the fact that no one spoke up for her. None of the girls who'd been at *Full House* that night offered evidence in support of her claim that she'd acted responsibly.

'What was the point of getting into a flap?' Eve had asked at one point. 'It wouldn't have helped him, would it?'

Had she been too proud to call for help? Hadn't she considered that it might be necessary, or at least prudent, to have one person on her side?

John Penshurst had been drinking before his visit to *Full House*. When asked whether she would describe him as drunk, Eve had replied, 'More or less.' When asked to explain what she meant by this, she said many of the clients she saw were 'tanked', or 'half tanked'. It struck me as a phrase the Margot I knew would not have used.

John Penshurst had collapsed on top of her. She'd thought it was the booze. She'd had to struggle to get out from underneath him, believing he'd passed out, and wasting valuable seconds wondering whether it would be better to leave him to sleep it off, or try and revive him. She'd fetched a mug of water from the bathroom and thrown it over him, but he hadn't responded. She'd checked to see if he was breathing, and tried to find a pulse, then walked to the front desk.

The coroner had questioned her closely, making her go over every detail several times. She said she didn't know what happened when a person had a heart attack. No one had ever told her, but she'd had plenty of experience with customers who'd had too much to drink. How was she to know the difference? Because the coroner could accept hearsay evidence, Penshurst's sister had said things that would not have been permitted during a trial, repeatedly calling Eve a slut, a whore, a murderer. The coroner had reprimanded her, but hadn't shut her up.

I imagined Eve replying, deferential to a point, but determined to stand her ground. I pictured the dead man's sister abusing her, and her colleagues snubbing, or perhaps abusing her as well. I thought of her getting up in the morning to newspaper headlines shouting, 'Guilty!'

The physical evidence – alcohol in Penshurst's bloodstream, extremely high cholesterol – had won the day. The matter had not gone to trial.

I needed to get outside, so I took Fred for a walk across the road. It was overcast and windy.

Back home again, I checked my mail. Andrew Glover had replied. He said that no one had approached him personally, but one of the other officers had received a request for information about *CleanNet*. I rang to ask if he could find out who, and he said sorry, he didn't think so. It would be a breach of client confidentiality.

I rang Brook, who'd glanced at the coroner's report, but not read it thoroughly.

We talked about it for a few minutes. Brook had already passed on the information I'd obtained from ASIC. I wondered if the police would apply for a warrant. I'd love to know who the other enquirer had been. I thought I had a pretty good idea.

'Whoever chased me on the highway was warning me to back off,' I said. 'My office was broken into, and my computer. *CleanNet*'s investors won't want it broadcast that McFadden put money into porn movies, and that makes it difficult for them because the information's sitting there. Anyone can find it, provided they've got the authority, and they know where to look. And I've been told by my contact at ASIC that there *was* another enquiry.'

'You're thinking of the Bishop girl?'

'Why not? Lawrence and Walewicz go back a long way, and recently put that website together. Now it turns out there's a business connection between Walewicz and McFadden. Jenny Bishop hated Lawrence. What's to stop her paying someone to do the research, then challenging him with it? Maybe she even tried to blackmail him.'

'But there's nothing connecting Lawrence to McFadden's company, is there?'

'Maybe I haven't found it yet. Could you get me Jenny's lab results and crime scene photos, do you think?'

There was a short silence, then Brook said, 'I'm not a solitary animal like you, Sandra.'

'I'm not a solitary animal either. Not by choice.'

'You put me in a difficult position.'

I bit my tongue. Be damned if I was going to apologise for that.

Nineteen

In front of me were Jenny Bishop's post-mortem results, plus the crime scene photographs and video.

The post-mortem was definitive. Jenny had died of asphyxiation caused by an overdose of heroin. All the outward signs were there – burst capillaries under the eyelids, blueness round the mouth. I'd never been close to anyone who'd been killed by heroin, but I knew that it was similar to death from suffocation. There'd been half a gram of the drug in her bloodstream, enough to kill a person who was using regularly. She had probably died within minutes of it being injected. There were also high levels of alcohol. The estimated time of death was between midnight and 2 am on Friday, December 31st. She'd been a healthy woman, if prematurely aged – no problems with her heart, lungs, liver, or any other organs.

The photographs taken in Jenny's bedroom made me feel sad, angry and helpless.

Her legs were wide open. That was the first surprise. It was hard to believe she'd died like that. In the thick summer light of that bedroom – I felt the heat again, increasing as I'd climbed the stairs – Jenny's spread legs, and the shadows they cast on the mattress, reminded me of angel's wings. It was terrible, that private space made public for the police photographer. I hoped someone had closed her legs as soon as possible. How sentimental, when modesty could no longer help.

Jenny lay on her back, arms by her sides, head resting on a pillow, face towards the window. She looked impossibly young.

Her prints and DNA were the only ones on the syringe. The needle had been new. There were old bloodstains on the sheets. Tests on the mattress had yielded a few more bloodstains whose type matched hers, and semen stains, that, as far as I could tell from the information in front of me, had not been matched to anybody. The only other fingerprints in the room – on a number of places including the door jamb and the bookcase – belonged to Ian and Francesca.

One partial print, possibly Jenny's, and another complete, but smudged one, had been lifted from the glass left in the kitchen sink. The bottle of Fosters had a number of overlapping prints around the neck. No other liquor bottles had been in the garbage.

The only piece of good news was that the Glebe police had taken out a warrant for her phone calls. Brook had told me when he'd dropped the package off. He hadn't said so, but I hoped he'd had a hand in pushing for some further investigation into the circumstances of her death.

I'd left the video till last.

There was the bedroom I'd looked into through an open doorway, conscious of Ian's thin, reluctant presence by my side. The camera caught a hand in a latex glove, then began a slow circuit of the room.

There was the mattress on its base underneath the window. The curtains were drawn back, exactly as I'd seen them. The camera swung past objects on the floor, a syringe and what looked like its crumpled wrapping next to the bed, the stack of three books with the top one open and face down, the bookshelf with its meagre assortment of literature texts.

Suddenly Jenny was there, sharply in focus, legs open to the world. I caught my breath and looked away, then forced my eyes back to the screen. Why were her legs open like that? The camera kept on moving, after it had established the position of the body, its relation to, and distance from, other objects in the room. And movement gave, for a few seconds anyway, the illusion of life.

...

Brook called round that evening as I was about to start my solitary omelette. I divided it in two, ignoring his protests that he wasn't hungry. He looked tired and drawn and I felt a stab of regret that I'd begrudged him his holiday.

Brook ate so fast, I was sure he'd missed out on lunch. In between mouthfuls, he told me Simon Lawrence had an alibi for the night of Jenny Bishop's death.

I began making a fruit salad, while I said that Lawrence had told me he'd been working on December 30th.

'But hardly in the middle of the night.'

Brook nodded. 'He was with a prostitute.'

'That figures.'

'It does.'

Brook sighed, stretching back in his chair, and said he'd questioned Stan Walewicz that afternoon.

'You know, I busted him a few times?'

'Really? Why didn't you tell me that before?'

Brook flexed his fingers with another sigh. 'Me and Bill McCallum. Before all this X-rated stuff was legal. God, it was tedious. And a waste of time. We'd drive away with a truckload of videos. They'd pay the fines, be back in business within twenty-four hours.'

'What did you do with the videos?'

'Buried them.'

'Did you watch them first?'

'A few.'

'Did Walewicz pay you?'

'I never took money off him. Nor did Bill. I'd swear to that.'

'Do you think he'll go offshore now?'

'Dunno. I get the feeling he likes the challenge of operating under the censors' noses.'

'But why would his service provider take the risk?'

'Money?' Brook suggested. 'You may or may not dismiss him as a scumbag, but he doesn't appear to have broken any law.'

'There's the rosebuds.'

Brook smiled.

I leant forward and handed him a bowl of fruit salad. I wanted to reach out my hand and touch his shoulder or his arm, test my fingers along his too prominent collar bones. It was suddenly ridiculous that I could not. How many women knew their men by bones? I'd learnt to know this one, when the hope of flesh returning had seemed as impossible as the act of stretching out my fingers now, to test that flesh was there.

I sat down opposite him and picked up my spoon.

'Did you ask about Richard McFadden's investment?'

'Stan didn't turn a hair. Said that Richard was a generous man, bless his heart. Denied having any more recent business dealings with him. Denied that McFadden was paying him to keep quiet. "Did me a good turn once, and I'm not about to cruel his chances with these filter gizmos now." Words to that effect.'

'What about business dealings with Margot Lancaster and Simon Lawrence?'

'Stan paid Lawrence for the use of his website. Said he did it for a laugh, and to prove how easy it is to get around the new law. Claims never to have done business with Lancaster.'

Brook picked at his dessert with a preoccupied expression.

'He reckons he's had nothing to do with the Bishop girl since that movie. He was at Mossy Point with his girlfriend on December thirty. Ditto January four.'

'That's convenient.'

'It is. On the other hand, half of Canberra was down the coast on those dates.'

Brook's glance at me was wary.

'Eat up,' I told him.

'I'm not hungry.'

'Just a few more mouthfuls.'

'You sound like my mother.'

'Pretend I am your mother, then. She who has to be obeyed.'

'What about Eden Carmichael?' I asked after we'd chewed together in silence for a while.

'Stan knew him by reputation.'

'But that's all?'

'He says so. Says he might have met Carmichael at some big social gathering, but he can't remember talking to him.'

It occurred to me that I was missing something obvious.

'Where's Sophie?' I asked.

'Gone back to her daughter's.'

'You had an argument?'

'Not really. I don't want to talk about it.'

. . .

Scarcely more than an hour after nightfall, and the temperature had already dropped fifteen degrees. The sky was clear, the air very thin and still. It seemed foolish to shut up the house soon after I'd opened it, but that's what I did. I spoke to Fred through the gate, telling him he was better off outside.

My car was low on petrol. I pulled in to the Lyneham service station. Even in my quiet suburb, at nine o'clock at night, there were plenty of people out and about, walking dogs, or just themselves. The tables outside *Tilleys* were practically full. I heard a sound like a small explosion, then a burst of laughter.

At the bar where I'd met Mieke, I bought a beer and sat by the open door to drink it. Though the ceiling fans seemed to be working well enough, the room was hot and stale-smelling. The barman was watching the soccer on SBS. At a break in the match, I pulled out Jenny's photo and took it over.

'Gone missing has she? What are you, a cop?'

'No.'

He peered at me more closely. 'Mother?'

'No. Have you ever seen her?'

'Why do you want to know?'

'She died just after Christmas.'

'Overdose, was it?'

'Why do you say that?'

The barman shrugged.

'Seen any of the girls from *Margot's* lately?' I asked.

'This one work there, did she?'

'For a while. Have they been told to stay away?'

'I wouldn't know.'

I finished my beer and left, glad to be out of doors again. I stood by my car and breathed in the long night breath of the city, thinking that Jenny may well have liked a liquid dinner, to fortify her for a night's work. But there were better, surer ways to blunt sensation. Why would she bother with a tacky, lifeless pub? I was surely on a wild-goose chase, an excuse to keep moving, in my imagination, away from Brook's house with its well-made curtains thrown back, covers off the bed, moonlight soaking down through layers of skin.

There were three cars parked in the street, but no one around. I was reminded how much Mitchell was a place of day trading. With the exception of the brothel and video hire customers, few people had a reason to be there at night.

. . .

The third bar I went into had a curly neon sign above the entrance that reminded me of Margot's club. The barman stared at Jenny's photo and asked, 'What's she done?'

'She died. I'm looking for her friends.'

'You don't look like police.'

'I'm not.'

'What did she die of?'

'I'm trying to find out.'

'If you're a cop you ought to say so.'

'I'm not.'

I pulled out my card and handed it across.

The barman read it without comment, then looked up at me.

'What did you say her name was?'

'Jenny Bishop.'

'She didn't come here that often, but I thought she was nice – nice smile, knew how to enjoy herself.'

'Who did she come with?'

'Different people.'

'Was there a regular night of the week?'

'Monday. Tuesday sometimes.'

'Who with?' I asked again.

'Girls from *Margot's*. That Dutch girl.'

I asked the barman to call me if any of Jenny's friends came in. His answer was an almost imperceptible nod.

Energy drained out of me. I sat in my car, arms crossed over the steering wheel. Who hung around in Canberra, in January? Surely Jenny's friends were down the coast, at Batemans Bay or Ulladulla, surfing, partying, smoking dope and having sex on bunk beds, drinking in crowded, salty, effervescent beach hotels.

I could knock on Margot's door and give her an excuse to complain again. I could turn my back on Canberra, head down the coast myself. The impulse to drive, and keep on driving, seemed to come from the blue-black-purple of the hills beyond Belconnen. The bush had its fingers up everyone's backyard. Bush capital – the resilience of that – the sense of moving on and out, of highways running through. Belconnen. Civic. Urban cul-de-sacs. Burley Griffin's mazes that infuriated newcomers with one dead end after another, tracing and re-tracing an outdated geometric pattern.

Perhaps the fluid boundary between bush and capital city had appealed to Jenny. Those mountains out beyond Belconnen – how they teased perspective, how we called them mountains, knowing that, in wider contexts, they would be regarded as no more than tree-covered rocks. I recalled driving out to them, to the Ginninderra Falls – another euphemism since the falls were usually dry from September to May – with Peter and his father, one spring when there'd been a lot of rain. The climb was too steep for Peter, and very slippery. We could hear water in the distance, and he kept asking where they were. Derek carried him on his back, while I took the food and rug, though I knew by then that Derek had no intention of sitting down in such inhospitable surroundings. As we slipped and slithered, dirtied our clothes and scratched our hands, Peter had begun to cry, not only with discomfort, but taking in, as he often did, the lack of accord between his parents. Derek had snapped at him. There could be nothing worse, sometimes, than half-knowing what was wrong.

I started my car, thinking that if Carmichael in his blue dress had made himself into a patch of Canberra's night sky, then so had Margot, with her helmet of black hair. I could feel Margot's story beginning to unravel, the story she'd carefully constructed with Denise. That morning in the carpark, when she'd been sitting in her car with her arms on the steering wheel, and I'd dropped by on impulse on my way to Sydney – I wondered where she'd been going, at that hour. Had she been planning to sit in her club all day with only the crossword for company, listening in the silence to the phone that didn't ring, the customers who obstinately stayed away?

Margot's camouflage had served her well, much better than Carmichael's, but then he'd died, leaving her to fit together what pieces she was able to, make a story plausible enough for the police and press. And she'd done all right. She would have done all right if it hadn't been for Jenny Bishop.

At home, I opened all the doors and windows, then sat with Fred panting on the front step beside me. The house breathed out heavily behind our backs. I was tired, but afraid of the faces that would appear as soon as I lay down – Carmichael's ghost, stepping out of the photograph I'd finally cut from the newspaper and pinned up in my office. I would see Jenny's flung open body. Then that other man – I'd see him clearly too, waiting for an opportunity to slam my car into a concrete wall.

I pictured Sophie returning from her daughter's, Brook and Sophie making up. Sophie would throw back the curtains she'd made, those clever curtains of Brook's illness, which had kept the scorching day at one remove. Her opening would be an expansive, graceful gesture. Coming up behind her, Brook would put his hands around her waist, then move them higher. His movement, her response, would be as normal and expected as two masses of air meeting one another after a day apart. I winced at how simply a woman could turn to face a man, after he had cupped her breasts with his hands.

Twenty

Bryant's list of recommended filters was in the morning papers. *The Canberra Times* listed the lucky top scorers on page three, together with brightly coloured pictures of their products. *CleanNet* was not among them.

The phone rang as I was pouring myself a second cup of tea. Gail was pissed off. 'You knew they'd been scrubbed,' she said.

'I didn't.'

Gail didn't stay on the phone long enough to debate the point with me.

. . .

I took Fred for a token walk across the road, then decided to pay Stan Walewicz a visit.

He came to the door of his studio looking a little the worse for wear.

'Did you know *CleanNet* was going to be left off Senator Bryant's list?' I asked.

'You're flattering me – Ms Mahoney isn't it? I'm blushing.'

'Did you?'

Walewicz smiled and rubbed his chin. He hadn't shaved that morning. 'I wish I could say yes.'

'How do you feel about it?'

'Feel?'

'A shame to see an old friend's company passed over in favour of imports from America.'

'Old friend?' Walewicz looked puzzled, then he smiled. 'A crying shame. Now, if you'll excuse me, I'm sorry, but I have things to do.'

. . .

I rang Richard McFadden's office. While I waited for him to come to the phone, or perhaps decide not to, I pictured again the 1930s decor, those chandeliers weighted with yellow light, the red velvet and the mirrors. More revealing, in terms of its reflections, had been the shop window on the other side of Castlereagh Street, where I'd glimpsed Simon Lawrence's watchdog for the first time, his large brown eyes and stubbly jaw, his manner that was bumbling and yet predatory.

'Were you disappointed that *CleanNet* was left off Senator Bryant's list?' I asked when McFadden finally came on the line.

'It's a loss for the Australian public,' he replied politely, 'because our product is the best available. But it's not the end of the world. Of course, the minister acts according to his own discretion. *CleanNet* will beat the competition hands down. The market will sort out the sheep from the goats.'

'Do you know what happened to make Senator Bryant change his mind?'

'No idea at all. The senator is an intelligent man. He was impressed by our presentation. If *CleanNet*'s not to carry a government recommendation, then that's a loss for Australian consumers, and the Australian Treasury as well. That list. Know how many Australian companies are on it? None. Zero. Zilch.'

'Eden Carmichael would have been disappointed.'

'I believe he would have.' McFadden sounded genuinely sorry.

'Did you know that Carmichael was on his way to meet Senator Bryant on the day he died?'

'On his way?' McFadden repeated. 'No, I didn't.'

'Was Carmichael ever a shareholder in your company?'

'I can't imagine you need that information for your thesis, Ms Mahoney.'

'What about Margot Lancaster? Was she ever given shares?'

'Who?'

'She owns the brothel where Carmichael died.' I pressed on, ignoring McFadden's irritation. 'What about Ken Dollimore, Carmichael's former colleague?'

'The one with the coiffure? He paid me a visit. I was staying in that hotel next to the casino. Great spot, great atmosphere. He lectured me about my sins.'

'Is that all?'

'It was enough. Quite enough.'

'And Stan Walewicz? Has he been helpful too?'

'I'm not –'

'That would be fair, wouldn't it? Seeing as how you helped him out.'

'How –'

'When Mr Walewicz was getting started in the movie business. You lent him a generous amount of money.'

'Who told you that?'

'I paid for the information, the way any member of the public can. I wasn't the only one, was I Mr McFadden?'

McFadden's sharp intake of breath told me that I'd hit a nerve.

. . .

I rang Brook who told me he'd paid a visit to my friend.

'Which one?' I asked him.

'Seems Lancaster wasn't telling the whole truth about the Bishop girl. Glebe faxed her phone calls down. She made eight to the club after she's supposed to have left.'

'What did Margot say to that?'

'Didn't turn a hair. Says Bishop rang about money that she claimed was owed her.'

'But Denise told –'

'She covered that as well. Admits there was some disagreement between her and Bishop over money. The other girl – Denise – didn't know the details.'

'But Margot was definite about the lack of contact. And Denise was definite about the money. She said Margot paid Jenny by cheque.'

Brook had persisted, in a way that let Margot know he had the list of phone calls, and finally Margot had admitted that Jenny had wanted more money than she was owed.

'How much more?' I asked.

'Five hundred.'

'Did she agree to pay it?'

'Yes. But then Bishop wanted another thousand. Payment for "pain and suffering", she called it.'

'Did Margot agree?'

'She did. She apologised for not having told us before. She said she hadn't wanted to admit that she'd given in to Bishop.'

'Who else was Jenny ringing in December?'

'Stan Walewicz and Denise Travers.'

'Simon Lawrence?'

'No match for him so far. And –' Brook went on, in a voice that said he'd saved the best for last, 'three calls to Eden Carmichael in the second half of December.'

'I knew there was a connection.'

'Yeah, well,' Brook said dryly, 'pity they're both dead, and they can't tell us about it.'

I agreed it was.

The fact that Denise had lied about her contact with Jenny didn't surprise me. As for Walewicz, Brook told me Jenny had made numerous calls to his studio. He also said that Jenny's bank transactions included a five hundred dollar deposit, and then one for a thousand dollars dated three weeks later – Margot's "pain and suffering" payout.

Twenty-one

Denise Travers was missing. When she hadn't shown up for work, Margot had been worried, but not excessively so. When Denise hadn't answered her phone in the morning, and Margot hadn't been able to reach her on her mobile, she'd decided it was time to tell the police.

Denise had last been seen leaving her flat at eleven o'clock the morning before, Brook rang to tell me. A neighbour had seen her walking down the street, and getting on a bus. He'd watched her till the bus came. His observations were precise. She'd been carrying a small backpack, but no other luggage. When Brook phoned me, he'd just come back from questioning the man, who'd said Denise was a nice woman. He noticed when she came and went.

Brook and a Detective Constable went round to Denise's flat, and interviewed her neighbours after they found it empty, with her red Valiant parked outside. It was Denise's daughter's week for staying with her father. He told Brook that the girl had spent most of yesterday at Civic Pool. Her mother hadn't rung, or left a message.

Margot had no objection to the club and her own flat being searched. While this was underway, the driver of the 11.03 bus, which had picked Denise up according to her neighbour, was tracked down and questioned.

When shown a photograph of Denise, the driver remembered her. Denise had had no change. He'd had to give her change for ten dollars, which annoyed him. She'd got off the bus at the Civic Interchange. She'd been alone, as far as he could tell.

. . .

My mobile rang. It was the bartender at *Klim's*. One of Jenny Bishop's drinking mates had just come in, if I was interested.

Inside the bar, it was very still and hot.

The bartender recognised me, and indicated a young woman sitting by herself.

She wasn't anyone I'd seen before, pale and thin, with short, dark hair dyed red in streaks, and small, sharp features.

When I walked over to her, she glanced at me indifferently, as if she was used to being accosted by strangers. She looked round to catch the bartender's attention, but didn't call him over.

'Who are you?' she asked.

'My name's Sandra. I'm trying to find out what happened to Jenny Bishop.'

'Jen was ace. I can't believe she's dead. Are you the one been asking questions about that politician?'

'That's right. Do you know Denise Travers? She's missing.'

The young woman shook her head.

'Did you work with Jenny?'

'I'm not into all that shit. They can keep their money. Jen and me, we like went to the same college.'

'What about Jenny's other friends?'

The young woman gave me a sharp look. 'You know, I seen that polly here one night? He was with a guy who Jen said was giving her a hard time. Good-looking guy. Dark hair. Owns some sort of flower shop.'

'Simon Lawrence. He was with Eden Carmichael?'

'I recognised the old guy from the telly.'

'Was anybody else with them?'

'Another guy came in. He went and sat with them. Muscled-up guy.'

'Did you recognise him?'

'Jen told me he makes fuck flicks.'

'What did they do?'

'Drank, talked, what anybody does in a bar.'

'Did Jenny speak to them?'

'Oh yes. She yelled out to the old guy.'

'What did she say?'

'She said she'd got his picture. It was really pretty too, she said.'

'And then?'

'He said something to the other two, and Jen called out, "Hey guys, want it for your family album?".'

'What happened after that?'

'The old guy, the politician, he stood up. His face was like all red. The dago guy tried to calm him down. Jen burst out laughing. I go, "What's so funny?" And she goes, "Him with the curly hair? He's the biggest bastard." I go, "So?" "So, I just figured out a way to get him." Then they got the old guy out. He was looking pretty sick.'

'And Jenny?'

'She told me the story, about what the curly-haired guy done to her.'

'Did she say how she was going to get even with him?'

'Nah.'

'Do you know if they met again?'

'Who?'

'Jenny and any of those three men.'

'I never saw Jen after that night.'

'Did you speak to her on the phone?'

'Only once. She rang to ask if I'd seen the politician.'

'Had you?'

'No.'

'The others?'

'Not the flower guy. The other one come in.'

'Who with?'

'Margot, who Jenny used to work for.'

'You recognised her?'

'She had her picture in the paper.'

'What was Jenny doing in Canberra in the middle of December?'

'Visiting, I guess.'

'Anybody in particular?'

'She never said.'

'Did Jenny see Margot when she was here?'

'I dunno.'

'Was Jenny using heroin?'

'No.'

'How do you know she hadn't started again?'

'I just know, that's all.'

'She died of an overdose.'

'That's bullshit.'

'Why would anybody want to kill her?'

'Jen had a big mouth, and she liked to use it. She made enemies.'

'Do you know who?'

'That flower guy, for one.'

'Do you remember when you saw the three men? What date?'

'It was a Monday. Round like maybe the sixteenth. I don't remember exactly.'

'How did Jenny arrange to meet you?'

'She messaged me and said she was coming down, and maybe we could catch up.'

'What about Denise?'

'I don't know nothing about her.'

I asked the young woman for her mobile number, but she wouldn't give it to me.

. . .

Something made me linger after she'd left the bar. It was very quiet. The bartender looked as though he had time for a chat. I bought myself a drink and went over what I'd just been told. The bartender nodded warily, but said he mustn't have been working that night. He would have remembered if Jenny had got into a shouting match with someone. I asked him if he recalled any other occasions when Eden Carmichael had come in. He nodded again, even more reluctantly. Proceeding carefully, I asked him if Carmichael had been in with anyone at the end of December, or the beginning of January. After a few moments, the bartender said he was there one night with a young guy, not the kind of guy he would have expected to be keeping a politician company.

'Do you know who he was?'

'Well by sight, kind of.'

'He makes porn movies?'

The bartender nodded.

'And Eden Carmichael?'

'He looked terrible. I wasn't surprised when he had another heart attack. He looked like he was about to have one then.'

. . .

I rang Brook back. He'd obtained a warrant and was supervising a search of Denise's flat. Her bed was made, and there was no sign of disturbance or forced entry, no note, or messages on the answering machine, and no hint as to where she might have gone.

Stan Walewicz's studio was closed and he wasn't answering his phones. Neither was Simon Lawrence. I told Brook I'd found a witness who claimed that Jenny had been in Canberra in the middle of December, and that she and the witness had been drinking in *Klim's* when Lawrence had come in with Walewicz and Carmichael. The net was shrinking, the gaps in the mesh getting smaller. But I was afraid it was too late for Denise.

Brook said that the search of Margot's premises had drawn a blank.

'What about the wig box?' I asked.

'I don't know what happened to it. Does it matter?'

'It might,' I said, then told him I was going to drop by the club.

. . .

I found Margot alone, with all the blinds drawn, sitting in the dark. No one had answered when I rang the doorbell, but her car was parked outside. I'd tried the door, found it locked, but heard a faint scraping sound when I put my ear to it. I knocked and waited, knocked again, called out.

Margot's voice came through the closed door. 'Go away.'

'I need to talk to you.'

'Just go away.'

'Please,' I said.

Margot opened the door a crack. Seen from above, I thought we would appear to be two anxious women meeting clandestinely, playing out an awkward scene. The pressure of the hot day released itself through the slightly open door. I felt the air's movement gently at first, then more strongly, the way children sometimes push each other experimentally, then find that they like it.

I put my foot in the opening, and, when Margot didn't try to stop me, opened the door wide and walked in.

Her figure was darker than the club's small foyer; her face was one smooth shadow. The air-conditioning wasn't on, and the heat leant with its massive breath against the walls. The desk, the chair, the simple furniture of the reception area seemed to swell.

'What is it between you and that cop?' Margot asked, each word distinct.

'We're friends.'

Margot laughed.

'Where's the wig?' I asked her.

'The wig is mine. I bought it. It belongs to me.'

'Where is it now?'

'Ed had a bad heart,' Margot said.

'What about the one in Sydney?'

'He had a bad heart too.'

'Did you know his heart was bad?'

'Nobody did.'

'Jenny was young and healthy.'

'She was a junkie.'

'She'd given up. Can I switch the light on?'

'No.'

'Where were you the night Jenny died?'

'I've been having trouble sleeping. Sometimes I spend the night here.'

'Were you here that night?'

'Yes.'

'On your own?'

'After Denise left.' Margot's voice rose out of the darkness, sadly, but with steel in it. 'Rebecca's a great kid. She makes you think about kids who have everything handed to them on a plate.'

I swallowed, then thought, okay, if you want to talk about Rebecca, I'll go along with that.

'Will her father take good care of her?' I asked.

I could feel Margot looking at me sharply, trying to gauge what I meant.

'Denise would never do this to Becky. Never. If she got it into her head to go off somewhere, she'd take her daughter with her.'

'What if Rebecca didn't want to go?'

'That wouldn't come into it.'

'You mean –'

'She would go. I've never seen a mother and daughter as close as those two.'

'If Denise has gone somewhere on her own, do you think Rebecca knows where?'

Margot didn't answer. I took her silence to mean it was a possibility, and that she understood the danger Rebecca was in better than I did.

I knew the relationship between Margot and Denise was many-layered, and that they were both intelligent, brave women. Yet what I felt most strongly at that moment, as a pull between myself and the two of them, was not female competence and capability, but Margot's need for someone to reach out to, or what I imagined was that need. I wanted to be that person, yet I was afraid of crossing a boundary I would not be able to step back over again, once I had.

'Why did you lie to me about Carmichael seeing Jenny Bishop?'

'I didn't want to complicate things any further.'

'You told Denise to lie to me as well.'

'Ed died of a heart attack. What difference does it make?'

'You lied about Jenny's phone calls too.'

'She wanted money.'

'Did you see Jenny when she was in Canberra in December?'

'No.'

'But you knew she was here.'

'I heard about it afterwards.'

'Who from?'

'Stan Walewicz.'

'What did Walewicz want?'

'What do you mean?'

'When you met him at *Klim's*. He wanted something, didn't he?'

'Stan was reminding me of my obligations.'

'Obligations?'

'If I wanted Lawrence to take the club off my hands, I had to stay sweet.'

'How?'

When Margot didn't answer, I said, 'By giving him other girls for free?'

When she still didn't answer, I asked, 'Who killed Jenny?'

'She killed herself.' Margot reached for her bag, suddenly crisp and decisive. 'Come with me.'

. . .

We drove around streets the night was beginning to claim, streets that mocked the disappearance of a single woman who'd left behind a beloved daughter. Neon advertised used cars, sex, used cars. The flags of the second-hand car lots shone wetly, as though it had been raining. The streets were empty of people, though filled with their artefacts, and the promise that tomorrow more shoppers would appear to buy them. I remembered pulling up in a rag of shade, looking across at *Margot's* for the first time. I thought of lights in the main streets of country towns, how they clustered round the service station and the pub, how the brothel, if there was one, would advertise itself discreetly.

Every few minutes, Margot's guard seemed to slip a little. It was more a feeling I had than anything she said. What were we looking for, a body pushed against a wall, long legs protruding from a dumpster, a fingernail the colour of used blood beckoning from a pile of leaves? At any rate, a body. Eden Carmichael, in his finery, was proof that the suburb could absorb a violent death.

'What's that?' Margot said.

She pulled over to the curb. We got out, but left the engine running. What looked like a heap of clothing piled against a wall proved to be just that. It was near a big Smith Family clothing bin, but not against it, back in the shadows, leaning against a wall advertising Better Bricks. There was a coat, old tracksuit pants, a T-shirt.

Margot lifted them, put them back again.

She straightened up and stared at me. I stared back, waiting. This search, this using up of time, was her idea. I felt it was important to stick with her, go where she went, find nothing, or false alarms. Her concentration might lapse further. She might let something slip.

We cruised past deserted buildings. When Margot was too tired to drive any more, we returned to her club.

. . .

Once again, I entered a space that had been carefully preserved, rooms that felt more like a shrine than ever before.

I asked Margot what she thought had happened to Denise.

'You think if I knew that, I'd have spent the last two hours driving round with you?'

'It depends on how close I am to a lucky guess. You knew what Carmichael was upset about the day he turned up here. Denise did too.'

Margot stared at me with narrowed eyes. 'Denise is afraid of Stan and Simon. Afraid of them coming after her.'

'Why would those two come after Denise, and not you?'

'I'm useful to them still.'

'Where's your wig? Do you still keep it here?'

'Why do you want to know?'

'What about the box?'

'What about it?'

'Why was it taken out of the room before the police came?'

'It wasn't.'

'Where is it now?'

'The wigs are mine.'

Margot moved over to a chair, but didn't sit on it. She stood with her hands resting on its back.

'Why had Carmichael made an appointment with Senator Bryant for that day? What did it have to do with you?'

When Margot didn't reply, I said, 'Jenny Bishop worked it out. What's the connection between Lawrence and Carmichael? Did Lawrence do him a favour at some low point in his career? Did he lend him money, help him the way he offered to help you out by buying your club?'

'Lawrence never lifted a finger for Ed,' Margot said harshly. 'I want you to leave now.'

. . .

One set of headlights passed me on Flemington Road. I was startled by the brief, distant recognition of lights on a road otherwise as dark as a highway through the bush. My hands began to shake. The presence of the dead weighed heavily.

A cluster of red neon along Northbourne Avenue advertised Canberra's cheap hotels. They brought to mind the roses in Lawrence's window, and the buds that he'd selected for me. I wondered at the absence of red lights in Mitchell, the pragmatic, low-key approach to sex for sale, and how this approach, its legal, sensible surface, had been cracked wide open.

Disoriented, I peered through the windscreen, looking for signs of daybreak, reminding myself that it was at least six hours away. I recalled running for home down the Federal Highway, a wash of light across flat paddocks, the familiar signals of dawn arriving way too soon.

Trees picked up the street lights' definition, threw it back. I was relieved to be alone, but sick of empty streets. I thought of my house shut up against the night, as still and hot as the inside of a rotting fruit. I thought of the times I'd crossed the city, back and forth. That bundle of clothes by the brick wall had seemed so right in its placing, in the expectation it created, and in the suddenness of disappointment and relief. It seemed as though its sole purpose in lying there had been so we could find it.

Twenty-two

I dozed until it started to get light, then rang Brook. No news of Denise, but I wasn't expecting any. Lawrence still hadn't turned up either, but the New South Wales police had a warrant to search his apartment and his nursery, and, at long last, for *CleanNet*'s financial records as well.

The day passed excruciatingly slowly. I listened to the news reports and watched Brook being interviewed on television. I re-read all my notes, hoping something would jump out at me that might point in Denise's direction. But the words dissolved in front of my eyes and, after a couple of hours, I stopped being able to take them in at all.

Brook was too busy to talk to me for more than a couple of minutes when I rang in the late afternoon, but he did tell me that a search of Lawrence's nursery and flat had turned up nothing that threw any light on Denise's disappearance, or Jenny Bishop's death.

When he knocked on the door, it was obvious that he'd eaten nothing all day. I added a bit more tomato paste to the simple sauce I was preparing, and an extra handful of spaghetti to the pot.

Brook had tracked down Stan Walewicz at his girlfriend's flat in Braddon. But Walewicz had claimed not to know Denise at all, and insisted that he hadn't seen or heard from Jenny Bishop since she'd appeared in his movie. He also claimed never to have had a personal meeting with Eden Carmichael, but when Brook put it to him that he'd been seen with Carmichael and Simon Lawrence at *Klim's* bar in December, he acknowledged that he'd been there. He said he'd just happened to drop in. When Brook had brought up the point about Jenny being in the bar as well, Walewicz hadn't denied it. He'd said Jenny was drunk. Brook had pressed him for details of what had happened, but Walewicz simply kept repeating that he'd left the bar and didn't know where Eden Carmichael or Simon Lawrence had gone. In answer to why he'd met Margot Lancaster in the same bar a few nights later, Walewicz had said she'd wanted him to put in a good word with Lawrence in relation to buying her club. Asked whether this had been successful, Walewicz had replied, 'Simon does what's best for Simon. He wouldn't do something because I asked him to. Not in a blue fit.'

Then Brook had brought up the matter of Jenny Bishop's calls to his studio: eleven between December 16 and 28.

'I got him to admit that Bishop was after money, but that's all. He was down the coast with his girlfriend the night she died, and he's adamant about not knowing Denise. The only good news is that the magistrate's approved a warrant for his financial records, and his studio. I'm going over there now to supervise a search.'

I persuaded Brook to eat something first, but his phone rang when we were halfway through our meal. The manager of the holiday camp where Denise's daughter had stayed had contacted the police to say a woman on her own had checked in the night before.

'She doesn't look anything like Denise, apparently,' Brook said, shrugging on his jacket. 'She's blonde, with a foreign accent, but the manager saw the news and thought he should report it anyway.'

'The blonde wig,' I said.

'Someone from Jindabyne will check it out.'

'How long will it take them to get there?' I asked.

'An hour. Maybe a bit less.'

'What about you?'

'I'll head to Fyshwick as planned.'

'What can I do?'

'Nothing.'

I was careful not to meet his eye.

...

I stood on my front porch, picturing Jenny on the esplanade, waiting for Simon Lawrence to show up. I smelt again the oil and seaweed floating across La Grande Parade to meet high-rise hotels, flats and terrace houses, the brothel painted white, secure within its row. I wondered if they'd promenaded up and down, or sat on a wooden seat and watched oil tankers cross Botany Bay, the 757s overhead, beautiful hyperbolas if you shut out the noise. Unless Lawrence confessed to the meeting, or another witness turned up, I did not think that I would ever know the details. I hoped Rose had somewhere safe to stay.

Making the decision almost without thinking about it, I drove to Eden Carmichael's block of flats and parked around the corner.

The garage roller door was closed. It wasn't locked, but the garage was empty, no sign of Carmichael's car. I wished I'd thought to ask Brook what had happened to it after the forensic people had finished their tests. For now, its absence was enough to confirm my suspicion. I circled the flats to make sure it hadn't been parked somewhere else, then returned to my car, and home again to look up Margot Lancaster's address. The phone book listed only one Lancaster M, whose address was a block of units in the new suburb of Gungahlin. I called the number. When there was no answer, I felt pleased, as though chance was on my side.

Again, I parked away from the building and walked around it. A line of acacias gave good cover, growing right up against the wall of number 9, on the side where I'd located the bathroom. All the blinds were drawn. I found the garage, each space marked with a number. Margot's black Nissan was there.

I went back to the bathroom. The window catch was level with my nose, the sill about shoulder height. Working away to loosen the catch, I was surprised that Margot hadn't thought to have her windows fitted with deadlocks.

I succeeded in forcing it, scrambled up one of the wattle trees, balanced on the sill, then jumped down to the floor. My hands were sweating, and a headache that had been building up since early morning hammered at my temples.

I entered the pressure-cooker feel of closed, still rooms, sighing with relief once I'd made sure the flat was empty, realising how intently I'd been listening for footsteps, watching for that extra length of shadow. With half my mind, I was aware that Margot could walk in any minute. But within me was a growing certainty that she'd taken Carmichael's car and gone after Denise.

Her living room was neat and everything appeared to be in order, though the shadow of a ceramic giraffe gave me a fright. I stood still.

After a moment, a door slammed, and I heard two unfamiliar voices arguing.

I made my way to Margot's bedroom. The bed was made, and there were no clothes lying on it, or on the chair beside it. The built-in wardrobe held several of the suits I'd seen her wearing, as well as winter coats and skirts. There was a shelf above the clothes rack. I stepped back and saw what looked like jumpers on one side, a pillow and two folded blankets on the other. I fetched a chair. Nothing was under the blankets, but right at the back of the shelf, hidden by them and the pillow, was a medium-sized cylindrical box. I pulled it out and set it on the bed. It was empty, except for a receipt. The name *Julia's* curled around the box in ornate lettering. Below it, in much smaller writing, was the address of the shop in Parramatta Road. The receipt was for a black wig, dated November last year.

. . .

I was on the Southern Highway out of Canberra before I thought of ringing Brook. He didn't waste time asking questions once he knew where I was going.

'Turn around now, Sandra.'

'I need to see for myself.'

'The car from Jindabyne will be there any minute. You won't be able to do anything. You'll just be in the way.'

'I talked Denise into meeting me.'

'Don't argue.'

'I found another wig box. Margot's wearing a long black wig, and she's driving Eden Carmichael's car. But I doubt if she'll still be on the road. She's figured out where Denise is, or else she knew all along.'

I settled my hands on the steering wheel and tried to will my muscles to relax. I was afraid of fast cars coming up behind me. The clock on the dashboard said 7.17. I had another three hours driving, and no map of the area. I hoped there'd be good signs. At least my petrol tank was almost full.

Twenty-three

They were log cabins of the sort that had never been built by Australian settlers, certainly not in the Snowy Mountains. The paths between the cabins were well lit, and the Jindabyne police had powerful torches. Under them, the cabins looked like they'd been copied from a nostalgic Hollywood movie set in the Appallachians. Made of treated pine that had been grown and harvested in the foothills, each had an identical chimney at one end, and one door in the middle of a wall, with small square windows either side.

The cabin that had been taken by a blonde woman on her own, speaking with a European accent, was on the side furthest from the main road, closest to the river. She had signed the registration form 'Mrs A Prideaux', and paid cash in advance for three nights. The manager hadn't seen her at all since her arrival. In the same building as the office was a kiosk which sold basic groceries and toiletries, but she hadn't been in there, according to his wife. Neither of them had seen her arrive. She'd simply appeared, carrying a small backpack, at the office door. Since she'd walked to the cabin after paying, they'd assumed that she hadn't come by car. It had been busy, and they hadn't given Mrs Prideaux another thought, until they'd seen a news item which included a photo of Denise. The woman had looked nothing like Denise, but she'd arrived alone and apparently on foot, and this had been enough to make them phone the police.

Constables Gleeson and McNamara had already searched the cabin by the time I arrived, and the section of trees and river closest to it. There was no sign of forced entry. A backpack on one of the cabin's bunk beds held a purse containing Denise's driving licence, and her mobile phone. As soon as he found it, Constable Gleeson had rung Queanbeyan and asked for reinforcements. He'd been surprised by my appearance, but instead of ordering me to leave, he told me they'd identified Denise's belongings and questioned me concerning what I knew about her and Margot Lancaster.

Widely spaced eucalypts and acacias marked a path to the river, where the trees and undergrowth were thicker. This was the area that had already been searched. By the time Constable Gleeson had finished questioning me, a car-load of police had arrived from Queanbeyan, and a more thorough search was being organised. I learnt that Carmichael's car had been found a few hundred metres from the camp gates, off the road, behind some trees.

Twenty minutes later, the search was underway. The manager and his wife joined in. I attached myself to a group led by one of the Queanbeyan police. We chose a strip of river frontage and moved through it about a metre apart. I tried to imagine what Denise had done when Margot turned up. How much of a start had she had? Had she seen Margot coming? Why had she run off – if indeed she had run – leaving her bag and phone behind?

My group scoured its bit of bush, and moved on to another. My head was throbbing. At least I'd had the presence of mind to bring a water bottle. My feet were beginning to drag when there was a shout up ahead.

Strong torchlight picked out two bowed heads, two wigs shining and well cared for, the blonde and the brunette.

Denise's attempt at a disguise had slipped sideways, lending her an air of disarray. She was awake, though dazed-looking, and obviously in pain. Margot was lying on her back.

The officer in charge moved quickly, checking Margot's pulse, ringing for an ambulance, working out a way to get both injured women back to the cabins. The branch that Denise had used to attack, or to defend herself, was carried back as well.

'Is Rebecca all right?' Denise asked, before lapsing back into semi-consciousness.

After the ambulance arrived to take them to Cooma hospital, I was forgotten again. I curled up in my car and slept for a couple of hours, then drove back to Canberra.

. . .

Over the next few days, I pieced together what remained of the story. Denise's ankle had been badly sprained, but not broken. She was released from hospital into her ex-husband's care. Margot was kept longer. Brook forgave my dash to the holiday camp sufficiently to let me read their statements, and to show me a copy of a loan agreement drawn up by Richard McFadden's solicitor, which the police had obtained with *CleanNet*'s financial records.

The agreement was dated October 5, 1996, and stated that Simon Lawrence, Stanley Walewicz and Margot Lancaster pledged to lend half a million dollars to *CleanNet*, in return for seventy-five per cent of the profits. McFadden named his house at Potts Point as surety. I read it through a couple of times. There was no date by which the initial loan had to be paid back, and no mention of McFadden having to pay interest.

When I pointed this out to Brook, he merely nodded, waiting for me to see what probably ought to have been obvious a long time ago. McFadden was the front man, *CleanNet*'s public face. It was the other three who'd invented the company, and who'd made all the decisions. A private loan agreement did not have to be declared to ASIC. If it hadn't been for two deaths, Eden Carmichael's and Jenny Bishop's, there was no reason why the police would ever have learnt of its existence.

It seemed that Margot had been expected to work hardest for her share of the profits, while McFadden coasted along on the surface, smiling and looking concerned about the safety of the young and vulnerable in cyberspace. He'd been quick to condemn the others, and present himself as an innocent businessman with money to invest, who'd been drawn into a quicksand of deceit and cruelty. He'd quickly spilled everything he knew about Lawrence and Walewicz, while remaining adamant that he had never connived at, much less committed, murder.

Lawrence had finally turned up, with an alibi for the last forty-eight hours. He'd been with a woman in a Sydney hotel. His staff hadn't known where he was, only the escort agency the woman worked for.

He'd been outraged to discover that his apartment and nursery had been searched in his absence, and had denied any involvement with

CleanNet. But when the loan agreement was read out to him, and it was made clear that McFadden had fully implicated both him and Stan Walewicz, and that Margot had confessed as well, Lawrence had decided to cut his losses.

Walewicz had admitted to taking the photograph of Carmichael that had appeared in *The Canberra Times* after negatives and a Pentax MZ-50 camera were found in his studio. He'd taken the shots through a window of Margot's club. He'd spoken of Carmichael with contempt, saying something like, 'I don't think the old fool even realised the blinds were open.'

Other photos had been found in his studio, of Carmichael in bed with Denise Travers, which Walewicz, once he realised that his partners were holding nothing back, described as their insurance policy. The threat of publishing them had kept Carmichael in line, and Denise silent. Carmichael might have put up with the indignity, but humiliating Denise Travers in public, in the eyes of her daughter, was a different story.

The meeting at *Klim's* in December, the one Jenny Bishop had interrupted, had been arranged to discuss Carmichael's appointment with Bryant, and to make sure Carmichael understood what he was expected to do – offer the senator a generous campaign donation. They'd grossly mistaken their target. Senator Bryant, the Federal Independent who'd made a name for himself on issues of morality and ethics, would have been outraged at the offer of a bribe. But it had never got that far.

The second meeting with Carmichael had been to let him know that one problem had been taken care of. Jenny Bishop wasn't going to cause any further trouble. But Carmichael didn't react to the news as he was expected to. Instead, it pushed him over the edge.

......
Twenty-four

When Denise had appeared at *Margot's* looking for work, a single mother with a small daughter, she already knew what it was like to be bullied by bosses who acted as though Rebecca didn't exist, who expected her to work most nights till very late, and, even when she wasn't working, to be on call.

Margot had admired Denise for her determination to give her daughter the best she could afford, and for her ability to live the contradictory lives of mother and sex worker. While Denise was saving for the deposit on a flat, Margot let her keep almost all her earnings. She learnt to trust Denise, valuing her ability to deal with nervous clients, and troublesome ones, too. Margot was choosy about the girls she hired. She hated addicts. No drugs was an unbreakable rule. The arrangement with *Sans Souci* was a good way of trying new girls out. If Margot liked them, and if they liked Canberra, she would ask them to stay. She preferred three or four girls she could rely on, girls who knew their job. Clients didn't complain about the lack of variety. Most regulars, the older men who made up the bulk of her business, would rather one skilled professional than twenty fumbling amateurs.

Then Jenny Bishop had turned up. Jenny was smart, and, though she'd been an addict, she wasn't any longer. She was fun. Denise had liked her, and so had the clients. But Jenny had a temper. And she knew her rights, even if she couldn't enforce them in a court of law. Simon Lawrence had hurt and humiliated her, and she wasn't about to let him forget it.

She'd pestered Denise for information about Lawrence, and anyone connected to him. She had the flyer made. Margot had paid her five hundred dollars, then another thousand, but Jenny wasn't satisfied with that. Once she'd seen Lawrence with Walewicz and Carmichael, she hassled Denise for information about Carmichael too. On the night Carmichael had seen Jenny instead of Denise, he'd been drunk and had told her the story of Margot and John Penshurst. He'd talked about his promise to Margot, and how much it worried him. Denise had lied to give Margot an alibi for the night of Jenny's death. But by then, Denise was frightened. She wanted to leave the club, and Canberra as well, but Margot made her stay. To leave at that point would have looked suspicious.

. . .

Margot had recorded her statement while she was in hospital. It began with a complaint.

I couldn't stand Jenny Bishop. She was brash and crude. Her sense of humour, if you could call it that, was tasteless. I wanted to send her straight back to Sydney, but she was stubborn. She said she was entitled to try out, so I kept my feelings under control. I should never have let Simon anywhere near her. I didn't know about the movie then, I only found out afterwards. The girl could pull them, you have to give her that. But then she made that awful fuss. You'd think the sky had fallen in. At least it gave me an excuse to get rid of her. I had to pay her double what I owed her to stop her going to the cops. Was she grateful? She blamed me as well as him. She asked for four times the amount again.

I had no idea that Ed had talked to her about me. Up till then he'd respected my wishes, and even though he drank too much, he knew when to keep his mouth shut. That Tuesday when he turned up, he told me Senator Bryant's office had cancelled the appointment. He said Stan and Simon had told him Jenny Bishop wasn't going to give them any more trouble. I told him she'd died of an overdose, but he didn't believe me. He thought Simon had killed her. He wanted me to go away with him while we had the chance. I told him I was sorry I'd asked him to front up to the senator. He should go home, relax, take a nap. We'd talk about it tomorrow. But he wouldn't listen. He started raving about getting married. He'd brought it up before, but this time he was insistent. He kept on repeating that his days were numbered. He had this plan that we'd go away together, buy a place in the country. He'd made up his mind to retire, and he knew I wanted to leave Canberra. He'd look after the money. Why couldn't I give him a few months' happiness? He'd brought everything he'd kept relating to me, letters, newspaper articles, a diary he'd kept while he was looking for me in Europe. It made me sick to think he'd hoarded them all those years. I couldn't make us young again, any more than I could have stopped that other fool from dying on me. I was angry and I just wanted him to leave. I fetched the photos of him and Denise and told him I'd send them to the newspaper if he didn't leave me alone. I don't think it had dawned on him that I had copies. Up till then, it'd been Stan who'd put the pressure on him. He grabbed the photos and began ripping them up. Then he collapsed. I called out for Denise. Denise started dressing him while I gathered up all the papers, then her daughter rang. I didn't realise she'd forgotten the underwear till she finally had the dress on him. I put it in the wig box with the other things and took it out the back.

. . .

Margot's statement had been typed up, copies made. A distancing process had begun, one phase of which would end with her conviction and sentencing, since she'd already confessed to murder. But as I sat there reading, I recalled another Margot, the Margot I believed I'd been getting to know. I pondered the moment when she'd decided to admit to killing Jenny, rather than to continue lying. Had it been when she woke out of her concussion, and realised that Denise had told the truth at last? Or before that, when she'd run past the cabin, after Denise's fleeting, gold-topped shadow, her own false hair streaming out behind?

I stopped reading, and went to fetch a glass of water, thinking, as I did so, of Jenny and Margot in Jenny's kitchen, that single glass that had been left in the sink. I wondered, not what had been going through Margot's head, for I had a fair idea of that now, but through Jenny's. Had she died believing she was more than a match for Margot? There was the money Margot had already paid her – enough to lull her into a false sense of security, perhaps. And Margot would have acted her part well.

. . .

Margot's confession read, in many places, like a statement of defiance.

'It never occurred to me that Ed would betray me to that scheming little bitch. My first decision was to tough it out. I could call anyone's bluff. I'd had years of practice. She rang me at the club and told me she knew about John Penshurst. She'd looked up old newspaper articles. She quoted headlines to me over the phone. They made me feel sick. If she made the information public, as she was threatening, it would have exposed and embarrassed me, but I told myself that that was all. I hadn't killed that man.

Then she saw Ed with Stan and Simon.

She knew about the photos Stan had taken. I rang Stan and we fought over the phone. I couldn't believe he'd been so stupid. He said she'd seen him with the camera. I asked why he hadn't told me earlier. We might have paid her off then, and been done with it. Stan infuriated me. By then, I also realised Simon had no intention of buying the club, and I hated him for leading me on.

Simon offered her money. He met her and gave it to her in cash. She just took it and went on as before. Simon underestimated her intelligence, and her perseverance. So did Stan.

She nagged Ed and frightened him by how close she was to guessing what I'd asked him to do.

As usual, the mess was left to me to clean up. It was then the idea came to me that I could get rid of her. It came to me all at once, like a movie in front of my eyes. I only had to blink, and there it was. At first I told myself not to be crazy, but I couldn't stop thinking about it. It was her life for mine. I woke up with those words, went to bed with them. I couldn't have got them out of my head even if I'd wanted to, but after a while I didn't want to.

She wanted fifty thousand dollars, in lots of ten grand each. I could have paid it. It wouldn't have broken me. But would it have ended there?

When she rang the last time, we arranged for me to go to her place on the Thursday night. She wanted me to send a bank cheque for ten thousand dollars. I said I wouldn't do that. We would have to meet. Thursday suited her because she wasn't working and those other two had been invited to a party. They would have thought it odd for me to suddenly turn up.

I bought the heroin and some whiskey here in Canberra. I'd have to give her the cheque, but if things went according to plan, I could retrieve it later. I wore my wig in case any of the neighbours saw me.

She thought it was weird, but she knew how much I liked them. Her housemates could have come home early, but I was willing to risk that.

She'd put away a good bit of alcohol by the time I arrived. She wanted me to leave as soon as I'd handed over the cheque, but I said I was exhausted with the long drive and I'd have to rest for a while. She watched while I opened the whiskey. She wouldn't have accepted a drink from me if the bottle hadn't been sealed. She smelt it too. I poured myself a glass first, but after that I made sure mine were mainly water.

While I watched her drinking, I planned how I was going to get back into the house. When she went to the toilet, I unlocked a kitchen window, and hoped she wouldn't notice. When it was my turn to go upstairs to use the bathroom, I took the opportunity to look around, and worked out which was her bedroom.

It was after midnight when she showed me out. I drove around the block and waited. I decided that if she was still awake when I went back, or woke up and challenged me, I could say I'd had enough of being blackmailed and I was going to the police. I could have abandoned my plan at any point.

I sat in my car for over an hour. I hoped she'd go to sleep, but I couldn't be sure. In the end, it was much easier than I thought it would be. I got over the back fence, and through the kitchen window. I made a bit of noise, but there were no lights on in either of the adjoining houses. I found her bedroom again without any trouble. She rolled over and muttered something when I put the syringe in her hand, but she never even came close to waking up. I retrieved my whiskey bottle, and washed and put away the glass I'd used. On the drive back to Canberra, I threw away the bottle and the gloves I'd put on before returning to the house.

Denise presented the greatest risk. I needed Denise. I promised her enough money so she could stop working, go back to study, get some qualifications. All she had to say, if she was asked, was that I'd been at the club that Thursday night. I was counting on the police accepting that Bishop had overdosed. But then Ed had to go and die.'

. . .

I stopped reading again and closed my eyes for a moment. The meaning of Denise's attack with the tree branch was beginning to sink in. Margot hadn't gone after Denise to threaten her. She'd gone to persuade her to come back, be brave, hang in there. They were through the worst. Her reward was waiting.

. . .

'I didn't notice the blonde wig was missing until Denise failed to show up for work. I rang her flat. When there was no answer, I went round there. Her car was in its usual spot, but there was no answer when I knocked. I had no idea what state I'd find Denise in. I only knew I had to talk to her. By the time she was three hours late, I realised the wig was missing, and I guessed that she'd be wearing it. I closed the club and drove back to her flat. The car was still there. She could have hired one, but to do that she would have had to fill in forms, and show her driver's licence. I thought she was more likely to have taken a bus. I couldn't decide whether or not to tell Simon and Stan, but in the end I decided against it. She didn't trust either of them, and she hated Simon.

Next morning, I drove to the Jolimont Centre, and asked, first of all at Greyhound, then at Murrays, describing Denise as carefully as I could, and saying she might be wearing a blonde wig. At Murrays I found a girl who was surprisingly helpful. She'd noticed a customer who might have been Denise. Her height and build were right. She'd paid cash for a return ticket to Cooma, which led me to think of the holiday camp near Jindabyne where Rebecca had stayed. I could have rung the camp and asked if a single woman had made a booking, but I didn't want to alert the manager. The best course, I decided, was to drive up there and see for myself.

To guard against being followed, I decided to report Denise missing, then to wait one more night. I decided to use Ed's car as well. It was hell to wait, but there was a good chance I wouldn't be followed if I stuck to my plan. Of course, I could have been wrong. Denise could turn up in the meantime. I wanted to allow for that possibility too.

I shouldn't have moved the wig box after Ed died. I should have taken the photographs and papers and left the box under the table. I knew as soon as the police started with their cameras that I'd made a mistake. I hoped nobody would notice, but that Mahoney woman did. It made her feel that she was onto something. I couldn't get rid of her after that. I did think it might prove useful to have Ed's car key. I broke into his flat one night after the police had finished their search, and found one in a drawer. I used the opportunity to check if Ed had left any old letters. He'd said he'd brought them all with him, but I wanted to make sure. Of course, the police could have found them and be holding onto them, but I felt better after I'd satisfied myself that there weren't any left lying around his flat.

I'm sure I could have talked Denise into coming back, if she'd only listened to me, if she hadn't run away. Why did she turn on me like that? She ought to have known I'd never do her any harm.'

. . .

I noticed that I'd aligned the pages very neatly, with all their edges matching, as though I believed that arranging them like this could provide some kind of antidote to the story they told. Margot's account fitted, the way a broken glass fits, scattered on a kitchen floor. You know the pieces go together. They've made a glass just seconds before. But you can never make it whole again.

. . .

Denise had agreed to testify against Margot, but refused to talk to the media. She didn't want to see me either. I sent her a message, describing how I'd found the wig box in Margot's flat. In the end, she told me I could have ten minutes.

. . .

Rebecca half sat, half lay against her mother, touching, massaging and stroking first one, then another part of her – her upper arm through her T-shirt, the small of her back. She looked like Denise must have at nine or ten, her fine, dark hair pulled back in a ponytail.

'Mum?' she whispered. 'Can I get you anything? Do you want a cup of tea?'

Denise smiled and said, 'That would be lovely.'

Her eyes, fixed on the top of her daughter's head, were tired but calm, the relief of not having to pretend any longer an almost visible cloud around her head.

Rebecca uncurled herself. I knew Denise would not give me a minute more than the allotted ten.

'Did you see Margot coming?' I asked. 'Why did you leave your phone in the cabin? Why didn't you ring for help?'

Denise turned to me and spoke reluctantly. 'I didn't think. Margot knocked on the front door. I ran out the back. It was practically dark. I hoped she wouldn't hear me. I planned to double back to the office and get help. But she was faster than I thought. I could hear her catching up. She called out my name, said she wanted to talk. I grabbed that branch, you saw it? I stopped running, and got behind a tree and waited.' Denise licked her lips. 'She just kept coming. I waited till she was ahead of me and hit her. Then I hit her again.'

'Margot defended herself.'

'She tried to, but I had the weapon. She's a strong woman. In the end, we went down in a heap.'

'What happened the night Jenny was killed?'

'Margot went home early. She said she was sick.' Denise was silent for a moment. 'I wanted to believe her.'

'So did Eden Carmichael.'

'He'd just found out, that day he turned up. Stan told him. Margot said it was an overdose. He *wanted* to believe her. Just like I did. But too much had happened by then.'

'What about the wig box? The one you said was in the room with Carmichael.'

'You gave me such a hard time over that. I didn't find out Margot had moved it till afterwards. She forgot to tell me. She was angry with me for telling you it was there.'

'What was in it?'

'Photos. Margot liked – she liked keeping them nearby. Ed ripped them up and threw them round the room. Then after, after he was dead – you see, Margot made me put his dress on him. She said it would look more convincing that way, but I forgot his underwear. She was collecting the photos. She was scared of not finding all the pieces. She kept on saying that we couldn't wait. We'd have to ring the ambulance. She shoved them in the wig box together with some letters Ed had brought. When he lost his temper, he threw those at her too. When he stopped breathing – it was terrible.'

'What happened to the letters?'

'She burnt them that night.'

'What about Rebecca's phone call?'

'You think I'd have made that up?'

'What were you doing when she rang?'

'Trying to put Ed's dress on him. That's why I ripped it. I was so upset!'

'Margot wore the dark wig when she went to Jenny's house.'

Denise said nothing to that. I wasn't sure if she was aware of the full implications of it. With a long dark wig, and at a distance, Margot could easily have been mistaken for her.

'When did you take the blonde wig?' I asked.

'The night before I left. Margot wasn't feeling well. She went home and left me to lock up. I saw it sitting there. That's what gave me the idea that I might take off.'

'Didn't you expect Margot to come after you?'

'She had to find out where I was first.' After another short silence, she said softly, 'I would have left as soon as I found out Jenny was dead. But I had Rebecca. Together, we were too conspicuous. Where could we have hidden without being found? I didn't want to leave Beck, but then Ed died. It was too much. I'm getting out of sex work. Beck's asked me to, and I've promised.'

As though responding to her name, Rebecca came in carrying a tray. She'd made tea in an earthenware pot. There was milk beside it, and a matching sugar bowl. She'd been gone longer than she needed to make a pot of tea, and I knew, from the look that passed between mother and daughter, that my role was now to drink it and leave.

'Great,' Denise said. 'Thank you.'

Rebecca smiled. I knew she wouldn't leave her mother's side again while I was there, and that Denise would not answer any more questions in front of her.

They said goodbye to me with their arms around each other. Neither tried to hide her relief that I hadn't overstayed my welcome.

. . .

I was driving back through Civic when I spotted Stan Walewicz sitting at a pavement cafe. I pulled into a side street, found a park, and approached him from behind. He was on his own, and I guessed that he was waiting for someone.

'Hello,' I said.

Walewicz swung around, scowling as he recognised me.

'What do you want?'

'Just a quick word. Did you break into my house?'

Walewicz's frown deepened, then he shook his head and laughed.

'So it was you.'

'You want to hang me for it?'

'You dressed up as a woman.'

'How did you know?'

'Your wigs have a particular smell. Do you like dressing up?'

'Now and again.'

'What were you looking for?'

'What do you think?'

'I think you were trying to find out how much I knew about *CleanNet*.'

'What's it matter now?'

'Before that you'd tried hacking into my computer. When you couldn't find what you wanted, you got angry.'

'If the cops ask me, I'll deny it. You can't prove it was me. And I never touched either of those girls, Bishop or the other one. If it hadn't been for bloody Simon –'

Walewicz broke off and offered me another scowl.

When he spoke again, his voice was distant and deflated.

'I can't stand junkies. Never use them in my movies. Girls turn up, I can see they're on something, doesn't matter if they've got the best tits in the world, straight away I show them the door.'

'But Jenny –'

'Not in those days, she wasn't. Jenny was a great kid when I met her, full of life. The world was her oyster.'

'That movie title.'

'What about it?'

'"Jane Springs the Trap." She almost succeeded.'

Walewicz gave a snort and glared at me through narrowed eyes. I took it as my cue to leave.

. . .

Brook turned up as I was pulling into the driveway. I was pleased to see him. I knew better than to expect him to apologise for ordering me to turn back off the highway, and for the way he'd kept his distance since.

'You're looking well.'

Brook nodded, not rejecting the compliment, not quite accepting it either.

'You didn't end up getting much of a holiday,' he said.

'My choice.' I heard an unintended sharpness in my voice, and felt myself recoiling a little, as spectators must, who cannot sustain a gesture of anticipation. I thought how desire could be forever suspended, forever about to be acted on. How long had I gone on wanting this man, behaving well, and not so well?

Brook followed me into the house, and through to the kitchen, where I poured us both a beer.

'Cheers,' he said. 'Well, it seems young Picoult's clean. Apart from stalking you, that is.'

Brian Picoult had finally been interviewed and a copy of the interview sent down. Lawrence had paid him to follow me when I was in Sydney.

I sipped and listened, while Brook continued with his summing up.

'And Simon Lawrence has confessed to that business on the highway. After Picoult dobbed him in, he didn't have much choice. Picoult's willing to testify that Lawrence was with him that night. He waited in a bar while Picoult followed you out to the Esplanade. But the boy had had enough after that. Lawrence left him behind while he tailed you on the highway. Picoult refused to go along.'

'He might have had enough, but he still didn't go to the police.'

'He was scared.'

'Lawrence might have killed him? He tried to kill me.'

'Lancaster was the killer, Sandra.'

'She wouldn't have put her money into *CleanNet* if the other two hadn't persuaded her.'

'You don't know that.'

Brook spoke sharply, but I could feel his interest in the case dissolving. He'd taken it on reluctantly, and was more than prepared to let it go.

Ken Dollimore had announced his retirement. He'd decided not to wait until the next election. When I'd tried to ring his office, I'd been told he was in Townsville with his daughter. His PA refused to give me any contact details. I'd rung his home phone just to make sure. There was no answer and no answering machine.

Brook and I agreed that Dollimore would probably go on blaming himself for warning Senator Bryant's office on January 4, and precipitating the events that had led to Carmichael's second, fatal, heart attack.

'I regret never having seen Richard McFadden in a cowboy hat,' I said.

'Yeah, well. There are worse things to regret.'

I put my glass down carefully and turned to face him. 'Don't say I disobeyed you and betrayed your trust.'

'I wasn't going to.'

'What then?'

'Just – perhaps you shouldn't push yourself so hard.'

'Why not?'

When Brook didn't answer, I said, 'Maybe pushing ourselves is something we have in common.'

When he still didn't reply, I said, 'Don't feel sorry for me. Canberra in January turned out to be far more interesting than I expected.'

'*I* thought I'd keep an eye on you.'

'I know you did. Thank you.' After a moment's hesitation, I added, 'You never liked Margot, did you?'

'Never had an opinion one way or the other. Don't look at me like that. I know that look. You're wishing she'd never laid a finger on the girl. You're wishing it was those other two – dimples and muscles.'

'And number three. Don't forget Aces-Up-His-Sleeve.'

Brook finished his beer and said, 'I best be going, then.'

I kissed him on the forehead, just below the hairline.

'I'll be seeing you,' he said.

I scrunched my mouth up, not trusting myself to speak, nodding goodbye instead.

I thought of phoning Gail, but suspected she was annoyed with me for not contacting her as soon as I got back from the holiday camp. I didn't feel up to dealing with her annoyance just then. I'd talked Gail into writing an article implicitly praising Margot and her business. This seemed a relatively small thing, but to Gail it might not be. I realised that her friendship was important to me. I wished I'd confided in her more, instead of keeping half the things I'd done a secret. I hoped she'd hang around in Canberra, for a while at least.

I wrote my last report for Lucy. In publicity, if not in legal terms, her organisation would have a good case against *CleanNet*. How they used it would be up to them. But I wondered what difference it would make in the long run, even if they succeeded in tarnishing the company's image. It seemed to me that Richard McFadden would most likely ride out the bad publicity. Walewicz and Lawrence would be charged with attempting to blackmail Eden Carmichael, Lawrence at the worst with attempted murder, at best with dangerous driving, though I had a feeling expensive lawyers might argue their way even out of that. All three men would continue making a profit at whatever they turned their hands to, whether it was filters, or red roses, or eighteen-year-old college girls being filmed for sex.

I sent the report, then took Fred to the oval, apologising to him for the walks he'd missed over the last few days. I told him Peter would be home tomorrow, saying the words aloud to make them true, though I found the idea of his return, and Ivan's and Katya's, impossible to get my mind around. Fred wagged his tail at the sound of Peter's name.

Back at the house, I lay down for a few minutes and fell asleep without meaning to. The last light was leaving my bedroom when I woke up, a glow all yellow and lilac, as though my dreams had been peaceful.

Wakefield Press is an independent publishing and
distribution company based in Adelaide, South Australia.
We love good stories and publish beautiful books.
To see our full range of titles, please visit our website at
www.wakefieldpress.com.au.